YOU'LL NEVER ESCAPE ME

JACQUELINE BEARD

BOOKS

Vinci Books

vinci-books.com

Published by Vinci Books Ltd in 2026

1

The publisher and the author have made every effort to obtain permissions for any third party material used in this book and to comply with copyright law. Any queries in this respect should be brought to the attention of the publisher and any omissions will be corrected in future editions.

A CIP catalogue record for this book is available from the British Library.

Paperback ISBN: 9781036703974

The EU GPSR authorised representative is Logos Europe, 9 rue Nicolas Poussion, 17000 La Rochelle, France contact@logoseurope.eu

By Jacqueline Beard

Denman & Tallis Cotswold Crime Thrillers

The Girl in Flat Three
You'll Never Escape Me
The Devil Comes to Bylands

Prologue

September 2019

The boy stood, hands on hips, with a steely glint in his eyes.

"Chuck it over here."

"No way. If you want it, come and get it, big man."

Luke rolled his eyes. "Give it a rest, Jam. My mum will go mental if I get another detention."

"Calm down. It's only a bit of fun." The tall, dark-skinned boy roughly shoved the bright red rucksack into his companion's midriff.

"That hurt, you muppet."

"Serves you right for supporting a rubbish team."

"Give over, you two." The smaller of the three boys spoke up.

"Who rattled your cage, Charlie?" Jamal lunged at the boot bag slung over Charlie's shoulder.

"Grow up."

"Make me."

"Oi. Leave it alone." Charlie cast a protective hand over the bag, but it was too late. Jamal had grabbed it before sprinting into the distance, across Rotherleigh Road and towards a small copse of trees.

"Ah, crap. I've got football practice tonight." Charlie threw his schoolbag to the ground in disgust.

"Jamal's only playing. He's too unfit to keep that pace for long. We'll catch him in no time. Follow me." Luke sped off with Charlie at the rear, soon gaining ground on the taller boy in the distance.

By the time they caught him, Jamal had strung up the boot bag from a tree branch an inch too high for the shorter boys to reach.

"Idiot," scowled Charlie.

"I'll get it." Luke jumped, grabbed a handful of fabric, and the bag crashed to the floor.

"Thanks, mate."

"You're welcome. Now can we just go home with no more dickery from you, Jamal?"

"Where's the fun in that?" Jamal grinned and raised his hand. "What's over there?" he asked, pointing to a distant building.

"It's a cottage," said Luke.

"I can see that. Who lives in it?"

"How should I know?"

"I thought you knew everything."

"Well, I don't, and I don't care either. Can we go now?"

"Mrs Ballinger lives in the right-hand cottage," said Charlie confidently.

"Who?"

"Mrs Ballinger. She cleaned for us before she retired."

"Ooh, posh boy. I keep forgetting you have staff."

"Leave him alone, Jamal," said Luke.

"Does she live alone?" Jamal's eyes flashed mischievously.

"Yes. Why?"

"We haven't played knock down ginger for a while, and I vote you batter the door."

"No way. She knows me. I'd be in all sorts of crap."

"Coward."

"You do it then." Charlie stared defiantly, hands on hips.

"No point in keeping a dog and barking yourself."

"It's getting late. I'm off," said Luke, checking his phone. "And, Charlie, you'd better move sharpish, or you'll miss football practice."

"It's an hour later tonight. Mr Pearcey's got a council meeting."

"Good. Then you can still tap Mrs Ballinger's door," Jamal persisted.

"No. I'm not getting grounded to please you."

"Then try the one next door."

"No point. It's empty."

"Are you sure?"

"Positive. The Drewits left years ago."

"Double dare you to go inside." Jamal raised an eyebrow, and Charlie sighed.

"Why me?"

"It's your turn."

"When was it your turn?"

"I make the rules."

"For crying out loud." Luke scowled. "I've got better things to do, even if you two haven't."

"Run along home then," sneered Jamal.

"It's not like that."

"Isn't it? Sounds like you're scared."

"Like hell."

"Then prove it. Wait five minutes for Chazzer to get inside. We'll watch from the window to make sure he doesn't sneak off, and then you can go."

"Must we?"

"Yes," said Jamal firmly. "Otherwise, we're as boring as Freddie and his dragon-slaying nerds. He can listen to a real adventure next time he starts boring off about his stupid dungeon elves."

Charlie shrugged. "Do what?"

"He means Dungeons and Dragons," explained Luke.

"Whatever. Get on with it, Charlie. We haven't got all day." Jamal gestured at the stone path leading towards the cottages. "Talk about primitive. Don't they have cars around here?"

Charlie ignored him and stepped cautiously down the path. He advanced a few yards and glanced over his shoulder, hoping Jamal would call off the dare. But the taller boy stood grinning, casually sweeping a hand through his dark, curly hair, watching until Charlie was almost out of sight.

"Looks like he's going in," Jamal said excitedly.

"You didn't leave him much choice." Luke shifted uncomfortably, wishing he was anywhere else but there.

"Come on."

"Where are we going?"

"To the cottage, like I said. Charlie will weasel out of the dare if we don't watch him."

They sauntered towards the left-hand side of the shabby property ahead, Jamal narrowly missing a broken tile near what remained of the front garden. Two years of neglect had left the stone building covered with weeds while ivy crawled out of control across the front aspect.

The boys squeezed past a large bush and pushed open the gate to find Charlie leaning against the wall on the other side.

"I knew you wouldn't go for it," said Jamal.

"Something's wrong."

"Yes. Your sense of adventure. You should be inside by now."

"The house is open," said Charlie, pointing to the unlocked door.

"Big deal. Nobody lives in it."

"But the door should be secure."

"That's no excuse for welching on a dare."

"He's right," said Luke, stepping forward. "Nobody leaves their house open for anyone to enter. Did you move the door at all?"

Charlie shook his head. "No. It was already ajar. I didn't touch it. And I'm not going to. We should leave well alone."

"Don't be daft. We're here now. Let's finish what we started."

"You bloody do it if you're so brave?" Charlie wiped his hand over his eyes, hoping Jamal wouldn't see his trembling fingers.

"It's just an empty house, chicken shit. Fine. I'll go." Jamal dropped his schoolbag by the door and strode inside. He returned moments later carrying a dusty milk bottle.

"Here," he said, thrusting it towards Charlie. "It's just an empty house with a few crappy bags of litter and stuff. Not worth wetting your pants over."

"Then let's go," said Luke, rechecking his mobile. "Crap. Message from Mum. She wants me to pick up a box of tea bags on my way back."

"I'll come with you. I want an energy drink."

Charlie smirked. "You're not allowed."

"What Mama don't know she don't care about," said Jamal.

"What was that?" Luke cocked his head to one side as Jamal pulled the door to.

"I didn't hear anything," said Charlie.

"Listen."

The boys stood quietly for a moment.

"Must be the wind," said Jamal. "Or at least the hot air coming from Charlie."

"Do one."

"It's there again. Shut up for a moment and listen properly."

A faint metallic tap reverberated from below.

"It's just the pipes," said Jamal.

"No. It's a regular noise. Listen."

The clanging continued between long silent gaps but with an undeniable rhythm.

"Something's down there," said Luke.

"Don't be an arse."

"Call me all the names you like, Jamal. Something's not right. We should check."

"Er, no. I've been inside. It's your turn."

"We'll all go. There's safety in numbers."

"It's getting dark." Charlie thrust his hands into his jacket pocket and tried to ignore the menacing sound.

"It'll only take a minute," said Luke. Then we can run home. The last man back is an arse."

Jamal glanced at Charlie, who closed his eyes and nodded.

"Okay then. Lead the way."

Luke licked his lips, pushed past Jamal, and headed into the tiny hallway, the other two trailing like shadows behind.

"Have you got a light?" he whispered.

"No. But look over there." Jamal pointed to a shelf running the length of the rear wall, housing boxes of light bulbs and a torch.

"It better bloody work," said Luke, clicking the button. A powerful beam swept across the hallway.

"Watch out," yelled Charlie, shielding his eyes. The clanging stopped, and the boys exchanged glances.

"They've heard us," hissed Jamal.

"Then let's get the hell out of here." Charlie stared owl-like, transfixed with fear.

Thud, thud, thud. The noise slowly resumed, every stroke sounding laboured.

"Not without checking. It's our duty," said Luke solemnly.

"I need a wee."

"Alright, Charlie. Go outside, empty your bladder, and stay put. If we're not back in five minutes, fetch our parents."

"Okay." Charlie disappeared, and Luke turned to Jamal.

"Ready?"

"Let's do it."

They followed the sound into the kitchen and towards a wooden door standing ajar.

"What's that awful smell?" Jamal raised the front of his hoodie over his nose.

"Over there. On the table."

"What is it?"

"It was milk. It's more like yoghurt now. I'm surprised you didn't smell it earlier."

"I didn't get this far," admitted Jamal. "The bottle was by the door."

"Never mind. Stand back." Luke approached the basement door and pulled it towards him before directing the flashlight beam down the stairs.

"What can you see?" Luke felt Jamal's warm breath on his neck as he hovered behind.

"Nothing yet, but the noise is louder."

"Jesus. We should never have started this. Let's call your dad."

"Not until we know what's down there." Luke's breath came in ragged gasps as he tried to conceal his fear.

Jamal wordlessly reached for Luke's trembling hand as they advanced downstairs. The groans began before they reached the bottom, a pitiful moan of despair keeping time with the metallic beat.

"Who's there?" whispered Luke, his voice rasping as Jamal shivered behind him.

The voice moaned again, this time more urgently, as if trying to speak.

Luke tensed, fighting the urge to turn tail and tear upstairs. He took a deep breath and composed himself, and then something clattered to the ground.

Jamal screamed. "What the fuck was that?"

"It's okay. I dropped the torch."

"It's not okay. I'm done here."

"Wait." Luke scrabbled on the earthy floor and retrieved the flashlight before switching the beam back to full. He swept it behind him, catching a glimpse of Jamal's wild-eyed face and flaring nostrils, and patted him on the shoulder. He was about to speak, to reassure his friend when another weaker moan stopped him, and he shone his torch to the side of the room. It flickered over a white-washed wall, illuminating an old paint-spattered table with the desiccated remains of a plate of food and onwards to a camping stove. Luke swallowed and slowly shone the light to his left, moving inch by inch, frame by frame. And there, at the end of the cellar, the torchlight settled on the iron-barred door of a man-sized cage, where it glinted against the metal. Hand in hand, the boys approached as the beam picked up a shadowy form on the dusty floor. A skeletal shape lay huddled in the corner, clutching a rusty chain, his hand moving like a clockwork automaton as it beat the link against an iron bar in a last desperate attempt to survive.

Chapter One

Three years later

"I won't do it, and you can't make me." Sean narrowed his eyes and glared at me across the desk.

"Are you serious?"

"Deadly."

"Then we might as well shut up shop."

"It's tempting."

I sighed and pushed against my wheeled chair, steering it towards the water cooler Sean had reluctantly installed the previous month. I grabbed a plastic cup and filled it before scooting back again without spilling a drop.

"I can't help but admire your determination not to stand if you can help it. But I doubt your physio would feel the same way," he said smugly.

"Don't nag," I replied, anger welling inside me. Sean's supercilious recommendations were all very well, but he wasn't the one suffering excruciating back pain caused by the dead weight of a suicidal psychopath. Not only had I suffered multiple knife wounds, but my attacker had the poor grace to fall directly on top of me with his dying breath. The injuries had kept me in Cheltenham General for the best part of a month and although I could walk and probably run at a push, standing up often brought a particular brand of agony I was keen to avoid.

"You know I'm right." Sean winked as he flashed the okay gesture, and I fought to contain my irritation.

"Going back to the matter at hand," I said.

"It's still a firm no."

"Fine. I'll do it."

"Callie won't see you. She's far too busy and important."

"I don't want to hear it, Sean. Since you handed over the accounting, you've taken your eye right off the ball. Are you bored with getting paid? Or shall we just live off credit cards for the next few months?"

Sean's face fell. "Don't exaggerate. We've only just banked Doll Murphy's cheque."

"It paid the rent, your car insurance, and the electricity bill, which wasn't pretty, Sean. They weren't kidding when they said prices were on the rise."

"Hold fire." Sean tapped his mouse, and his PC sprang to life. A couple of clicks later, he was staring at the accounting software with a look of disgust.

"Fine," he said. "I take your point. But I would rather eat my spleen than go cap in hand to Callie."

"You say that as if we hadn't earned the money. It's not our fault their centralised accounts department can't get its act together."

"You could always speak to them again."

"Speak to who? I never get the same person twice, and the only one who sounded remotely competent said she'd need permission to expedite our payment from someone senior at Truscombe nick. And with Kim on long-term sick and the new inspector not yet onside, that's Callie."

"But you know what happened last time."

"Yes. Your ex-wife asked you out to dinner, and because you didn't have the guts to say no while you had the chance, you spent the next three months avoiding her. Which now makes everything harder. I'm only surprised we're still getting the work."

"They're overloaded," said Sean. "Another round of cutbacks. I haven't seen Tom in weeks."

"I wonder how he is?" I asked, despondency creeping over me. Although Tom had grown irritated with us during the final days of the Skin Thief debacle, he had been a good friend afterwards, visiting me in the hospital and texting regularly until last month. I'd messaged him a few times since to tumbleweed.

"I don't know," muttered Sean, staring distractedly at his computer. I shuffled my chair a few inches towards him as he quickly minimised a screen looking suspiciously like an online pet store.

"You don't need any more lizards," I said.

"No. But the ones I own require feeding."

I swallowed a snappy retort and changed the subject. As a guest in Sean's house, it wouldn't do to get between a man and his geckos.

"So, when are you going to the station?" I asked.

"How about when hell freezes over?"

"And back in the real world, where we still need to eat?"

"Oh, God. Tomorrow, I suppose," he said, putting his head in his hands. "It's just excruciating. I never minded the difference in rank while we were married. But being beholden to Callie is not high on my list of aspirations."

"It's up to her to play the game," I snapped. I'd never

met Callie, but she was already an irritant. Sean lost all sense of rationality in any dealings with his ex-wife, and I had a low tolerance for people who didn't pay their bills. And yes. Assistant Chief Constable Callista Hart might hold too high a rank to get down and dirty with BACS payments to third parties, but she carried responsibility for the smooth running of the southwest offices. As far as I was concerned, it was her bad.

"Fine. I'll eat my toad tomorrow first thing. But I warn you, Sass. If Callie gets snarky, she might pull the funding again."

"I'll take her to small claims."

"Don't be silly. I'll sort it out. Now can we do something more productive?"

"Such as?"

"What have we got?"

"A backlog of research for the station, which I'm unenthusiastically ploughing through, as it's not bringing any money in."

"I told you. I'll sort it."

I ignored him and continued. "A potential missing boyfriend, a couple of background checks on dodgy claimants for the DWP, and a request to quote for covert surveillance from the Truscombe bookies."

"I'll take that," said Sean.

"It's not a done deal. They've asked Jez Marley too."

"Bloody hell. He's only been in town five minutes, and he's getting all the decent jobs. There's not enough work for two PIs."

"It's not worth worrying yet. Doug Parmenter said he'd decide on Friday."

"I know Big Doug. Perhaps I should pop by."

"If you think it will help."

14

"I'll do better than that. Thorny Devil is running in the three thirty at Prestbury Park on Friday. It's about time I had a bit of luck on the gee-gees."

I rolled my eyes. Sean had a long list of fixations, starting with lizards and ending with virtually any sport, particularly those with gambling opportunities. Personally, I didn't get the excitement of horse racing. I'd only been once, finding the so-called atmosphere ruined by the tortuous car journeys at either end. I didn't do queuing. It simply wasn't worth it.

"Go for it," I said unenthusiastically.

"Right. That's a plan."

"For tomorrow," I said. "It's only two o'clock. I've got plenty to do. How about you?"

"Shopping, I suppose. What do you fancy for tea?"

I lowered my pen. "Anything you like, but you don't need to cater for me. I can do it." I took a deep breath and let loose the question I had been trying to avoid all week. A negative answer would be tricky to deal with, but it couldn't go unsaid for much longer. "I've been living at yours for a few months, Sean. Isn't it time I found somewhere more permanent?"

"Do you want to?"

"I really should. I'm paying a small fortune in storage costs. And you must be fed up with me by now."

"I don't mind. And it works for both of us. I appreciate the extra rent, and you are paying a damn sight less than you did at Bosworth House."

I shuddered at the mention of my former flat. After Sean had collected me from the hospital, I never went back. He'd packed and stored my possessions, made up his spare room, and I'd moved into his house in Carling Drive. Every few weeks, I went through the motions of volunteering to leave, but it suited me better to stay. We rubbed along together reasonably well, and I wasn't as lonely as I'd been in my flat.

"As long as you're sure?"

"I'd tell you if I wasn't. Now stop fishing and give me a steer on food, or we'll be dining on fish and chips again. I don't mind, but I know your aversion to brown food."

"Oh, I don't know. Just grab me a healthy ready meal. Or a quiche and salad."

"Gross," he said, pulling a face. "You're as fussy as Dhruv."

"That's unfair. Dhruv's not a fan of takeaways. He prefers to cook for himself."

"I wouldn't know. We pass like ships in the night, considering we work in the same building."

"Ah. Haven't you called round to see him?"

"No. Have you?"

"Not to his flat. I meant to the office."

"I'm not sure I'd be welcome. Dhruv's boss is a strange one."

"I know. We've met."

"When did you visit?"

"Last week. I probably should have said something, but things aren't straightforward, so I left it for another time."

"Said what? Is Dhruv alright?"

"More or less." I considered my words carefully. Sean had many positive attributes, but tolerance and understanding were not among them.

"What's that supposed to mean?"

"Look. It's not a secret, but best not to mention that we've spoken if you see him, right?"

"Mention what?"

"Dhruv is in therapy."

"Big deal. So are you."

I scowled. With great reluctance and after much persuasion from the hospital, I had consulted a therapist shortly after I was released. I attended once and studiously avoided his secretary's calls over the following weeks. I wasn't against therapy. Not at all. But it wasn't for me. I can only process my feelings with peace and quiet. It doesn't work if other people get involved.

"Dhruv is pretty much reliant on it," I explained. "He's going weekly."

"Blimey. That doesn't sound like him at all. Dhruv's always been pretty upbeat."

"Yes. Well, that was before Mill went off the rails."

Sean pushed his mouse away and looked directly at me, fully concentrating for the first time since we'd started the conversation.

"I don't understand."

"You know Mill's been in and out of hospital since contracting sepsis. He's lost a chunk of his foot, and it's badly set him back. Psychologically, I mean. Anyway. He's started drinking heavily, which isn't a good look for a teacher. God knows how it's gone undetected by the school. Dhruv tried everything to set him right, but Mill isn't listening, and their relationship is on a knife edge. Dhruv is gutted. He's in therapy for his sanity and hopes to arrange some relationship counselling."

"Doesn't that need both parties?"

"Exactly. And Mill won't have a bar of it. It breaks my heart. Two lovely guys, and they're tearing each other apart. More casualties of the bloody Skin Thief."

"Should I have a word?"

"I'd rather you didn't. Dhruv was open about everything. You know what he's like. He wears his heart on his sleeve. But I'd rather he told you himself."

"He might if I drop by."

"Sure. On a pretext. But don't mention me."

"That would seem odd."

"I mean, don't say I told you."

"Copy that. Might be better if Mill was out."

"He's always out, according to Dhruv. I—" But I didn't get to finish. Sean's mobile vibrated across the desk. He picked it up and smiled.

"Bloody hell. It's Tom," he said, accepting the call. "How are you, my old friend?"

Chapter Two

I went to the toilet while Sean took the call and returned to find him animatedly rifling through his desk drawer. "Where are my keys?" he asked.

"They're your keys. How should I know?"

"Doesn't matter. Yours will do."

"House keys or office keys?"

"Don't you keep them together?"

"No."

"How on earth do you remember them? Don't answer. It doesn't matter. Have you seen anything odd in town today?"

"Odd, how?"

"Police. In West Street."

"No. But we've been together all day. I've only seen what you've seen."

"Hmmm." Sean wasn't listening and continued opening doors and half-heartedly moving files as if overwhelmingly distracted.

"What is it, Sean?"

"We need to leave."

"When?"

"In about ten minutes."

"Then why the drama? You've got plenty of time to find your keys."

He stopped in his tracks and faced me. "Good point."

"Where are we going?"

"To see Tom."

"Business or pleasure?"

"Murder."

I stared goggle-eyed. "Wow. Where?"

"Grosvenor Street, last night. And that's all I know."

"Male or female?"

"As I said, I don't know any details."

"They must be sure of their facts to involve us."

"It's off the record, strictly off the record. Tom doesn't know how the new inspector would view our little arrange-ment, and it's not a straightforward question to ask. So, he's playing it as if Kim were still the boss. We must be careful not to press him too hard."

"I can't believe it—another murder in our sleepy little town. We've only just seen off one psychopath. Presumably, this is a domestic matter?"

"Presume all you like. I don't know, and I'm not pre-judging."

"Are we meeting Tom at the usual place?"

"Yes. Assuming Fat Vi will still serve me. That trouble-making new waitress told her about our little nickname, and she wasn't impressed."

"I'm not surprised. It's rather childish."

"I think you mean humorous."

"I don't."

Sean raised an eyebrow. "Desist. I'm still the boss."

I smiled sweetly. "Glad you think so."

"Come on then," said Sean, grabbing his coat. He slid his hands into the pockets where they closed over a large bunch of keys.

"Found them."

"I never doubted you would."

Chapter Three

Fat Vi wasn't there when we arrived at the cafe. Instead, a young man stood uncertainly behind the counter, his eyes flicking between us and the doorway as if he might flee in fright. A heavy fringe flopped over his face, and he sported a raging bull tattoo on his scrawny white arm. His protruding Adam's apple wobbled in anticipation of our imminent conversation.

"Hello, hello," muttered Sean, evidently disapproving of the new staffing arrangement.

"Be nice," I whispered.

"Two flat whites and a sausage roll. What do you want, Sass?"

I eyed the unsavoury contents of the chiller cabinet and chose the least worst option. "One of those," I said, pointing to what I hoped was a croissant.

"Take a seat, and I'll bring it over," squeaked the young man in a voice an octave higher than I expected.

We scanned the room and saw Tom in his usual position at the back.

"Mate," said Sean, offering his hand while clapping Tom on the arm. I upped the ante and went in for a hug. Tom responded, holding me that little bit longer than necessary. I glanced at his tense jaw and bitten fingernails and wondered where the happy-go-lucky Tom of last year had gone.

"Must we?" asked Sean, wrinkling his nose at Tom's choice of table.

Tom went through the usual ritual of explaining why the nearby toilet was less of a problem than being seen from outside, and Sean, as ever, accepted his reasoning.

"Right. I haven't got long," said Tom. "And you'll hear about this soon enough. I thought you should have some context before Miles Savage hears the news and wrongly speculates in his rag."

"This meeting is unofficial, right?" asked Sean.

"Yes, and no. Unofficial from the point of view that you're not supposed to know, and official because Kim rang a few minutes ago. She's heard all about the murder and wants to return to work. And if Kim's back, she might need your help."

"Did she say so?"

"More or less. Kim has given me the green light to call you, and I didn't tell her I already had. There are many barriers to successful investigation these days, and your cavalier approach to the law can be helpful."

Sean beamed.

"If contained," continued Tom icily. "But don't get too carried away with that thought just yet. Kim may want you, but she's not on the case, and old ferret face is well-entrenched for now."

Sean raised an eyebrow. "Not a fan?"

"The man's a fool. Except that he isn't. Kevin Finnegan

is highly intelligent. You know the type, all brains and no common sense. Finnegan has a doctorate in psychology. God only knows why he joined the police. He should be lecturing at a university somewhere, but no. We get him. Deep joy."

I leaned across the table and reached for Tom's hand, trying to make sense of his furrowed brow and sagging cheeks, making him look like a depressed bloodhound. "What's wrong?" I asked.

"Apart from the murder," he said, snatching his hand away.

"Yes. Apart from that."

"Don't get me started. Now is not the time."

I banked the sentiment and let Sean change the subject, determined to call Tom later for more details and to offer a friendly chat.

"So, about this killing. Who is it, and how can you be sure he met his end through nefarious means?"

"It's she, not he, and keep your voice down," snapped Tom as the waiter arrived with our drinks. He placed the cups on the table, rattling them in the saucer as if the weight was too much for him to bear, before emitting an audible sigh of relief as he departed.

"Poor chap," I said, thinking aloud.

"Why?" Sean's tone was abrupt. He didn't appreciate the interruption.

"There must be something on his mind. Either that or he suffers from anxiety."

"Or girl trouble," said Tom.

Sean shook his head. "That one hasn't got a good shag in him."

"How very profound." I tried not to snap, but Sean, who was generally kind and well-disposed to humanity, was always at his worst in front of other men, having an inherent need to show off his alpha male credentials.

Tom slid up his sleeve and looked pointedly at his watch.

"Listen, and don't interrupt," said Sean, fixing me with a glare. Fighting the urge to respond, I smiled encouragingly at Tom.

"Yesterday afternoon, we received a call from a householder in Grosvenor Street," said Tom. "He'd heard noises in his garden the night before. Well, he's elderly and can't easily get around. So, it took him until after lunch to find the energy to go down to the bottom of the garden for a closer look."

"Left side or right of Grosvenor?" I asked.

Tom disregarded Sean's pointed glare.

"Right."

"The long gardens then?"

"Exactly. So, the householder dragged himself outside, sat on the bench at the bottom to catch his breath, and noticed a ginger wig. Except it wasn't. On closer inspection, it turned out to be human hair, attached to a human scalp, on a human body."

"Was she dead?"

"That's how it usually works in murder cases."

Sean raised an eyebrow at Tom's sarcasm. "It's a reasonable question, mate. They might have found the girl alive, and she died soon after."

"Alright. Accepted. No, she was already dead by the time we arrived. And before you ask, we don't know the time of death. Dai Davies is conducting the autopsy now."

"Vlad himself? Getting the big guns in then?"

"Yes. No choice, but I'll get to that."

"Before you do, who called it in?" I asked.

"I can't tell you."

"Once Miles Savage hears, it will be in the papers, and the whole county will know by tomorrow. Savage knows everyone in Truscombe and will knock up every resident in the street until he finds out."

"Does it matter?" asked Sean, flashing another irritated glance my way.

"Perhaps not. But Brendan's uncle lives in Grosvenor Road. You know the chap I mean. Colin Marshall."

"You're acquainted with Colin Marshall?" Tom leaned forward, suddenly interested.

"You know I am. We've discussed him before."

"Look. I can neither confirm nor deny his involvement. Particularly the latter."

"So, it is him." Memories of my uncomfortable visit to Colin Marshall's house flashed through my mind, and I shivered. Marshall was precisely the sort of person to find himself in this kind of unsavoury situation, with people loudly proclaiming they were not in the least bit surprised.

"You can remind me about it later," said Tom. "Time really is pressing."

"Okay. I'll summarise. You found the body of a young woman yesterday at the bottom of Colin Marshall's garden." Sean said quickly. "How did she die? Was she put there? What else do you know?"

"Cause of death as yet unknown, but the victim had extensive head injuries consistent with being hit by a heavy object. She may have succumbed to her wounds or died of exposure."

"Surely it isn't cold enough for that?"

"Ordinarily, but the girl was in a poor condition. We don't think the attacker carried her there. Her feet were bare and covered in mud with the cuts and abrasions you might expect to see in someone covering ground quickly with no care for what they were treading on."

"As if she were running away?"

"I thought so."

"Were you at the crime scene?" asked Sean.

Tom nodded but did not embellish.

"No wonder you look shattered," I offered. "Not a pleasant experience."

Tom sighed and stared directly into my eyes. For a moment, he looked like a lost little boy who needed a friendly hug. "I've seen worse," he muttered.

"Anything else?" asked Sean, tapping his phone in note-taking mode.

"There's not much more I can say."

"I suppose a name is out of the question?"

"I'd rather not."

"It'll be public knowledge in no time."

"Give me twenty-four hours. I'll tell you more tomorrow. I just wanted you to have the heads-up before Miles. Okay?"

Sean turned his phone face down and sat quietly for a moment. Then, taking the last bite from his sausage roll, he chewed thoughtfully, his eyes never leaving Tom's face. Tom and I watched and waited for Sean to tell us what was on his mind.

He licked his fingers, cleaned the plate of pastry flakes, and wiped his hands on a napkin. "Poor condition," Sean said. "The girl was in poor condition. What do you mean by that?"

Tom swallowed. "She was skinny and undernourished."

"How thin?"

"Emaciated."

"Anorexic?"

Tom shook his head.

"Dirty?"

"Very."

"Any other marks?"

Silence.

"Come on, Tom. I know you. What are you holding back?"

"Bloody hell, Sean. Whenever I stick my neck out like this, I wonder where it will end. Probably with my sacking."

"Well?"

"Yes. There was a mark. A deep mark, like a cuff."

"Where?"

"On her ankle."

"Jesus. Are you saying someone held her captive?"

"I'm trying very hard not to say anything at all."

"But you think so. And that's why you're telling me. You're worried this is like the Adam Harding case?"

Tom nodded imperceptibly.

Sean placed his hands over his mouth, staring far into the distance.

"Who is Adam Harding?"

"An old school friend," said Sean. "Otherwise known as the man in the cage."

Chapter Four

Sean was avoiding me. He'd walked away from Fat Vi's with a cursory, over-the-shoulder remark about visiting the chemist and didn't reappear in the office for the rest of the day. This was good news on the one hand, as working alone was always more productive, but also distracting, as I spent too much time wondering what he was up to. Sean was obviously upset about something, and it was unusual for him not to voice his concerns. But unlike me, Sean had plenty of friends and was no doubt leaning against the lounge bar in The Martingale Arms with one of his many confidants.

By the time four thirty arrived, I was growing impatient and annoyed at the lack of contact. Sean could at least have sent a quick text message to stop me from worrying. My eyes wandered between my computer screen and phone every few minutes until five o'clock arrived, and I locked the office with relief and made my way home, rehearsing what I would say to Sean when I next saw him. But the walk brought clarity, and I had a quick word with myself, recognising that I was behaving like a paranoid girlfriend. Sean was my boss. He'd been kind when I was at my lowest ebb, but he owed me nothing and certainly not an explanation of his whereabouts. It was his right to use his time as he pleased. And in fairness, he was always ready to work over the weekend while not expecting the same from me. Just because I hadn't yet made friends and Sean was drowning in them was no reason for jealousy. But I was envious, even if I didn't want to admit it, and reluctant to go home to Sean's house in case he wasn't there.

The closer I got to Carling Road, the slower I walked. Something about the prospect of approaching a house bathed in darkness, its occupant elsewhere and enjoying the company of others made my stomach lurch. My skin crawled with the realisation that I had become dependent upon my boss for friendship, which wasn't a healthy state of affairs, even though we got along. I needed to find ways of meeting new contacts before my solitude became permanent.

I mentally tallied up the number of people I knew well enough to call and invite myself in for a coffee. The list was short. It would have been longer had Velda not fallen victim to the Skin Thief, and now it was down to a doubtful two. Doubtful because one of them was Tom, and his friendship wavered depending on his mood. I decided not to chance rejection with him but throw myself on Dhruv's mercy and selfishly hope he hadn't made it up with Mill. I dialled his number and waited, my heart thumping as it rang out, disappointment growing with every ring. As I was about to give up and trudge dejectedly to Carling Road, Dhruv answered breathlessly. "Hello, Sass. What do you want?"

Charming, I thought. "Just called to see how you are," I said.

"Fed up."

"Me too. What's wrong?"

"Mill's gone out and left the flat in chaos. It's a mess, and now I'll be cleaning all night."

"Fancy some company?"

"I thought you couldn't face Bosworth House."

I swallowed at the thought of it. But the awful memories were no match for the prospect of being alone. "It's about time I got a grip," I said.

"Don't be too hard on yourself. Come over, and I'll clean the flat later. Have you eaten?"

"No. Be with you in five."

I turned into Prescott Street, where Bosworth House loomed ahead like a half-blind beast. Someone had boarded up the left-hand downstairs flat, and the brickwork beneath the window still bore traces of orange spray paint. No doubt some bright spark had sprayed choice words over the living accommodation, with little effort spared to remove it. Dhruv, always a stickler for tidiness, would no doubt have an opinion on the subject. Ignoring the frisson of fear snaking down my spine, I swallowed and practically ran towards Dhruv's flat before meeting resistance at the front door. Quite why I supposed I could wander in when I didn't live there anymore, I didn't know. But it took a few moments for me to remember I no longer had a key before ringing the buzzer.

"Come in, Sass." Dhruv sounded tired, and I hoped he wasn't going through the motions out of politeness.

I turned sharply left, unwilling to cast even a sideways glance at the opposite flat, and pushed Dhruv's door open. I found him in the kitchen, doing whatever one does to make lentil dahl.

"Smells good," I said, examining the kitchen and failing to see any signs of mess. "You tidied up then?"

"Not yet. No time," said Dhruv abruptly.

I didn't delve deeper. One man's mess is another's tidy space. The kitchen looked in good order to me, but now was not the time for nitpicking, so I let it go.

"Is Mill out?"

Dhruv nodded his head.

"Things still tough?"

"More than ever. It sucks. I never thought it could happen to us What we had was so strong. It's barely imaginable."

"I'm so sorry, Dhruv."

"Red or white?"

"Either. I thought you'd sworn off alcohol."

"I only drink socially. And not at all if Mum asks."

"I won't tell anyone."

Dhruv filled the best part of a pair of outsized wine glasses with an Australian Merlot.

"Good thing I'm not driving," I said.

"Whatever. What's wrong then?"

"I came to see you."

"That too. But there's more to it."

I paused, wondering what to say. Strictly speaking, Sean and Dhruv were friends. I just happened to live in the same building as Dhruv for a while. So, I could hardly expect his sympathies to lie entirely with me, and for a moment, I floundered. I needn't have worried. Dhruv understood.

"You can tell me anything," he said. "But be honest with me. I don't mind you offloading, Sass. Sean's not the easiest man to live with. But don't pretend you're here to see me when your needs are just as great."

"How do you know?" I asked, irritation welling inside me. I hadn't realised I was that transparent.

"You didn't reply to my last text, and that was several days ago, after another fight with Mill."

"Shit, I'm sorry. I meant to."

"I'm sure you did. And I could have picked up the phone too. Don't stress about it."

Dhruv fussed silently around the dahl for a moment, then took a couple of bowls from the cupboard. "Okay to eat off our laps?"

"Perfect," I said.

We took bowls and glasses into the living room. Dhruv reached behind the sofa and removed a matching pair of lap trays. He handed me one with a swan motif, eyes distant and sad. I guessed it belonged to Mill.

"Tell me about your troubles," said Dhruv, picking unenthusiastically at the lentils.

"No. You first. I sense your need is greater."

"That's why I have a therapist."

"Is it helping?"

"Not really. Tim says I'm too accommodating, a people pleaser. And, like any therapist, he wants me to talk things out. But Mill isn't interested. He won't admit there's a problem."

"Tim?" I said, momentarily distracted by the name.

"Yes. Tim Gibbons. Why?"

"How strange. I've seen him too."

"Really? Why are you under a therapist?"

"The hospital was keen, and Sean practically made me."

"I'm surprised. He's the cynical type."

"Me too, but it's a throwback from his police days. I should have been back for a second appointment with Tim by now, but I can't see it helping. I'm not good at unburdening myself to strangers and didn't feel any connection with him."

"Give it time, Sass.

"Why, when it's not helping you?"

"I can't solve my problems. That's down to Mill."

"Then why bother with therapy?"

"Some guidance, I suppose. And it helps to talk even if Tim's suggestions are impractical. And because I don't know what the bloody hell else to do."

"I assume you've tried talking to Mill?"

"Endlessly. He either agrees to change but doesn't mean it or refuses to face facts."

"What do you want from him?"

"To stop drinking and spend a bit of time at home."

"And when you put it like that, does he listen?"

"I just told you. Mill glosses over the drinking and promises not to go out so much. And sometimes, he succeeds for a day or two."

"Any chance of Mill seeking therapy?"

Dhruv laughed hollowly. "No. None at all."

"I'm so sorry. I don't know what to say."

"Why would you? There's nothing further to add. It's a mess."

"Do you want me to talk to Mill?"

"And say what?"

"That his behaviour is making you unhappy."

Dhruv blinked and turned his head away. His voice wobbled as he spoke. "I don't think he cares."

I placed my tray on the table and joined Dhruv on the couch, leaning my head on his shoulder as I held his hand. It was too much for Dhruv, and he burst into tears, sobbing loudly. I cried too, touched by his distress. Eventually, the wracking gulps faded, and his shoulders stilled.

"Take this," I said, handing him the glass of wine. He gulped deeply.

"Distract me, Sass. Make me feel better about my crappy life. I want to hear all your problems, every sordid little one of them," he said, brushing the last tears from his face.

I sipped my wine, collected the tray, and finished my last mouthful of now-cold lentils before answering him. My issues seemed minor in comparison, and the prospect of whining to my desperately unhappy friend made me feel like a fraud.

"It's nothing, really," I said.

"Yes, it is. And you're allowed to tell me. I don't own all the problems."

I smiled at his words, now a little lighter, less angsty. The old Dhruv. "Okay. But this is super lame. If you asked me to sum it up in one word, I would have to say loneliness."

"You're lonely?"

"Yes, I am."

"But you live and work with Sean. He's a handful and very loud."

"I know. And entertaining, vain, pushy and often unexpectedly kind. But what would I have left if there was no Sean?"

"Me?"

"That's kind, Dhruv. But I truly believe you and Mill will sort your problems out."

"Do you?" asked Dhruv, his face momentarily alight with hope.

"Absolutely. And then where will I be? Who would you go to if the worst came to the worst?"

"It's different for me. I'm friendly with a few of my work colleagues, and my sister's only a few train stops away. Mum and Dad don't shout at me if I accidentally Skype India in the early hours of the morning. But it would still be hard without Mill."

"I don't have a Mill," I said.

"Sean's your Mill, in a manner of speaking."

"He's really not. We're not; I hope you don't think... What I'm trying to say is our friendship has no hidden bene-fits. It isn't even a friendship. We're work buddies."

"I think you'll find it's more than that. Sean doesn't normally share his home with colleagues."

"As I said, he's been good to me. But we'll never be more than friends. So, I don't have a Mill or any other workmates. My brother, with whom I have no genetic connection, lives in Belfast. We only speak on high days and holidays, and I haven't got a clue who my parents are. For all I know, they grew me in a lab."

Dhruv nodded. "I get it. Fair point. You really should speak to Tim about your feelings. I tell you what—"

But I never got to hear his pearls of wisdom. The door flew open and slammed against the hallway. Dhruv shot up and darted through the living room door. Moments later, he returned an expression of resignation across his face. "You'd better go. Mill's back, and he's off his head on something. We'll catch up another time."

Chapter Five

"Where the heck were you last night?" sniped Sean as I mooched into the kitchen, too tired to shower before breakfast.

"At Dhruv's," I replied, searching the cupboards for oatmeal, and drawing a blank.

"Nice of you to let me know."

"Why would I? You were out, and I'd heard nothing from you all day."

"Probably because I went shopping and picked up your tea, as we discussed. And not a microwave meal. I made a risotto, now languishing in a plastic box in the freezer."

"But you hate that sort of food."

"Yes. But you don't. I thought I'd make an effort for once. I won't bother again."

"Sean. I'm so sorry. I assumed you were out. And anyway, I came home to a dark house, so you must have left again."

"Of course, I did. I wasn't in the mood to sit around in an empty house alone."

"Neither was I, hence my visit to Dhruv."

"Hmm. We must have crossed paths. I suppose I should have texted."

"Me too. Did you have a good night?"

"Not particularly. You?"

"It was fine until Mill came home and passed out in the hallway."

"Jesus. It's getting worse then?"

I nodded. "Dhruv's barely coping. Ah, the post. I missed it last night," I said, making for a small pile of mail on the kitchen worktop.

"Wait one," said Sean, snatching the envelopes away. He rifled through them, placed an open handwritten white envelope in his breast pocket and offered me the remaining letters.

The dull brown envelopes suggested they were all bills, and I opened them unenthusiastically. "Yours looks far more interesting," I said.

Sean placed a protective hand over his shirt. "Yes, well. It's from my friend, Jack. We'll talk about it later."

I raised an eyebrow, but Sean turned his back and poured another cup of tea.

I responded with an exaggerated cough.

"Sorry. Do you want one?"

"Yes, please. And while you're at it, is there anything for breakfast?"

Sean hit his forehead with his palm. "Damn. I forgot your bloody porridge."

"Never mind," I sighed, opening the fridge, and retrieving a yoghurt several days out of date. I unpeeled the lid and sniffed before taking a tentative mouthful.

"Can I ask you something?"

Sean placed his tea on the breakfast bar and hopped onto the stool. "Anything."

I tightened my dressing gown cord and joined him. "Adam Harding," I said. "The man in the cage. How come I've never heard of him?"

Sean's expression sharpened into a frown. "Ah, Sass. I don't know if I can face this on a Saturday morning. I want to relax."

"You said anything."

"Anything but this."

"Fine. Don't worry." I moodily stirred my yoghurt, no longer hungry. If Kim Robbins reappeared and asked us to help with the murder, I didn't want to be ignorant of a crime with possible connections to it.

"Are you being snarky?" Sean challenged me, a steely glint in his eye.

"No. I'm eating my breakfast."

"You've gone very quiet."

"There's not much to say. You clearly don't want to talk about it. Hopefully, you'll change your mind by the time Kim instructs us."

"If, Sass. If."

"Tom seemed very sure."

"I suspect it's wishful thinking on his part."

"Whatever." I dismounted the stool, tossed the yoghurt pot into the ostentatious steel bin far too big for the kitchen, and proceeded towards the door.

"You've left your tea."

"Thanks. I'll take it upstairs."

"Sit down, Sass."

"Why?"

"You're right. You should know about Adam."

"Look. Tell me on Monday at work. That way, you get

an uninterrupted weekend. I mean, it's not normal living with your staff, is it? If I had my own place, I couldn't ask you awkward questions at inappropriate times."

"I said, sit down."

"Is that an order?"

"Don't be like that. I'm trying to get it right. This is uncharted territory for both of us."

I grabbed an apple and a knife from the drawer, sat down and started chopping while Sean explained.

"Before I tell you what happened, you should know something about my family."

I looked up, puzzled. I hadn't expected this.

"You've met my brother Mike."

I nodded.

"And you're MyPerfectLife friends with Kev."

"Yes. His posts are hilarious," I said. "And his private messages about you make me laugh out loud."

I smiled, expecting Sean to respond accordingly, but he stared downcast at his plate, his grey eyes distant and sad.

"You may not know that we started life as a foursome. I don't talk about my middle brother Bryan if I can help it. It's still too painful for my family."

"Oh, Sean. I didn't know."

"You wouldn't. It happened a long time ago."

"Only tell me if you want to."

"I can't give you any context if I don't. Let's just do it and get it over with."

Sean sipped his tea and marshalled his thoughts. "So, the four of us were quite close in age. Mum popped a child out almost every year. Four under-fives. It must have been hell. But she loved her boys and wasn't bothered about not having a pink one."

"Bless her."

"Yeah. Well, my brothers and I often hung out together. Not so much, Kev. He's the baby. But the rest of us..." Sean drifted away momentarily, lost in thought.

"You played together," I said gently, trying to ease him back on track.

"Often. Then one day, we were messing around by the Washpool, playing hide and seek with a bunch of school friends. There must have been a dozen or more of us. I was twelve, Mike eleven, and Bryan a little younger. Kev stayed at home that day, thank God. Anyway, there weren't many places to hide around there, and we were all a good distance away when Graham Strong shouted, 'Coming ready or not?' I hid behind a gorse bush and Mike behind another. I could just about see Mike, but Graham couldn't. Not that it mattered. Graham was useless at games, and I remember being stupidly bored by the time he finally found Mike. I couldn't face any more time squatting on my haunches, patiently waiting for Graham to track me down, so when he turned away, I crept up behind him and dug my fingers into his ribs. Graham jumped a mile. He was super ticklish, and I swear to God, he must have pissed himself. Mike and I laughed our backsides off. And that was pretty much the last time we smiled for a good few years after."

Sean gulped, and I debated whether to reach for his hand. But I didn't know how he would react, and it wasn't the time to take risks with unfamiliar displays of tactility. "Go on," I said.

"As we walked towards the others, Morgan Williams tanked up, screaming at us to fetch help. They'd found Bryan face down in the Washpool with a great cut on the side of his head. He'd slipped, cracked his temple, and passed out with his face in the water. Mike ran to fetch Dad, and I sprinted over to Bryan. By the time I arrived, Adam had pulled him out and was performing CPR. And he did it, Sass. Bryan lay there, grey, and unmoving, without a breath in his body. But Adam wouldn't give up. He kept going and going, and it was like a miracle. Bryan twitched, coughed a river of water and started breathing unaided."

"Wow," I said, relieved. "I thought you were going to tell me he died. Where is Bryan now?"

"In Truscombe cemetery," said Sean. "He didn't make old bones. Bryan suffered severe oxygen deprivation. We don't know how long he lay there before we found him. It could have been ages. But he was out long enough that he couldn't function properly again. An anoxic brain injury, they called it, a bit like a stroke. Bryan could move, blink, and make eye contact, but he couldn't speak or walk. And his lungs were shot to pieces. He was in the hospital for a year, and we converted one of the downstairs rooms and had him home for another year after that. But despite a full-time carer and Mum's undivided attention, he couldn't survive—too much damage. But thanks to Adam, we borrowed Bryan for a little longer and got used to the idea of losing him. It wasn't a shock when he died. More of a relief."

"Your poor parents."

"Yes. It's not the natural order of things. Mum still keeps Bryan's room exactly the same, even all these years later."

"I'm sorry. So sorry. I get why you didn't want to talk about it."

"But do you understand why I must?"

"Not really."

"I owe a debt to Adam Harding I can never repay. He gave us hope. And he didn't have any formal first-aid train-ing, only sheer willpower and dogged determination to keep going. When I think back, I feel so ashamed. I was the elder brother and the one in charge that day. I should have saved Bryan. But I was a trembling wreck, benignly watching as if it were happening to someone else's family."

"That's because you were too close. It's not a failing, Sean."

"It is to me. You need to understand that Adam is my hero. Almost like a blood brother."

I hesitated before asking a question that would not lay still in my head.

"Then why have I never heard of him? You talk about your other friends."

Sean bit his lip. "That's a tricky question to answer. It's fair to say that Adam became a recluse after the cage incident. But to tell the truth, I hadn't seen him for a few years before it happened."

"How strange. Can you tell me why?"

"Not really. It doesn't paint me in a good light."

"Then don't."

Sean faltered. "My relationship with Adam was fine while we were in school. We saw each other daily. Then he went to university, and I joined the police. We'd occasionally meet when he came home but saw less of each other as time passed. And if I'm honest, it suited me. I couldn't see Adam without visualising Bryan. And it got to the stage that whenever we met, all the feelings of guilt and inadequacy supplanted any pleasure in seeing him. Adam was my hero but also my tormentor. Not through any fault of his own, but by being in the wrong place at the wrong time and making me feel like a coward."

"So, Adam is a bad memory?"

"Exactly."

"You must have had mixed feelings when you discovered what had happened to him."

Sean's head snapped up, and he glared. "Of course not. I was gutted for him, poor bloke. My God. None of this was Adam's fault."

"I didn't mean that."

"I know. But it's a complicated situation. I would never wish ill on Adam. And as much as I would have happily avoided seeing him, I was as good a friend as possible, given the circumstances. As soon as I heard, I went straight round to his house. And I know as much as any man about what happened during Adam's imprisonment. He gave me a first-hand account of his time in the cage."

"Care to share?" I asked gently, unsure whether Sean would embellish.

"Yes. That's the point of this conversation. I'll tell you everything I know, and when you hear the inevitable gossip, you can make a rational judgement. I don't buy the alleged connection between the dead girl and Adam, whatever Tom says, especially now we're three years on. But if someone imprisoned her, that's the tree they'll go barking up. So, do you want to make another brew and crack on, or would you rather get some clothes on?"

My half-dressed state was making me feel uncomfort-able, but I didn't want Sean to go off the boil. "More tea," I said, sliding from the bar stool while double-checking the state of my dressing gown knot before reaching for the milk. Sean sat silently, staring at the work surface as I skittered around the kitchen, trying to make tea before he changed his mind. As soon as the kettle boiled, I slammed a cup in front of him, sloshing the tea into a ring on the counter and receiving a frown.

"Sorry," I said.

"Not important. Right. Let's do it."

44

Chapter Six

"Think back to pre-covid times when we were coming and going normally with no concerns about germs or working from home," said Sean. "I hadn't seen Adam for a while and wasn't the only one. His brother had lost track of him too. Now, Adam lost his mother many years ago, and his father met an American widow and moved abroad, leaving the boys in the house. And when I say boys, I mean full-grown men. After all, Adam's my age. Then Alex Harding left when he met his wife, and Adam bought him out of his share of the house, which their dad had signed over by then. Adam added space and value by extending the property, and all seemed rosy. Long story short, Adam lived alone, and nobody noticed when he vanished."

"Not even his employer?"

"That's the thing. Adam was working from home long before Covid made it fashionable. He's an architect, you see, and takes on private jobs. His house is one of those big buggers on the edge of town with plenty of room for an office. So, he went missing, and literally, nobody realised."

"It's hard to believe. I know barely anyone in Truscombe, but someone would miss me after a week or two."

"Ah, but yours is a different working pattern. Things might have been different if it had dragged on, but it wasn't unusual for Adam to come and go from the property, staying away for a few nights if the mood took him."

"What exactly happened to Adam?"

"A calculated plot to harm him, and he never found out who was behind it. Adam's not short of a bob or two, and his house has all the mod cons. You'd think an architect's job was a pretty safe bet in terms of personal security, but you'd be wrong. The year before he vanished, Adam was working on a project, getting heavily involved with the planning application for a complex, expensive job near Tewkesbury. The development was in a small, sought-after village involving the type of job planners usually run a mile from. But despite much protest from a well-organised group of activists, they unexpectedly passed planning permission. The decision went down like a lead balloon, and the villagers formed a pressure group cyber-stalking all the parties involved. For some unfathomable reason, they became fixated on Adam, who they blamed for an outcome they hadn't anticipated. Typical nimby's, Sass. The worst kind. All upset about their properties being downvalued."

"Perhaps they had a point?"

Sean grunted. "Either way, it wasn't down to Adam. Sure, he knew a few people, but the planning permission was above board."

I badly wanted Sean to get to the point and swallowed down a retort to that effect. Chewing his lip, Sean continued.

"Anyway. The protesters got hold of Adam's contact

details, making his life hell for a few weeks. I'm sure you can imagine what they did, spamming his emails and telephone calls at all times of the day and night with only silent breathing at the other end. He changed his phone number, but that didn't help, and just as he was considering calling the police, it all stopped. Things returned to normal, and he carried on with his life. By then, he was on another job somewhere in Cheltenham, and he thought that was that."

"But it wasn't?"

"Nope. Adam opened his post one day to find a letter threatening to kill him. And not your normal run-of-the-mill letter, but something straight out of a mystery novel. You know the kind of thing, words and letters cut from magazines."

"A poison pen letter?"

"Something of the kind. Well, Adam ignored the first one and put the second through the shredder. He said there was a third, but I don't know what happened to it. Not that it matters. He assumed it was fallout from the planning application and didn't stress about it. It's a lot easier to ignore post than phone calls and emails. So, he carried on regardless. Then one night, his dog disappeared."

"Oh, no. I don't want to hear this," I said, putting my hands over my ears.

"Why?"

"I can't bear cruelty to animals. And I don't want to know if his dog died."

"Don't worry," said Sean. "No dogs were hurt during this event."

"But it disappeared."

"How about I ruin the punchline and tell you it returned? The dog pitched up of its own accord and was taken in by a neighbour. It was a little thin and had been wandering in the woods. But it's safe, well, and was reunited with Adam as soon as he left the hospital."

"Thank goodness," I said, relieved. "But how did they get the dog?"

"Adam didn't know but assumed someone had wandered into the back of his house. Quite reasonable when you consider it borders open fields, has an unsecured back gate, and he never locked the doors while he was at home. Anyway, they pilfered the dog, and Adam realised it was missing pretty quickly, but before he could go out and look, he noticed a white envelope on his doormat."

"What time of day was this?"

"I don't know. I didn't ask. Does it matter?"

"It might do," I said, feeling aggrieved at the lack of detail.

"Whatever you say. But what was inside was more important than when it arrived. The letter, looking much like the others, directed Adam to an abandoned property on the edge of Truscombe Woods. They told him to hightail it over quickly if he wanted his dog back. So he went, without delay."

"I'd do the same if it was my dog."

"It wasn't a smart move though," said Sean. "Adam should have told someone and, better still, asked them to join him. He admitted that himself."

"You must have felt odd hearing this story when you hadn't seen each other in years."

"Yes. But only briefly. It's one of those friendships that picks up fairly easily, as long as I don't think too hard about Bryan and my colossal lack of courage."

"You're too hard on yourself."

Sean ignored me. "Adam talked more than I thought he would. But the poor guy was completely traumatised. He'd barely eaten for ten days when they found him. Fortunately, his assailant left a pail of water in the cage. But for that, he'd have died."

"Did Adam tell you the details?"

"Most of them, I think. He said he'd struggled to say anything to the police, and it was easier chatting to me."

"I guess he didn't realise how hard it was for you to see him after losing Bryan," I said, my words trailing lamely away as Sean steepled his hands.

"I hope not. Adam must have noticed my absence over the years, and I hate the thought of upsetting him. But there was no awkwardness that day."

"Where did you meet Adam?"

"At his home. The weather was decent, and we sat on the lawn. By then, he'd had a few good meals, but I could still see the weight loss. He was a shadow of his former self, and it was hard to carry on as normal. You know what I'm like. I don't take life too seriously. But I chose my words carefully that day, like I've never done before, to avoid giving any offence."

"You'd be unlikely to hurt his feelings."

"But I could have inadvertently upset him with a nervous joke or lack of sensitivity. Sometimes I'm brash, but I value Adam too much to risk saying the wrong thing. I was on my best behaviour, Sass. And I think that's why he revealed so much of his ordeal."

"How did it happen?"

"He arrived at the empty building, and whoever took his dog had left the cottage door ajar. Adam looked around the ground floor and saw nothing. He climbed the stairs, and all the rooms were empty. So, against his better judgement, he went down to the unlit basement and found a large iron cage in the corner big enough to hold a man."

"He should have run the hell out of there."

"Under any other circumstances, he would have done. But remember, he was looking for his dog. And the dog was like a surrogate child. Adam wasn't married, and his family was away. The dog stayed with him day and night, and he'd take it to his appointments where opportunity allowed. He and the dog made a regular pair. We live in the Cotswolds, after all."

"But if the dog eventually found its way home, it couldn't have been caged."

"Correct. It wasn't. But Adam didn't know that. He saw a large lump in the corner of a poorly lit metal box and thought the worst. No way was he leaving without Ludo."

"Ludo?"

"The dog, Sass. Keep up. He had no choice but to go inside. So, he did and found, to his relief, that the lump was just a rolled-up blanket. Then suddenly, the cage door slammed shut. Adam turned to see a man in a balaclava pocket the key and sprint up the steps."

"God, how awful. He must have been terrified."

"Not at first," said Sean.

I shrugged. "Why not?"

"Because he thought it was revenge for the planning issue. Someone wanted to teach him a lesson and would return to let him out when they thought the time was right. Adam said he'd been furious and had raged through the night. But as the next day passed, and he grew hungry, he started to worry about what would happen if they didn't let him out. By day three, he had screamed himself hoarse and rationed the water to a few daily sips. And by the time the boys found him, he was at death's door, doomed to starvation and literally hours from death."

"I can't bear to think about it," I said, shuddering. "What boys?"

"A few likely lads from school, involved in some dare or other. Thank God, though. Or he'd never have been found."

"Too isolated?"

"Oddly enough, it's one of a pair of semis. But the old girl next door is hard of hearing. And the basement is solid stone. She wouldn't have heard a jackhammer, never mind a human being."

"But your friend recovered?"

"Yes. And was in good health the last time I saw him nine months ago. Still, if Kim and her crew are going to pick this apart, or God forbid Miles Savage gets to it, then I'd better pay him a visit to warn him."

"Are you sure you can face it?"

Sean's lip wobbled momentarily. "I owe him," he said.

Chapter Seven

I slept poorly that night for worrying about Sean. His happy-go-lucky nature had vanished on Saturday and was still missing in action by Sunday breakfast. Visions of Bryan face down in the sheep dip woke me twice in the night, and I wondered how Sean ever slept, having seen it first-hand. Sean thought of himself as a coward, but his revelation about Bryan gave me a growing respect for my boss. I couldn't imagine handling the rest of my life as well as he had after such a trauma, and once showered and dressed, I went downstairs to pass on my newfound regard. But the carefully rehearsed words stayed in my head. Sean wasn't there and must have quietly left the house while I was getting ready.

Sighing, I boiled the kettle, opened the ready-made oats Sean had purchased sometime yesterday and cursed as the foil top tore. I stirred it, balanced a saucer on top, and returned upstairs for my laptop. In the absence of a scintillating conversation from Sean, I picked up my emails at the kitchen counter. There were disappointingly few, considering I hadn't checked for a day or two, and most were too dull to open, but one from Root and Branch DNA testing caught my eye. I gave it a cursory glance, feeling the usual swell of disappointment at a routine email telling me to check the website for a new message. But as I had nothing better to do, I went ahead. I was keying in a password change after a scatty moment when I completely forgot it when Sean arrived, laden with two plastic bags.

"Dinner?" I asked, hopefully.

"Yep."

"Yum. What is it?"

"Lizard food. Help yourself. They're a generous lot and don't mind sharing." Sean hefted the bags onto the kitchen island.

"Must you?" I grumbled.

"A few dead insects won't do you any harm," he replied.

I averted my eyes as he decanted the bags and finished my password reset while he fussed over the lizards in the living room. Once on the website, I clicked on a highlighted bell symbol indicating a new message.

I was about to read it when a browser notification pinged on the screen from my therapist. I clicked the message to find another email reminding me that my second appointment was overdue. "No bloody chance," I said, deleting the email.

"Of what?" Sean reappeared in the doorway.

"More therapy."

"I think you should."

"So, you keep saying. But it's a big fat no from me."

"Right."

Sean loitered in the doorway as if waiting for me to say something. I raised an eyebrow. "What is it?"

"We need to talk," he said, clutching an envelope.

But I wasn't listening. I'd finally opened the Root and Branch message to find a wholly unexpected communication and stared open-mouthed at the screen."

"Oh my God," I said.

"What's wrong?"

"A DNA match. Listen to this."

"Not now, Sass. We need to talk."

"But this is important."

"My news is too. And as it's imminent, I should let you know before it happens."

"Hell, Sean. Your timing is terrible."

"Concentrate," he said as I stared unblinkingly at the message, trying to take it all in.

"Come on, Sass." Sean gently pushed the laptop lid down.

"How rude."

"I'd like your complete and undivided attention for a few minutes. It's not too much to ask."

"Really? I've spent the last year trying to trace my birth family. This had better be good."

Sean pulled up the second breakfast stool and sat down before laying a handwritten letter on the counter.

"Ah. I recognise that. It's the mail you were so coy about yesterday."

"I was picking my moment," said Sean.

"I don't like the sound of that."

"It's no big deal. I just thought you should know."

"Know what?"

"My mate from my days at Hendon police college is coming to stay."

"Really? What mate is that then?"

"Jack. Jack Drake. You haven't met him."

"Yet," I said.

"Yet."

"When's he coming?"

Sean glanced at his watch. "In an hour or so," he said glibly.

"Wow. Nothing like a bit of warning. No biggie though. Any friend of yours is a friend of mine. How long is he staying?"

"Well, that's the thing. Jack's just split up from his wife. More accurately, she's kicked him out. So, a while."

"When you say a while?"

"Indefinitely."

"Poor chap. It must be a miserable time for him. And a long stay in the boxroom won't be comfortable."

"I'm glad you understand."

"Of course. If there's anything I can do to make him feel better, you've only to ask."

"Amazing. Then you won't mind swapping rooms."

I stared at Sean, shocked and unprepared. We'd only discussed my living arrangements a day or two previously, and now he wanted me to make way for one of his old friends.

"Seriously? I haven't found anywhere else to live yet. It could take a while."

"I realise that. And I'm not asking you to move out. Of course not. Stay as long as you like. But Jack's a married man with kids and weights, not to mention a large exercise bike. I can hardly ask him to cram it all into a tiny room. Most of your stuff is in storage. And you said you'd be happy to help."

"But he's about to arrive. Couldn't you have mentioned this yesterday?"

"I couldn't face it with all that stuff about Bryan. I didn't know how you'd react. Thank goodness you're being reasonable."

I crossed my arms to disguise my clenched fists and hoped Sean wasn't a closet mind reader. The thoughts swirling in my head were barely legal, much less reasonable. And my earlier admiration for Sean's fortitude in the face of adversity crumbled. But I was in no position to decline. "Sure, I'll move rooms if it helps," I said through gritted teeth.

"That's my girl," Sean grinned, visibly relieved. "You'll love Jack. He's a good laugh. We'll get on famously, like the three musketeers."

"Great. Tell me where I can find the spare linen."

"No need. I made up the boxroom bed yesterday."

"How kind." I grabbed my laptop, tucked it under my arm, and stomped upstairs to pack. It didn't take long. As Sean said, most of my effects were nestling in a box in the Truscombe storage centre, and I'd only brought what I needed to get by. I had debated collecting more of my things but couldn't face it then. A pity, as had my room been full, Sean wouldn't easily be able to evict me now. And that's what it felt like to my sinking heart. Sean had turfed me out for a well-regarded friend because I didn't occupy that place in his life. I was someone he employed, no more, no less. Loneliness stabbed like an icepick through my heart for the second time that week.

I finished half an hour later and still feeling aggrieved with Sean, I grabbed a book and curled up on the bed for a read and a sulk. Then I remembered the partially read message on Root and Branch, flipped open my laptop and took a closer look.

From: Longfellow999#
To: SassD32

> *Dear SassD*
>   *Any chance I could access your family tree? I've recently tested my DNA and good news! We have 879 centimorgans in common. I'm no expert, but that sounds like a first-cousin match. Only I've no unaccounted-for cousins! Drop me an email and let me know your thoughts. Better still, open up your tree if you have one.*
>   *Have a nice day now. CL.*

I stared at my screen, open-mouthed at the unexpected match. I'd always hoped for news of my genetic family, but this was big. A first cousin match was a dead cert lead to my parents. My hands shook as I typed my reply.

To: Longfellow999#
From: SassD32

> *Wow. Thanks for your email. I'm still in shock. I can't let you access my tree because I don't have one. Being adopted with no information about my birth parents has made it impossible. Please tell me more about you. Do you know my parents? Where do you live? I'd be grateful for anything. Sass.*

I felt slightly sick when I pressed send, and the message disappeared into cyberspace. And I rocked backwards and forwards on the bed, wondering about the Longfellow handle. The word fellow indicated a chap, but it might be a female cousin interested in poets. What did Longfellow write? I quickly typed the name into Google. Ah, yes. Henry Wadsworth Longfellow was the author of Paul Revere's Ride. Did that mean my cousin was American? Could I be from the USA? My mind swarmed with possibilities as I stared vacantly into space. I was still staring when a car pulled up and tooted loudly outside. The door slammed open, and a jumble of voices filled the air. I knelt on the bed and watched from the window as Sean bear-hugged a tall, stocky man wearing aviator glasses and a black bomber jacket.

"Mate," said Sean, loudly enough for half the street to hear. "Give me your bags and get yourself inside."

I sighed as I turned around, feeling more than a little envious of their bonding ritual. Short of flying to Cyprus, I had no female friends to offer an equivalent girly hug. And my old friends had doubtless been posted away by now. My fault for not staying in touch. I contemplated emailing to find out who was where, but dreading the response or potential lack thereof, I decided against it. Luckily, another browser notification drew my attention to a further message. I eagerly refreshed the screen and headed back to Root and Branch.

From: Longfellow999#
To: SassD32

> *Hi, Sass. Well, that explains that. Somebody in my family hasn't been entirely truthful. This situation is complicated and might be easier to discuss in person or on the telephone. I live in Gloucester-shire. How about you? How do you feel about giving me your phone number? Or call me if you like. Say the word, and I'll send my mobile number to you. All the best, Callum.*

Callum. I repeated it aloud, practising as if I had never heard the name before. After all the years of nothing, I had a cousin called Callum. My only known living genetic relative, well, currently, at least. I hoped all would soon become clear and I'd encounter many more. But first, I needed to compose a reply.

From: SassD32
To: Longfellow999#

> OMG - me too. I live in Gloucestershire. Can we meet up? I'm free any night this week if you are. BTW, I live in Truscombe.

I waited with bated breath, but Callum replied almost immediately.

From: Longfellow999#
To: SassD32

> I'm in Dursley, so a bit of a trek. For reasons I won't bother you with, I'd rather not meet in Truscombe. How about Woodmancote? There's a friendly little pub on Stockwell Lane. Is Friday week at 5.30 any good for you?

From: SassD32
To: Longfellow999#

> Perfect. I'll be there. See you then.

I sat quietly for a while, taking it all in and fantasising about being part of a family again. Perhaps I had a loving mother and father and siblings to go along with my newfound cousin. I bolted for the door, desperate to share the news with Sean, then stopped short, remembering Jack was here. But perhaps he would understand and be happy for me, even though I was a perfect stranger. I stepped downstairs, listening to their easy conversation punctuated with laughter, and sat on the stairs waiting for a gap to arise. I didn't mean to eavesdrop. It just happened. Jack asked about Callie, and Sean's voice dropped to a conspiratorial whisper. "I called her about an accounting matter, and now she's started texting me in the wee small hours about her marriage problems," he said. "It's a pain in the arse. I'm happy to listen, but it's not what Callie wants, and I can't lead her on. Not sure what to do, if I'm honest."

I crept back upstairs, not listening to Jack's reply. Sean hadn't told me he'd spoken to Callie, yet he'd just confided it to Jack as if they were the best of friends and saw each other daily. And despite the welcome news about my cousin and a potential new family, I had nobody to share my news with. I had never felt more alone in my life.

Chapter Eight

I recovered from my hurt feelings overnight, spoke sharply with myself in the shower, and consigned my misery to oblivion. I had a cousin I would meet in a few couple of weeks, which trumped any in-your-face macho friendships. So what if Sean confided in Jack? Why shouldn't he? I mentally pulled on my big girl pants and got a grip on the day.

Sean was dipping soldiers into a boiled egg when I waltzed into the kitchen.

"Want some?" he asked.

"An egg. I'd love one."

"Er, I meant a soldier," he said, offering a piece of buttered toast from a heap cut into identically sized slices.

"No. You're alright. I'll cook one myself."

"No can do."

"I'm not the best chef in the world, but even I can rustle up a boiled egg."

"You could if there was one."

I contemplated the second empty egg cup on his plate.

The greedy pig had already eaten one. Two for him and a big fat, nothing for me. And considering the amount I paid for my rations, it niggled. I made for the larder cupboard, hoping Sean had stashed another oat pot inside. I didn't want the day to start with an argument. Not when I had made peace with my wounded feelings. And to Sean's credit, three pots in varying flavours occupied the top shelf.

We ate our breakfast in companionable silence, Sean reading the sports page of the Truscombe Gazette and me snickering at talking dogs on TikTok. Then Sean's phone buzzed as a message came through.

"Ah, ha. The Robbins returns."

"Kim?"

"Yes. She's back in the nick," he continued, scanning the phone. "Wants us to come over. Good. Might get that money paid and a few more leads."

"Did you speak to Callie?"

"Kinda."

"Well?"

"Never mind Callie. We need more business, Sass. And Kim's the way we'll get it. Good old Tom knows his stuff. Why does Kim want us to keep a low profile?

"What do you mean?"

"Here," said Sean, sliding his phone down the counter.

I grabbed it and read the message.

Morning S. Back at work today. Are you free for a catch-up this afternoon? You, me, and Tom? Oh, and you can bring your girl if you like; up to you. I'm in my old office. Avoid FF if you can - he commandeered room 22 while I was away.

"How rude. I'm not your girl."

"Come on, Sass. She means nothing by it."

"Fine for you to say. I'll tag along like a spare part, shall I?"

"Like Tom, you mean? He's Kim's assistant, and I don't hear him moaning about it."

"Fine. Whatever. I wonder what Kim wants."

"I don't know. But it can only help us understand what's going on."

"And who is FF?"

"Ferret Faced Finnegan. You were there when Tom told us the other day. Pay more attention."

"She's very unprofessional."

"Like you don't talk about me when you're pissed off."

I rapidly replayed the recent conversation with Dhruv in my head. "Actually, no. I speak of you, but not disrespectfully."

"Good to hear, but unnecessary. I get on my own nerves at times. I'm sure you have some legitimate gripes."

"Morning campers." Jack Drake loped downstairs and bowled into the kitchen, barefoot with a pair of socks in his hands. I stared at his hammer toes, repulsed.

Sean spotted my expression and frowned. "Coffee?" he asked.

"Perfect. Two sugars and heavy with the caffeine."

"This is Sass," said Sean over his shoulder as he boiled the kettle in an introduction that felt like an afterthought.

"So I gathered. Pleased to meet you."

Jack's palm was warm, his handshake firm and seemingly sincere.

"I've heard a lot about you," he continued, his faint crow's feet wrinkling the delicate skin around his eyes. He clapped me on the shoulder as he spoke, and his blue eyes sparkled more than they ought, considering his circumstances. "And not all of it bad," he continued.

A sudden attack of shyness momentarily rendered me

dumb, and I cocked my head and smiled before it became awkward.

"Don't get on the wrong side of her," said Sean. "Sass can nag for England when she gets the bit between her teeth."

"Very funny," I said. Misogynistic bastard, I thought.

"He doesn't mean that," said Jack. "Sean says you're the best partner he's worked with in a long time."

"Only because I sacked the last three." Sean grinned as he handed me a cup of tar-like coffee while audaciously winking. My hackles would have risen at his laddish jocularity if I were a dog. Why did he think taking the piss was better than singing my praises? It was good to hear it from a third party, as Sean sure as hell wouldn't tell me himself. Sean Tallis had been a stalwart supporter while I was in the hospital. He couldn't have been nicer. But our living arrangements were bringing out the worst in him, and he was starting to behave like a husband of many years standing, routinely taking their poor beleaguered wife for granted.

"I'm off to work," I said, scraping the last of the oats.

"Don't go on my account." Jack seemed sincere, but he was hovering around the barstool I was sitting on. There were only two, and with Sean halfway through his breakfast, it didn't take a genius to realise I'd be the one expected to vacate.

"See you at the office," said Sean. "And grab some sandwiches on your way. Mustn't be late for Kim."

Chapter Nine

Far from keeping a low profile, we ran straight into Kevin Finnegan the moment we set foot through the door of Truscombe police station. He was standing at reception with his hands on his hips, lecturing a group of constables about the importance of misgendering.

He glanced up, and a flicker of recognition crossed his face. "Ah. Mr Tallis. Well, well. It's been a while. How are you keeping?"

"Decently well," said Sean. "You?"

"Promoted and running a murder investigation. I'm a busy man these days. I hear you've jumped on the private investigator bandwagon."

Sean pursed his lips, and I recoiled from the sudden testosterone surge. From the undisguised sneer on Finnegan's face and Sean's white knuckles, there was clearly no love lost between them. Some past history, no doubt. But to his credit, Sean let the barb pass.

"Yes, I'm a PI. We work for you guys now and then."

One of the police constables looked up sharply and anxiously glanced at his colleagues.

"I'll thank you for not using inappropriate language around here."

Sean stared at Kevin Finnegan, genuinely baffled. I could see him mentally considering whether a swear word had inadvertently slipped from his lips.

"What did I say?"

"Guys. We don't use that term. It is not a catch-all and is deeply inconsiderate. If you don't know someone's personal pronoun, then ask."

"It's just an expression."

"Not in this police station. Now, what do you want?"

"I have an appointment. Catch you later."

"With whom?" Finnegan took a pace forward until he was inches from Sean's face. Now firmly on the warpath, he wanted information and intended to get it.

"Nothing important. Nice to see you again."

"Where are you and the young lady going?"

Kevin Finnegan manoeuvred between Sean and the door, barring his way. Sean flexed his knuckles, and just when I feared he might hit him, he lowered his voice. "Young lady? Who are you calling a young lady? Have you asked Sass their preferred pronouns, or just made a crass assumption?"

A beetroot flush crept up Finnegan's narrow face, stopping at his temples. Even the comb-over didn't disguise the pink scalp through his thinning hair. He opened his mouth, floundering for an appropriate response.

"I'll let it go this time," said Sean. "But think before you speak in future."

Finnegan was still speechless as Sean led the way. He

strutted through the double doors to the foot of the staircase while the constables sniggered behind.

"So, now I'm gender-neutral?" I asked, feeling awkwardly disingenuous. I cared about fibbing even if Sean did not.

"That's not what I said. I'm not as blunt as you think, Sass. Sure, I'm not politically correct, but I'd never deliberately hurt someone's feelings either. I'm not against sensitivity, but old ferret face uses it for his own ends. If you live by the sword, you die by the sword."

"No cliches in there at all."

"You know what I mean."

"But it's the opposite of what Kim asked us to do. You know, avoid confrontation."

"What is?" Tom loomed up behind us and hissed loudly in Sean's ear.

"Give over. You nearly perforated my ear drum. And now it's covered in spit."

"What have you done now?" Tom was persistent.

"Nothing. Just gave Ferret Face a dose of his own medicine."

"Unwise. He's already gunning for Kim."

"Don't tell her then." Sean chewed his lip as he considered the consequences of baiting Finnegan.

"In you go." Tom opened a door at the far end of the corridor and ushered us through to a small, unprepossessing room overlooking the car park.

"How are the mighty fallen," said Sean.

"I heard that." Kim Robbins strode into her new office, dropped a pile of files on her desk, and sat behind it. "Shut the door, Tom. Sit down, Sean, and..." She tutted and clicked her fingers.

"Sass," said Sean.

"Sorry, Sass. Have you recovered from your injuries?"

"For the most part. You?"

"Yes. Better. I had a nervous breakdown. Best to get it out there. Then we don't need to pussyfoot around."

"I didn't realise. Sorry, Kim," said Sean.

"No reason you should. It happens to the best of us. But I'm fine now, and luckily, we have a psychiatrist on standby twice a week. It's helpful."

"As I keep telling Sass."

"Not here," I said, narrowing my eyes. Kim could wear her breakdown like a badge of honour but my mental health was private and not up for discussion.

"Right. Want to know why you are here?"

"More work?" asked Sean, hopefully.

Kim reached into her desk drawer and popped a few pills. "Ultimately, if I can get it past Inspector Finnegan."

"Must you answer to him?"

"For the time being." Kim's voice quivered with restrained emotion.

"What's his status?"

"He's heading the murder investigation, if that's what you mean."

"And yours?" Kim blanched. Trust Sean to be so forthright.

"No official title." Kim uttered each staccato word as if in pain.

"Are you in the briefings?"

"Of course."

"Hmmm. If it's up to Finnegan and you have no standing, we're unlikely to see much work coming through."

"Mind your mouth, Sean. It's not all about you." Kim's hands shook as she raised a glass of water to her mouth.

"He didn't mean it like that," I said, glaring at Sean for his indifference to Kim's humiliating position.

"Of course, you still have standing. Bad timing that you came back with an investigation in full swing. It must be frustrating."

"It is," said Kim, casting a rare smile in my direction. "My strategies are somewhat different to Inspector Finnegan's."

"You mean he has any?" Tom quipped and then bit his lip. "Sorry. Inappropriate."

"Enough. I haven't much time." Kim glanced at her watch and steepled her hands. "Callista Hart holds the purse strings, and Inspector Finnegan currently has her ear. I will get you involved. God knows we have insufficient staffing, which will become evident to him sooner or later. But there's a more pressing matter. Tom's briefed you about our murder victim, right?"

Sean nodded.

"And he's told you there's evidence of captivity."

"Not sure I agree, but you're the experts."

"Well, we need to speak to Adam Harding."

"I thought you might."

"Good. Then where is he?"

Sean's face crinkled. "You must know with all the resources at your disposal. Adam lives on Broadway Road."

"We know his address, but he's away. I want to chat with him, even if only by phone."

"Sorry, I can't help. I intended to visit myself, but Adam didn't answer my text."

"Pity. I knew you were friends and hoped he might have shared his plans."

"I haven't seen Adam for a while, but his dad lives

abroad. He could have gone for a visit. I can let you have his brother's address if that helps?"

"Thanks. It will save time. Let me know if Adam contacts you."

"Is it that important?"

"Yes. We're not making much progress with Ella Burton, considering her notoriety."

"Notoriety? Tell me more."

"Not now. I've promised to pop in and see our part-time psychiatrist, and he's off soon."

"On-the-fly therapy? A sign of the times, perhaps?"

"Not for me. He wants to pass on some pearls of wisdom about why a person might enjoy caging things."

"Sounds interesting?"

"Come and meet him then. It's a general chat and, undoubtedly, stuff you can find online. I'm sure he'll speak freely."

"Excellent. We'd love to."

I trailed behind Sean and Kim as they headed down the corridor. They might find it fascinating, but I was in no mood to hear about psychiatry so soon after encountering the resident psychopath in Bosworth House. Feeling more than a little queasy, I lagged behind, casting anxious glances towards Tom and trying to ignore the pounding in my temples.

Chapter Ten

I grabbed and dry-swallowed some pills from my bag as we entered a small office farther up the corridor. A swift glance soon revealed the station psychiatrist was Tim Gibbons, with whom I'd been playing cat and mouse over the last few months. I inwardly groaned at the sight of him at close quarters, but not a flicker of recognition crossed his face, and I breathed a sigh of relief, hoping I'd got away with it.

Kim introduced us and asked Gibbons if he would mind sharing his thoughts. He smiled broadly, seemingly pleased with a larger audience.

"No problem," he said. "Take a seat."

We clustered around a Formica-topped desk on plastic chairs that would not have looked out of place in a junior school.

"Do I know you?" asked Sean, cocking his head and regarding Gibbons suspiciously.

"I don't think so."

"Sure?"

"As I can be." A frown crossed Gibbons' face, and I

kicked Sean's leg under the table. He had driven me to my only therapy session and must have seen Tim Gibbons about the place. But for me to remain below the radar, he needed to keep quiet about it. Besides, I didn't appreciate the potential invasion of privacy. Sean looked up, startled, before mellowing as an expression of comprehension crept across his face. He shut up and listened.

"What are we dealing with here?" asked Kim, cutting to the chase.

"If only it were that simple." Gibbons worried at a Saint Christopher hanging around his neck, twisting the fragile chain between his fingers.

"Break it down then."

"I'll try. Can I speak openly?"

"I suppose so. But I was expecting some general psychiatry."

"You'll get it. But I need to know the circumstances surrounding the victim's captivity."

"You've read the report."

"From cover to cover. Just clarify something, please."

"Go on?" Kim tersely spoke as if she was already getting bored.

"The report mentions evidence of restraint on the female body together with a head wound. I'd like to know more."

Kim shifted uncomfortably in her seat.

"Shall we leave?" I asked as Sean flashed an angry look my way.

The offer seemed to calm Kim. "No. But keep this very quiet. I mean it. It'll all end up in the Gazette by the end of the week, but I don't want it getting there because of this conversation."

"Come on, Kim. Discretion is my middle name." Sean

spoke jocularly but with an undertone. He wasn't impressed that she needed to ask.

"Good. Well. The post-mortem revealed blunt force trauma to the skull."

"To what degree?" asked Sean.

Kim flipped open a brown file. "Abrasion, contusion and laceration of the scalp, cerebral contusion and a subdural bleed."

"Hmmm. Messy," said Sean. "Any chance she fell?"

"Unlikely, but not impossible," said Kim. "But factor in the restraint marks, and that's another story."

"Describe them?" asked Gibbons.

"Marks and abrasions to the lower leg. Swelling and bruising above the ankle with a three-inch indentation around the..." Kim broke off and scanned the page. "Around the left leg consistent with a shackle."

"A meaty shackle," said Sean holding up his fingers in an approximation of the size. "A big restraint for a small girl."

"How do you know?" snapped Kim.

"You just told me."

"No. That the victim was small."

"She was a young girl, and as I haven't heard otherwise, it's a reasonable assumption. Are you about to reveal she was of Amazonian proportions?"

Kim sighed. "No. She was slight, hadn't eaten for a while, and you'll already know about her drug use from the papers."

"Strangely, I didn't," said Sean. "But I'll take your word for it."

Kim ignored him and turned to Gibbons. "Is that good enough?"

"To go on with. Now, I know you can't be sure, but do

you think the two kidnapping crimes are linked?" Gibbons asked.

"We haven't categorised them as kidnappings yet," Kim replied.

"Then you should. Both show evidence of abduction and captivity."

"The reasons are self-evident when it comes to Harding. But the girl had an expensive drug habit. Who knows what lengths she might have gone to in order to fund it."

"Are you suggesting the victim allowed someone to shackle her?" Sean shook his head incredulously as he stared at Kim.

"It's possible if she needed the money."

"But unlikely. There must be better theories."

"Of course." Tim Gibbons jumped back into the conversation before Kim and Sean came to metaphorical blows. "There are many reasons to hold someone against their will."

"Go on?"

"Kidnapping generally boils down to financial gain which might be a ransom, extortion or involuntary servitude."

"Such as?"

"Slave labour, for example."

"Anything else?" asked Sean.

"The commission of a further criminal act against the person."

"Like sexual assault," I offered, grimacing at the thought.

"Exactly that," said Gibbons.

"Which theory best fits here?" Kim asked the question as if expecting an easy answer, but Gibbons frowned.

"No idea," he said honestly. "Either could apply to the

young woman, assuming involuntary placement of the leg restraint. The man in the cage is a different matter. If I've read the notes correctly, extortion or ransom could be a motive."

"Or revenge," said Sean darkly.

"It's possible but unlikely, in my opinion."

"Do you have much experience in human captivity?" asked Sean.

Kim shot him a sideways glance, but he raised an eyebrow and waited for the reply.

"Not much." Tim shrugged his shoulders candidly. "Helen, my colleague, has more. One or two recent cases, I believe. But she's in London for the rest of the week. Anyway, I know the principles, if not the practice, and it's the best I can offer you now."

"Mr Tallis was not questioning your credentials," said Kim, narrowing her eyes.

"Of course not." I hoped Sean's insincere smile wasn't as obvious to the others as it was to me.

"What kind of person enjoys restraining another?" asked Kim.

Gibbons stroked his chin. "I'll bypass financial kidnappings for now. That's an entirely different motivation. Let's focus on long-term captivity. Have you heard of Jaycee Dugard?"

"Yes. A young girl kidnapped as a child and held for eighteen years," said Kim.

"That's right. And sadly, there are others of that ilk. Elizabeth Fritzl, Amanda Berry, Natascha Kampusch and Colleen Stan all spring to mind."

"And Stephanie Slater," I said.

"You look too young to remember that case," said Gibbons.

"I was. I mean, I am. But I read about it."

"It's not quite the same," he replied. "Yes, Miss Slater was held and assaulted, but there was a financial element to the crime. Michael Sams intended to profit by blackmail."

"It doesn't make sense," said Sean, going off on a tangent.

"What doesn't?" Gibbons narrowed his eyes, and I detected a growing dislike between the men. Sean and Gibbons that is. Tom sat impassively, quietly absorbing the information without needing to contribute.

"All the cases you mentioned involve women who were seriously sexually assaulted. That didn't happen to Adam."

Gibbons raised an eyebrow and glanced at Kim.

"Harding wasn't attacked, just abandoned," said Kim.

"Are you sure?"

"If anything like that happened, he never said. I suppose it's possible."

"Or not. And there was a lot more to his imprisonment than you suggest." Sean spat the words angrily, his offence at the implication evidenced by a red flush inflaming his face.

"Calm down." Kim's words had the opposite effect, and for a moment, I wondered if Sean would storm from the room. But, containing his rage, he reiterated. "Adam's captivity was born of revenge. He told me that himself."

"That's rarer," said Tim. "And likely differentiates his case from the other. "Was the young woman assaulted?"

Kim did not answer, and Tim continued, taking it as read.

"We don't fully understand the motives for these crimes," said Gibbons. "Kidnappers follow a pattern, but not the same pattern. There are variations, naturally. But in the long-term captivity cases I mentioned, the kidnapper had some basic sexual need or fantasy that fuelled their behaviour. And this need, together with the natural assumption that the world revolves around them, indicates a personality disorder."

I bit down the temptation to say, *no shit, Sherlock.*

"And what causes this behaviour?" Kim seemed equally unimpressed, examining bitten nails as she asked the question.

"It might be a sense of powerlessness from an abusive childhood," said Gibbons. "And some psychologists will tell you it's from biological predispositions. I must disagree, I might add. But that category of kidnapper is dangerous because they don't have any guilt or feelings for the people they hurt."

"So, we're looking for a narcissist?" asked Kim.

"I'd rather not apply labels, but certainly someone with a personality disorder, perhaps an anti-social personality or a narcissist, as you say. And the abductor may have a paraphilic or abnormal sexual impulse."

"A deviant?" asked Tom, who had finally decided to participate in the conversation.

"Well." Gibbons hesitated.

"Not necessarily then?" Kim wanted details, not waffle.

"In the cases I mentioned, yes, for sure. And by that, I mean deviancy through humiliation, pain, abuse, and torture; behaviour that involves an imbalance of power. And another thing. They were all young women, so paedophilia may have been a factor. Essentially, the long-term kidnapper creates a false sense of reality, sometimes provoking Stockholm Syndrome in his victim. You know what I mean by that?"

"Of course," said Sean.

"Enlighten us." Kim was determined to get her pound of flesh.

"After a while, the captive may develop positive feelings towards their abductor like loyalty, or even affection."

"It doesn't fit well," said Sean, sliding his chair back and putting his hands behind his head. "We've every reason to suppose the young girl was fleeing, and at the risk of repeating myself, someone was threatening Adam long before they lured him to the cage."

"That's not in the report," said Gibbons.

"We'll need to talk privately." Kim glanced at Sean, and he imperceptibly nodded his head.

"But it's not necessarily deviancy?" I asked, replying to Gibbons' earlier comment.

"No. It wouldn't apply to Mr Harding, but in the right circumstances, the girl could be a victim of coercive control."

"I've had some experience of that," Kim replied. "But none with long-term physical restraint."

"That doesn't mean it can't happen. Depending on the girl's circumstances, it's worth considering."

"Well. Thank you, Dr Gibbons. You've been very helpful. That's all for now."

We left the room and walked a few yards up the corridor where Sean and Kim parked themselves against opposite walls, and Tom and I hung behind like shadows.

"Sorry. Not quite what I was hoping for," said Kim.

"Seems you're looking for a sociopathic, narcissistic, deviant with a personality disorder. Good luck with that."

"It's not cut and dried, though, is it?"

"Evidently not."

"Did you report back on your conversation with Adam Harding? You seem to know more than we do."

"I was one of you back then."

"Only just. You'd had one foot out the door for some time. It doesn't excuse withholding information."

"I didn't know what Adam had officially said. As you say, I was working my notice and not involved in the case. And we weren't talking murder anyway. You shouldn't be bandying these two cases around in the same context. It's not the same perp or MO."

"Okay. Calm down. We'll talk about it another time."

I left them bickering and accompanied Tom to the water fountain, where he poured me a cup before departing. I was about to wait for Sean in the car when Tim Gibbons strode up the corridor. I smiled and turned away but sensed that he had slowed. And sure enough, when I turned around, Gibbons was lurking motionless behind me. Then he pulled a white card from his top pocket, scribbled a note, and thrust it into my hand. I turned it over and scowled at an assumptive therapy appointment. The man was more aware than he looked. He had rumbled me.

Chapter Eleven

I spent the rest of the afternoon alone in the office, Sean having an appointment with a potential client in the more respectable of Truscombe's two coffee shops. Or, more accurately, the one with the real barista and not Fat Vi's greasy spoon. But I didn't mind. I was coming to the end of a fraud investigation involving a dodgy bookkeeper and had presented my findings in a well-constructed spreadsheet covered by a Word document. I slid it into a plastic spine, added an invoice and inserted my business card. Admiring the professionalism of my work, I popped it into an envelope and put it in my bag for posting on the way home. Feeling accomplished, I smugly shut the office. It's the small things that count in the end.

"Sloping off early, are we?" asked a familiar voice as I left.

"Dhruv." I flung my arms around him as he came down the stairs as if I hadn't seen him forever.

"Wow. You're almost as enthusiastic as Mill's mother's Labrador," said Dhruv.

"I'm just pleased to see you. How are things?"

"The same." Dhruv shrugged despondently.

"Ah, I'm sorry. What happened to Mill the other night?"

Dhruv checked his watch. "I'm running late, Sass. You going home?"

I nodded.

"I'll walk you to the end of the road; then, I must fly."

"Going somewhere nice?" I asked as we left the building.

"To check in with my therapist."

"I saw him today."

"Good. I'm glad you've finally seen sense."

"I mean professionally, not personally."

"Why?"

"Just police stuff. And not that helpful."

"Ah." Dhruv stared distractedly ahead, and we walked a few paces in silence. I missed the old Dhruv, whose words spilt from his mouth in endless chatter. The happy-go-lucky man I first met last year had been absent for some time.

"Things better between you and Sean?"

"They're certainly different. Two have become three."

"Sorry?"

"A new kid on the block."

Dhruv sighed. "Too cryptic. You'll have to spell it out. I don't have the time."

"Sean's moved an old friend in. Jack Drake."

"Good. That should ease the tension."

"Or make it worse."

"You'll just need to make the best of it, Sass." Dhruv's tone was curt. I inwardly considered whether it was the right time to tell him my family news, but the silence was growing uncomfortable, and I blurted it out with little thought.

"I've had a hit on Root and Branch with my DNA. I'm meeting my cousin next week."

Dhruv's eyes lit up, and he grinned. "Go you. Well done. That's fantastic news. You're only a few steps away from finding your parents."

"Hopefully."

"Are you excited?"

"More like terrified."

"All the luck in the world, my friend," said Dhruv, hugging me tightly. He held my hand for a few brief moments before releasing it.

"I must go. Catch you later in the week. I want to hear every little detail."

"You will," I said, waving until he was out of sight.

I arrived at Sean's house in good spirits. But they dropped as soon as I opened the door. The house was still and empty. Not a boss or a house guest in sight. I slung my handbag under the stairs, grabbed my phone charger, and slumped on the couch by the lizards while I read an online newspaper. The first few stories were the usual doom and gloom, but the fifth, a brief article about the Truscombe death with next to no detail, caught my eye. I hoped that the national press was a few steps ahead of the loathsome Miles Savage, lead rat of the Truscombe Gazette. But a glance under the coffee table disabused me of that notion. I could read the headline from the couch and, more importantly, realised that Sean had been home earlier and moved it from the mailbox to the lounge. Feeling grubby at the thought of reading anything by Savage, I nevertheless devoured the article, confirming Ella Burton's status as a drug user, her scandalous past, and an implied slip into prostitution. But the text, though heavy on innuendo, was light on facts, and I decided to make an effort to learn more about her. I placed the paper back under the coffee table and glimpsed one of the lizards with its feet against the glass casting a causal stare my way. I watched it for a few moments, feeling guilty. Was its fate any worse than Adam Harding's when he was caged? At least the lizard had food, but never one second of privacy. Perhaps lizards didn't value solitude like humans. Then I realised I was overthinking, dropped a couple of dried pellets in the cage and made for the kitchen.

A folded note greeted me, propped upright on the work surface between the salt and pepper pots. I opened it.

Hey, S. Hope your afternoon wasn't too boring. Don't wait up. Jack and I are out for the night. Going for a few bevvies with Tom. Boys at play and all that. Promise not to make too much noise when we come in. :) There are fresh gnocchi in the fridge and a stir-in sauce in the cupboard. Oh, and a KitKat for afters, you lucky thing. Who says I don't look after you!? Have a good night.

I balled the note and hurled it towards the swing bin. It missed and ricocheted onto the floor. Sean probably thought he was being kind when he purchased my tea. But kind would have not been disappearing with half of my friendship group, i.e., Tom. At least not without extending an invitation my way. Why hadn't he thought to ask me? I racked my brains and couldn't think of the last time I'd been out socially other than to visit Dhruv. Was I such a bore that they'd rather leave me behind to fester?

I opened the fridge and removed the gnocchi but was too apathetic to cook. Instead, I boiled the kettle, made a cup of tea and resumed my seat on the breakfast stool, cupping my drink and trying to remember what it was like to be out. I remembered days of old listening to the buzz of chatter, a little music and feeling slightly woozy from a glass of wine and good company. A tear slipped from my eye onto the imitation granite work surface. Feeling pathetic, I wiped it away, but I knew from the lump in my throat that it was too late. One tear followed another as the kitchen clock ticked loudly in the silent room, and loneliness engulfed me. I thought of Mum as she was before cancer took her, Auntie Doreen mouldering in the dementia home, and my brother Connor miles away in Dublin. And I let it all go, sobbing loud and long until I was too tired and empty to continue.

I located the KitKat, made another tea and went upstairs, thinking I might as well have an early night. Instead, I dived into the shower, which worked wonders for my apathy, if not my mood, pulled on a pair of tracksuit bottoms and curled up on top of my bed, intending to read. But I was too sad to concentrate, and as I pondered the day's events, I thought about Ella Burton. Now would be as good a time as any to learn a little more about her.

Heaving my laptop from under the bed, I balanced it on my knees, snapped the KitKat in two, and Googled her name.

Chapter Twelve

I was unprepared for the slew of results when I typed *Ella Burton, Evesham*. Line after line, page after page of newspaper headlines, filled my feed. I clicked on an article from one of the red-top papers, but the barrage of adverts almost crashed my computer, so I tried a more reliable news source.

The *Cotswold Courant*, a well-respected newspaper covering the North Cotswolds, Wiltshire, and, more importantly, Worcestershire, came to the rescue. Containing news without fabrication or scandal, it was as far away from slimy Savage's rag as humanly possible, and I knew I could expect a balanced story. I sorted the results into date order and clicked on one published late in 2015.

Cotswold Courant, Wednesday, March 18, 2015
Teacher on trial for schoolgirl abduction faces four years in jail.

Schoolgirl Ella May Burton, who turned eighteen last week, appeared in Worcester Crown court today to give evidence on behalf of her former lover, deputy head teacher Marcus Catton. The girl, whose name was not released until recently for legal reasons, said their relationship happened largely at her instigation. Catton, 45, had indulged in a harmless flirtation with the girl for several months, which eventually turned into a physical relationship when he drove her home following an after-school detention. Ms Burton claimed she kissed him goodbye while placing her hand in an intimate area. The following day, she waited for him after he covered an absent colleague's physics class, and they shared a kiss in the science lab a few hours later. Over the coming weeks, Catton tried to distance himself, but Ms Burton sent him emails, and they began sharing intimate tweets and texts. Ultimately, their feelings deepened, and Ms Burton successfully persuaded Catton to book a hotel room for the afternoon when she was only fifteen, although they stopped short of intercourse. But a sexual relationship developed after liaisons in his car, in classrooms after school hours, and once at her house while her parents were away.

Catton, a married man, knew their relationship was illegal and attempted to extricate himself on several occasions, fearing the loss of his job, reputation, wife and young family. But Ms Burton claimed she could always change his mind. Matters came to a head when Burton confided in a friend who told her sister. Rumours of the affair circulated, with Burton knowing it was only a matter of time until her parents found out. After a difficult Christmas at home, Burton persuaded Marcus Catton to leave his family and run away with her. They fled to Wales and embarked on a ferry to Ireland, where they rented a property in Cork, living together as man and wife for over a year. But the Garda was alerted after Burton contacted a friend and let slip their location. Catton was taken into custody, and Burton returned to her parents.

Ms Burton asked the court to show Catton leniency, admitting she had fully encouraged the relationship. But Clive Wentworth, QC, argued that the girl could not legally consent as she was underage.

Catton, from Ashton Under Hill near Evesham, denies abduction but pleads guilty to sexual intercourse with a minor.

Intrigued but keen for more detail, I searched again, finding, to my delight, an article from an online magazine with a first-person account by Ella. Though likely the work of a ghostwriter, it was full of interesting facts, potentially giving me an insight into how her mind worked. Now hungry and on a mission, I copied the article into Word, expanded it to a bigger font and sent it to Sean's printer downstairs. Then I took fifteen minutes to heat my gnocchi, poured a glass of wine, and settled back on my bed, eating as I read Ella's story.

Put Your Feet Up Magazine, Friday, 24th August 2018

Ella Burton made headlines in 2015 when she fled the country with her 45-year-old married science teacher, Marcus Catton. Now twenty-one and living close to Catton, recently released from prison, Ella reflects on the decisions that changed their lives.

I didn't fancy Marcus Catton when I first saw him. Miss Drury had taught science at Honeybourne Road High for most of my time there. She was laid back and didn't push us too hard. So, when Marky took over and started giving out detentions in his first week, we thought he was bad news. It didn't take long before I changed my mind.

I was always outgoing. It's not that I didn't respect the teachers, but I didn't see them as my betters. And if I wanted to say something, I did. So, when Marky attended a parents' evening in a new sharp suit, I told him he looked good in it, and he smiled. The next day, he gave us back our essays and marked mine with an A minus. I'm not saying he reacted to the flattery, but it was my highest grade in ages, and it felt good. A week later, I struggled with a physics question. I could have looked it up, but I was last out of class and figured asking Marky might be a better bet. He was short of time but told me to return at the end of the day, so I did. Long story short, he offered me extra tuition on Wednesday nights and I agreed. I followed his profile on MyPerfectLife, and he messaged me a few times, then thought better of it and unfriended me. I remember how hurt I felt when I realised he'd done this, even though nothing had happened between us. Then Marky suggested using Quickchat, and that's when things hotted up. At first, we messaged in the evening. All innocent to start with, but then I sent him a selfie of me all dressed up for a friend's party. Marky liked it, then changed it from like to love. My friend Francine had vodka and wine at her house. I drank a few glasses, started feeling brave, and sent Marky a picture of me in my underwear when I got home. He replied with a single word: more. So, I took my bra off and sent another.

School was awkward the next day. Marky looked embarrassed, and I felt hurt by his coldness. But when Wednesday evening came, and I went to meet him for extra tuition, science went out the window. I'd hardly been there five minutes when he shut the door and sat beside me. He pointed to something in the textbook, and our fingers brushed together. And that was it. Our lips locked, and my body burned with anticipation. Marky took my hand and walked me to the stationery cupboard, where we kissed until our lips were raw— but only kissing. Nothing more, even though I tried to instigate it by touching him.

Marky wanted to wait until I was sixteen, but I couldn't bear it any longer. One night after extra tuition, I asked him to drive me home. He wouldn't drive us directly from the school in case anyone saw him, so I met him in a layby a little way out of town. He picked me up and turned the car as if he intended to drive to my parents' house, but when I told him I'd lined up an excuse for being late, he changed his mind. I'd told Mum that my friend Nat and I had a late detention, and I was going to her house for supper afterwards. Mum had no reason to doubt me and wasn't the kind to check with Nat's parents. And Marky's little shrew of a wife, Abigail, had just started a pilates class. Usually, he'd have to babysit, but her sister was stay-ing, leaving Marky free for the evening.

They say your first time is the worst, and you must grin and get through it. But it wasn't like that for me, even though we did it in the back of his car. Marky was gentle and did everything possible to make me feel good. And if I wasn't in love with him before that night, I was his forever from that moment on.

We kept it on the down-low for ages. But things turned sour for a while when his wife wanted him to look after the kids in the evening. It wasn't like she had a proper job. She sold cosmetics from a catalogue and did all her work after school. Marky supported the family financially but said his wife needed her independence. And that was all well and good, but not on a Wednesday night, which was our only real chance to be together. Anyway, we started seeing less of each other, so I got friendly with a new group of people who knew how to have fun. Zed and Trisha lived on the other side of town and made their money running a line from a group in Birmingham. I hadn't much experience with drugs, but it didn't bother me if that was their thing. It soon became mine too. But as time went by, the inevitable happened. I got careless, and Marky found me on the top playing field, high as a kite and not giving a shit. He went ballistic, blamed himself and made me promise to stop. I said I would if he spent more time with me. I don't know what he told his wife, but from then on, we were closer, leading to more promises and sex, with Marky falling heart and soul in love with me. Everything worked for a while, but it didn't last.

Marky and I had taken to meeting in Cheltenham. The town was close enough to get to and big enough that we were unlikely to be seen by anyone we knew. But luck was against us, and we crossed paths with blabbermouth Kenzie Bailey in Yates wine bar just as we were kissing. Gossip flew around the school. Everywhere I went, they stared at me, openly asking if I was shagging the teacher. And I liked him, well, loved him by then, so although I said no, it was a half-hearted denial. Deep down, I wanted our relationship to be official, even though I knew our situation would never be acceptable.

It all turned sour one day when I entered the school library, where Marcus was supervising a lunch club. The librarian literally manhandled me from the room for fear that Marky's reputation would suffer from being around me. And I knew then that it was only a matter of time before things got out of control.

I worried about how it would go down at home. Mum was laid back and didn't bother me much, mainly because she didn't care. Not about me specifically. Just life in general. But Dad was big on disci-pline. And though he wasn't especially fond of me either, he'd have been furious at the thought of a teacher taking advantage. I didn't see it that way. If anyone had taken liberties, it was me. But Dad had a short fuse at the best of times. He'd make damn sure Marky went to prison, probably with a pair of black eyes.

We might have flown under the radar if we'd ended our relation-ship there. But I couldn't bear the thought of never feeling Marky's lips on mine again. I loved him with everything I had, and there was only one solution. We needed to go far away immediately.

Cork was Marky's idea. He had a friend who'd relocated there, who was pleasingly loose in the morals department and happy to shelter us until we found our own place. We fled late one night. I still remember tiptoeing past our sleeping dog as he snuffled in the hall-way. It was the only time I doubted myself. I could cope without my parents, my school, and my friends. But leaving my dog, Hunter, was painful. Karma bit back when Hunter died while I was in Ireland, but I didn't find out until I returned. Anyway, Marky got a job as a builder's labourer. It was a bit of a climb down, but he didn't mind.

He quite enjoyed the physical work, and I liked how he looked in tight jeans with horny builders' hands, especially when he lost the beginnings of his pot belly.

Marcus didn't expect me to work, but I lied about my age and got a job as a carer in a private home. I could have been a serial killer for all they knew, but their keenness to pay in cash and their blasé attitude to checking documentation suited both of us. Marky and I were happy even though he missed his kids. I dyed my hair, making me look older, and Marky's weight loss did the opposite for him. Somehow, nobody realised or mentioned our age difference. I honestly thought we'd make a life in Ireland growing old together. Then one day, I did something foolish.

It was early February, and I woke up to the realisation that it was Francine's birthday. She was my best friend at school, and I had an overwhelming urge to contact her and wish her a happy birthday. I was careful not to ring from either of our pay-as-you-go mobiles, so I called her from a payphone at the station. Francine's number was one of the few I remembered by heart. I'd stored most of them in my old phone, now languishing somewhere on the bed of the Irish channel where I'd thrown it from the ferry. She answered her mobile immediately even though she couldn't have recognised the number and was so pleased to hear from me she made me cry. We chatted for ages, but I didn't tell her anything about my life or give any clues about where I was staying. But she made me promise to call her back, and I did fortnightly for the next few months. Needless to say, I didn't mention the call to Marky. Then one day, while Francine and I were speaking, I let my location slip. I didn't mean to, not consciously, but the Garda arrived the next day, and that was that.

The court case was a horrific ordeal. Poor Marky took the brunt of it. I tried telling them it was my fault, but they insisted he'd taken advantage of me. The locals called him a paedophile and trashed his car. Marky got three years inside. He's out now, but only just. I thought he might get in touch with me when they released him. But then I found out he went back to his wife. It hurts like hell. I guess Marky feels he must go back for the sake of the children, but it's not right or fair. Marcus has ended up in a better position than me. I went home for a while, but Dad chucked me out, saying he couldn't have drugs around his younger children. I'm not a heavy user. I could have given it up if Dad had been reasonable about me staying. And no. I don't blame Marky. Not really. I wish we could meet up and talk it out. We could still have a future. I will always love him.

Do I have any regrets? Yes. I wish I hadn't contacted Francine. I'd still live in that little rendered cottage in Blarney Street, perhaps with my own children—a little boy like Marcus and a daughter I'd adore, faults and all. I still believe in love. I want someone to love me, to like me. But how did love cost us both so dearly?

Chapter Thirteen

"Sad isn't it," I said, slumping back on my office chair and feeling a twinge of pain from my old injuries.

Sean looked up, bleary-eyed. He'd arrived home in the small hours, woken me up as he bounced from every wall, and made it to breakfast as I was preparing to leave the house. Sean had arrived at the office an hour after I did, headed straight for the coffee machine and drunk three cups on the bounce. He was still a horrible colour and barely feigning interest in the papers I had ambushed him with at the earliest opportunity.

"More like inevitable," scowled Sean. "They couldn't have expected it to end any other way."

"Did you read the article?"

"Of course. You just watched me."

"Then you know Ella hoped for a happy outcome."

"But she was just a kid."

"And they had the life they wanted for a year."

"Is there a point to this?"

I swallowed an angry retort. "Only that I thought

learning more about the dead girl would be useful. After all, we are investigators."

"But not in this case."

"Yet," I said.

Sean sighed. "Fine. We'll get our turn soon but take a break in the meantime and do something we're likely to get paid for." He opened his desk drawer and reached for an aspirin. "And where has your inner accountant gone? This conversation usually happens in reverse."

"I was trying to get a few steps ahead of the game, Sean. Aren't you interested?"

"Not today."

"Did you have a good night?" I asked, despite myself. I had tried hard to feign indifference, but curiosity was getting the better of me.

Sean grinned. "Not bad. We might have hit the clubs."

"In Truscombe?" I literally snorted. The closest thing we had to a nightclub was Patsy's, a dingy bar with a tiny dance floor and a rotating supply of cheesy eighties music, bringing an otherwise excellent decade into disrepute.

"Yes, in Truscombe. There's nothing wrong with Patsy's. It's a good laugh. You should try it."

I clenched my fists but resisted the temptation to bite back about my exclusion from their boys' night out. "How was Tom?" I asked instead.

"Boring. He left at eleven o'clock. Said he needed a good night's sleep for his date tomorrow."

"Fantastic. Is he back on the internet dating circuit?"

"How should I know?"

"Don't you talk?"

"Sure, when it's quiet. But a wild night out isn't the time for it."

"So wild that Tom left early."

Sean ignored me. "How about Jack?" I asked. "Did he enjoy himself?"

"Mostly. When he wasn't wallowing in misery about his marriage."

"A night to miss then?"

"No. It was great once Jack got over himself. You should have seen him on the dance floor. That guy can move."

Out, as soon as possible, if I have my way, I thought, but I didn't say it.

"Moving on to Ella Burton. Are you really not interested?"

"I refer you to my previous answer."

"But the reason she died must be in her background. In the magazine article, she admitted she was running with a gang from the county lines."

"Way back when."

"Evesham is her hometown, and it's small. We know Ella was recently involved with drugs, and Savage implied she'd ventured into prostitution."

"Like he knows."

"He must have heard it from somewhere."

Sean sighed. "Recap for me again."

"I knew you weren't reading the article. Your eyes just glazed over."

"Recap or stop talking. My head is throbbing."

"Fine. Ella ran off with her teacher. They got caught. He went to prison; she returned to Evesham. They released him, and he returned to his wife with his tail between his legs. Ella's father kicked her out because she was using drugs. I've no idea what happened to her mother. I did a little more digging when I got to work this morning. Ella was still living in Evesham until three months ago. Nobody reported her missing, probably because they didn't notice.

Ella had been sofa surfing for some time. I can't see any evidence of employment. Savage may be right. Ella needed money for drugs and could have resorted to working on the streets."

"The police will be all over this."

"It's drugs. Nobody will fall over themselves to help the law."

"Except their snouts."

"Really?"

"Kind of. They'll have some. Not the same ones that I did."

"In Evesham?"

"Cheltenham too."

"I know the problem is universal, but I don't like to think of drugs in Cheltenham."

Sean cast a disdainful glance my way. "Get over yourself," he said.

"I know. I was only saying."

"It's a good point though," he mused.

"Cheltenham being too nice for drugs?"

Sean made the international sign for zip it. "I mean contacts in Evesham," he continued. "I could get hold of my guys at a push."

"Then do it."

"Slight issue."

"What?"

"Funding," said Sean, rubbing his fingers together. "Strictly *quid pro quo*."

"Ah. And Kim can't access a budget."

"Nope. Not while Finnegan's in charge. Still, it might be a short-term investment for us."

"Exactly what I thought. So, when are we going?"

"I haven't said yes yet. Wait on." Sean hunched over his

screen and lifted his head moments later with a sparkle in his eye.

"Yep. We'll fund it. Give me a few hours for this headache to pass, and I'll head off to Evesham."

"Great. What time?"

"When I feel like it. Why?"

"I need to clear my diary."

"Sass. You can't come."

"Why?"

"My guys won't trust you. They barely trust me."

"And they never will if I'm always left behind."

"Rein in your ego. That's not how it works. Don't worry. I have listened, and I know what to ask. I'll get the lowdown about Ella Burton. If she was involved in the drug scene, they'll know. And yes, I will discreetly find out how she funded her habit."

"Can I come along for the ride? I'll stay in the car."

"Absolutely not. There's plenty for you to crack on with here. I'll tell you how it went when I get home."

"If you're sure?"

Sean nodded, and I returned to the menial task of background checks until he left the office. As soon as he had shut the door, my hands closed around my car keys. I'd found another interesting morsel on the internet, which I would have told Sean about had he been more open to the suggestion of us going to Evesham together. Marcus Catton now worked in an insurance call centre but his wife was a self-employed bookkeeper who likely operated from home. They hadn't moved despite the scandal, and still lived in Ashton under Hill, a mere twenty-minute drive away. I diverted the phone and set the out-of-office notice before thinking better of it—no point in alerting Sean to an empty workplace. Whistling, I walked towards the car.

Chapter Fourteen

Abigail Catton was hostile from the off. I should have skirted around her husband's scandal and introduced myself in another way by pretending to be a potential customer. But she'd have had all kinds of sleazy journalists trying to ingratiate themselves into her life over the years, and I didn't want to insult her intelligence. So, I knocked on the door and came right out with it, asking if she'd heard of Ella Burton. Her second word was off, which didn't altogether surprise me. But she didn't shut the door in my face, and I felt some negotiation might be possible.

"How fucking dare you?" she offered after the initial exchange.

"I'm sorry to upset you, but I thought you should know that something's happened to Ella."

Abigail's white fingers clasped the door as if she were about to slam it in my face, but curiosity got the better of her.

"Good. I hope it hurt."

"You mean you haven't heard any rumours?"

"Like what?"

I swallowed an inconvenient frog in my throat, nearly spluttering as I asked, "Have the police called?"

"What here?"

"Yes, to see you."

"Why would they? And who the hell are you, anyway?"

"I'm Sass Denman, the better half of Tallis Private Investigators." She didn't raise a smile at my poor attempt at humour.

"So?" she challenged.

"We're looking into a death in Truscombe."

"I've heard. A dead girl in someone's garden, according to yesterday's news. I turned it off. The kids don't need to hear that kind of thing."

"Not just any dead girl."

"Oh, my God. Are you saying it's her?"

I nodded. "Ella Burton."

"How did she die?"

"I can't say."

"Not naturally?"

"No."

"Murdered?"

"I can't say."

"It wasn't me." Abigail's face was ashen, her top lip trembling as she spoke. Her eyes welled, and she wiped them with her sleeve.

"I know you weren't involved, and that's not why I came here. I just wanted to ask you some questions."

"But you're not the police."

"No."

"And you're not connected with them?"

"They haven't sent me. This is a private matter."

"Good. I won't give them the time of day without a

warrant. I'll talk to you, but I want some information in return."

"Fine. But I haven't much to offer. Why don't you tell me about Ella from your perspective, and I'll tell you all I know."

"Okay. Where do you want to start?"

"Do you mind if we go inside? We're a little conspicuous here," I said, watching the curtains twitch in the opposite cottage.

Abigail noticed too. "They're used to our little dramas," she said caustically. "We've provided plenty of entertainment over the years. I had their sympathy at first. But not when Marcus returned. The neighbours don't like it. I can't tell you how often we've repainted the door and resprayed the car. They'll get over it one day. I don't mind so much, but it's rough on our kids."

"Wouldn't it have been easier to move?" I asked, following Abigail as she led me through a low-ceilinged corridor into a stylish kitchen with full-width sliding doors to the garden.

"And leave this?" She gestured to the Tardis-like room, with up-to-the-moment contemporary fittings merging seamlessly with original stone cottage features.

"Nice place," I said, genuinely impressed.

"I love it. Dad left me some money when he died, and I used it for this extension. I'll never leave my home, and why should I? What did I do to deserve any of this?"

"Absolutely nothing, Abigail. Not from what I've read."

"Abi," she said.

"Appreciated. So, you don't have a high opinion of the police force then?"

"Would you?"

"It's hard to know what else they could have done," I

said, my ex-Royal Air Force Policewoman persona naturally coming to the defence of Her Majesty's finest.

"You'd understand if you were in my position," said Abigail. "I've been spat at, ridiculed, and lost most of my friends while my children suffered the same at school. But the police weren't interested in us. In fact, they made it worse by implying that I knew what Marcus was up to. I didn't. Not at all. At least not until I read the note."

"Ouch," I said, grimacing.

"Yes. Marcus didn't have the decency to tell me to my face."

"I don't mean to speak out of turn, but I'm surprised you're still with him."

"Only in a manner of speaking," she said cryptically. "Tea or coffee?"

"Tea would be perfect."

"Milk? Sugar?"

"Both, unless you have a sweetener."

"I do," she said, picking up a packet from the counter and rattling it by her ear.

Abigail made tea from a three-in-one boiling tap set on the kitchen island, which arrived beside me in record time.

"Nice gadget," I said.

"Never mind that. We'll sit in the snug where it's comfortable, and I'll tell you how that girl destroyed my marriage."

Chapter Fifteen

We retired to a compact but homely room off the hallway and sat on chintzy covered high back chairs in front of an unlit fireplace with horse brasses above. I cupped my tea in my hands while leaning back in the comfy chair, immediately resuming a perched position at the realisation I could easily fall asleep. Abigail smiled.

"I like to read here," she said. "The living room is too formal. But I rarely make it past the first few pages without dropping off. There's something soothing about this room."

"And the rest of your house," I replied. "I can see why you've tolerated so much to stay here."

Abigail's face changed into a rictus grin. She placed her cup on a low wooden side table, opened a cupboard beneath the built-in bookcase and produced a crumpled note which she thrust under my nose.

"Read it."

I unfolded the paper, which, at some point in time, had been retrieved from a bin, and cast a wary eye over a faintly written, spidery scrawl.

Abi

> *By the time you read this, I will have gone. Nothing I can say will make up for my behaviour and the humiliation you will undoubtedly suffer when the news comes out. So, I will keep it brief. I am leaving you and can't say where I am going. I have fallen in love with another woman, but it's complicated. I'll send money for the kids as soon as I find work. Tell them I love them, and it's not their fault. Find another man, Abi. I don't deserve you. Marcus.*

"Did he?" I asked.

"Did he what?"

"Send money for the kids?"

"Eventually. A couple of hundred here and there. It didn't scratch the surface of what we needed."

"What did you tell your children?"

"The truth. What choice did I have? It was all over the news within a day or two."

"So, Marcus didn't prepare you for the scandal. When did you find out about Ella?"

"The following day, when the headmaster unexpectedly arrived at the house. Tony Drummond was a few steps ahead of me. He realised what had happened when the teacher and pupil at the centre of school rumours I knew nothing about, didn't turn up for class. He was decent about the situation and came to see me before calling the police. One look at Marcus's note was all he needed to confirm his worst suspicions."

"I'm surprised you still have it. I'd have burned the bloody thing."

"It will stay with me forever," said Abigail, folding the note and carefully replacing it in the cupboard. "Whenever I start mellowing towards Marcus, I take it out to remind myself never to be so trusting again."

"Were there no clues?"

"Not one. Marcus was still attentive, still affectionate. We made love as much as we ever did."

Abigail visibly shuddered as she spoke.

"Then you weren't naive. How could you have known?"

"I feel like I should have done. And if I had, I wouldn't feel as dirty as I do now. All those months when he was sliding into me after seeing her. It's hideous. I'll never forgive him. It's taken years of therapy to come to terms with his betrayal."

"Then why are you still with your husband?"

Abigail sipped her tea and looked directly into my eyes.

"For the kids," she said.

"Is that healthy?"

"Not according to my shrink. But I'm doing what's right for the family."

I resisted the urge to ask her if she was sure, but I didn't need to. Abigail registered my sceptical expression and spoke.

"We're not together," she said. "It's all a front for the children. They love their dad. That's why I agreed when Marcus asked to come home. With conditions."

"To protect yourself?"

"Well, yes. And also, because my feelings for him vanished when he left me for a school child. Nobody appreciates being married to a paedophile."

"It must have been grim."

"It was. Anyway, we negotiated through a marriage counsellor, got some therapy and made a plan that worked for both of us. Better for me than him, but that's the price he had to pay for being a creep. You must think I sound harsh."

"Not at all. I couldn't be as selfless as you were."

"It hasn't been easy, and I sometimes wonder if I should have put my kids above the house. They've suffered the most, but I think it would have been worse for them if I hadn't let their dad live with us. And we sleep in separate rooms, if you're wondering. I don't know what he does outside the home, and I don't ask. But if he so much as looks at another underage girl, he's out for good."

"You must miss the physical aspects of marriage."

Abigail shook her head and cast a wry smile. "I'm fully satisfied in that department. I have a very nice single man friend, and we go out occasionally, sometimes with sleepovers."

"Does Marcus know?"

"I should think so. It doesn't take a genius to work it out. I hope he notices and suffers."

"Are you saying he agreed to what is essentially a love-less marriage?"

"Yes. Not at first. He railed against the idea but said yes after a bit of persuasion. I couldn't have coped with anything else. Helen, my therapist, was appalled by the idea. We emailed back and forth until she realised I'd set my heart on it."

"Email therapy?" I mused, wondering if it might be a way to appease Sean while keeping a healthy distance from Tim Gibbons.

"Sure. I could have met Helen face to face, but it seemed rather pointless when it was so easy to Zoom call or email. And it's much quicker than jumping in a car and driving. At first, Helen wasn't keen. She tried to persuade me to see her as she felt I was avoiding a robust discussion by hiding behind a computer. She said she was worried about my decision to take Marcus back and the potential long-term repercussions. She was right, of course. I knew it was risky, but I didn't want her to talk me out of it. And I'm glad she didn't. This is not a marriage made in heaven, but it works for me and my family. That's good enough."

"Can I ask you something delicate before we touch on Ella Burton?"

"Such as?"

"Bedroom stuff."

Abigail grimaced. "Must we?"

"You're not obliged to tell me anything. I'm just grateful for your cooperation."

Abigail reached into her shirt pocket and scanned my business card again as if satisfying herself with my identity. "Happy to help as long as you're not police or press."

"Neither. Honest."

"What is it then?"

"Confidentially, someone may have restrained Ella Burton before she died."

"How?"

"I don't know."

"And you want to know if Marcus ever did anything similar to me?"

"It might help."

"Will this nightmare never end?"

"As I said, don't answer if it makes you uncomfortable."

"Yes, he did. We did. Nothing weird. Just a pair of furry handcuffs and a hairbrush. It was nothing, just horseplay. It wasn't sexy, at least not for me. Oh, fuck. I've just remembered what he asked me to wear. White high socks and a tennis skirt, the lowlife paedo."

"Sorry. I didn't mean to stir up bad memories."

"They weren't. It was nothing and only happened a few times. But I guess he liked the schoolgirl look even back then."

"Before Ella?"

"Before our kids were born, actually. We just got pissed one night and messed around. It happened a few times after, but not often."

"So, he didn't have a thing for restraint?"

"Not with me. I don't know what he did with her. And I don't want to know."

A red blush crept over Abigail's neck as long-dormant shame took hold. She put her head in her hands. "You see, I should have known," she muttered, still covering her eyes.

I waited for her to compose herself. "Did you ever meet Ella?"

"No."

"Were your kids at the same school?"

"God, no. They weren't old enough, and Marcus wouldn't have wanted it anyway. He disagrees with the idea of parent-teachers in the same school as their offspring. He's quite a stickler. Why are you asking about his love life? Surely you don't think Marcus hurt Ella?"

"No. The investigation is in its early days. But there's a history between Marcus and Ella. The police are bound to ask sooner or later."

"Great. That's all we need," said Abigail, staring at the floor as if it held the answers.

"Get in first," I suggested. "Call them. Say you read all about it in the newspapers and if they want to see you, you'll be happy to come to the station. Then the neighbours don't get the satisfaction of a doorstep meeting."

Abigail nodded. "Perhaps I will," she said morosely. "And I'll talk to Marcus about it. But he wouldn't have hurt the girl, would he?"

"You know him best," I said.

"Not anymore. When did it happen?"

"A few days ago."

"Not Tuesday, I hope. I was out. Marcus should have been babysitting, but Kayla's twelve now, and Toby eleven. He sometimes leaves them to pop out for cigarettes. No more than that though. Not long enough to restrain and murder someone."

"Understood." I was lost in thought when Abigail cocked her head, listening as a car pulled up outside.

"Hell. I forgot my mother was coming," said Abigail, making for the window.

I opened my phone and quickly jotted a few notes while she investigated the disturbance.

"The bastards," she exclaimed, swiftly drawing the curtains and returning to her seat. Abigail shut her eyes and gently rocked for a moment while she processed what she'd seen.

"What is it?" I asked.

"A fucking police car just crawled up the road and is doing a three-point turn."

I rose and peered around the curtains just in time to see Finnegan emerge from the car, standing with his hat under his arm. Tom switched off the car engine and joined him.

"Scruffy git," I muttered. "Sorry. They're heading this way."

"Why didn't they just take out an advert in the Evesham bloody Standard."

"I'm so sorry," I said.

"Not your fault."

We swapped sympathetic glances as three knocks belted out from the front door.

"Mind the bloody wood stain," Abigail hissed.

"I shouldn't be here. Might get into a spot of bother if they see me."

She gestured towards the kitchen. There's a gate in the fence at the bottom of the garden. Turn right and right again to get back to the main road.

"Thank you, and I will. Call me if you think of anything else."

Abigail nodded, and with a thunderous face, she strode towards the front while I bolted for the kitchen door and sprinted down the lawn.

Chapter Sixteen

From: Id47291 (Jem.Wright@werewolfmail.com)
To: Tim.Gibbons@GibbonsGreyPartnership.co.uk
Date: Wednesday, July 14, 2021, 23.11
Subject: Enquiry

> *Dear Mr Gibbons*
> *Please advise your prices for online therapy after the initial consultation. How many sessions do you recommend, and how long does it usually take to see results?*
> *Kind regards*
> *Jem*

From: Tim.Gibbons@GibbonsGreyPartnership.co.uk
To: Jem.Wrights@werewolfmail.com
Date: Thursday, July 15, 2021, 10.46
Subject: Enquiry

> *Dear Jem*
> *Thank you for your mail. Our prices are £70 per session for*

most therapies. Concessions are available for block bookings of 10 sessions or more. Special rates may apply if your insurer is paying. Most of our clients report an improvement in their condition after about three months. The number of sessions required varies depending on the nature of your treatment. I have attached a questionnaire for you to complete should you wish to proceed. These confidential questions are to ensure that online counselling is right for you. If you return the form but do not proceed with our service, rest assured we will destroy your answers immediately.

Yours sincerely
Timothy Gibbons
Practitioner Psychologist

From: Id47291 (Jem.Wright@werewolfmail.com)
To: Tim.Gibbons@GibbonsGreyPartnership.co.uk
Date: Thursday, July 15, 2021, 21.35
Subject: Enquiry

Dear Mr Gibbons
Thank you for your quick reply. I have a few more queries before deciding whether to complete your questionnaire. You refer to online meetings, but I'm only interested in non-visual therapy. Is that an option? If so, how does it work?
Kind regards
Jem

From: Tim.Gibbons@GibbonsGreyPartnership.co.uk
To: Jem.Wright@werewolfmail.com
Date: Monday, July 19, 2021, 14.02
Subject: Enquiry

Dear Jem
I assume you would prefer not to be seen in person or via a

webcam, in which case email therapy might suit you best. We would ask you to write down any problems or concerns before emailing them to your therapist for consideration. This allows you time to reflect on your thoughts and feelings and may, in itself, prove therapeutic. We offer email therapy at a reduced rate of £60 per session and undertake to reply to your email with a detailed response within a few days and no later than one week. Please note that email sessions will not be suitable for all types of therapy. For your further information, my colleagues Helen Chalmers and Scott Stevens deliver this service. Please complete and send the questionnaire if you wish to proceed in this manner.

> *Yours sincerely*
> *Timothy Gibbons*
> *Practitioner Psychologist*

From: Id47291 (Jem.Wright@werewolfmail.com)
To: Tim.Gibbons@GibbonsGreyPartnership.co.uk
Date: Thursday, July 22, 2021, 11.57
Subject: Enquiry

> *Dear Mr Gibbons*
> *Please find my completed questionnaire. I wish to start email therapy as soon as possible. Let me know the process going forward.*
> *Regards*
> *Jem*

Attachment:

Name: *Jem Wright*
Date of Birth: *n/a*
Gender: *n/a*
Email: *Jem.Wright@werewolfmail.com*
Telephone Availability: *n/a*

Reason for Counselling: *Emotional solitude*
Have you ever tried counselling before? *No*
If so, was it online or face-to-face? *n/a*
Are you taking any medication or anti-depressants? *No*
Would you like to add anything further? *No*

From: Tim.Gibbons@GibbonsGreyPartnership.co.uk
To: Helen.Chalmers@GibbonsGreyPartnership.co.uk
Date: Friday, July 23, 2021, 12.02
Subject: New Enquiry

> *Hi Helen*
> *How's your diary looking? Can you fit in another email therapy client? Please see the attached and let me know your availability as soon as possible. If you can't fit it in, I'll ask Scott.*
> *Thanks*
> *TG*

From: Helen.Chalmers@GibbonsGreypartership.co.uk
To: Tim.Gibbons@GibbonsGreyPartnership.co.uk
Date: Friday, July 23, 2021, 13.29
Subject: New Enquiry

> *Hi Tim*
> *Yes, I can squeeze him in. Is it a him? The form is not exactly brimming with information. I hope the emails are more substantive. I'm still not sure about email therapy. As you know, I prefer to see the whites of their eyes! FYI, the halogen bulb popped in the kitchenette earlier. Any spares?*
> *Best*
> *Helen*

From: Tim.Gibbons@GibbonsGreyPartnership.co.uk

To: Helen.Chalmers@GibbonsGreyPartnership.co.uk
Date: Monday, July 26, 2021, 11.16
Subject: New Enquiry

Hi Helen

Sorry, I'm afraid I don't know. According to the internet, Jem is a diminutive of James, Jeremiah, Jeremy, Jenna or Jemima. They haven't stated their gender on the form. Should we be asking clients about gender in this day and age? I can see it becoming an issue. Get Claire to rehash the paper into something more palatable for the times we live in.

God, not another blown bulb. There must be a fault. Claire can look at that too. Perhaps try a different supplier. Will you respond to Jem Wright?

Thanks

Tim

From: Helen.Chalmers@GibbonsGreyPartnership.co.uk
To: Tim.Gibbons@GibbonsGreyPartnership.co.uk
Date: Monday, July 26, 11.34
Subject: New Enquiry

Will do :)

From: Helen.Chalmers@GibbonsGreyPartnership.co.uk
To: Jem.Wright@werewolfmail.com
Date: Monday, July 26, 11.38
Subject: New Enquiry

Dear Jem

Thank you for your completed form, and I am pleased to say you will be a suitable subject for email therapy based on the contents. It would be helpful if we established a routine from the outset. Ideally, you should email me on the same day each week. Your initial email should be in the region of 1000 words, and I will respond to you within two days. Don't worry if your word count is slightly below or above the recommended number. It is purely a suggestion designed to help you in the early days. You may find you can express yourself in far fewer words. If so, feel free. If you're unsure what to write in your initial email, a description of your problem would be an excellent place to start, particularly noting how it makes you feel. Don't worry about grammar or spelling. Write what feels natural.

I will password-protect my responses to you to maintain your privacy. You should find a quiet, private area to read my answer, and I would ask you to treat this session as an appointment as you would if you attended in person. Please be assured that we will take your confidentiality seriously.

I would like to propose Monday as your day for emailing, with my response arriving on Wednesday afternoon. Please feel free to offer an alternative if this time does not suit you. If I do not hear to the contrary, I look forward to receiving your first email this coming Monday.

> *Yours sincerely*
> *Helen Chalmers*
> *Clinical Psychologist*
> *For Gibbons Grey Partnership*

Chapter Seventeen

"Where have you been?" Sean burst through the front door as I walked up the path to his house, still reeling from my close encounter with Kevin Finnegan. Fortunately, Abi Catton had delayed him on the doorstep long enough for me to escape undetected. But several hundred yards of tall weeds and grasses on the seldom-used cut-through impeded my progress to the main street. A forest of burrs now covered the floor of my car where I'd picked them from my clothes while driving, my mind whirring about all she had said.

"Out," I said lamely, noting Sean's florid face.

"Obviously. Which would be why you didn't pick up Callie's call."

"And why would your ex-wife be ringing me?"

"She called the office. You work there, supposedly."

"What did Callie want?"

"I don't know. But she's left a message on my mobile to inform me it's poor business practice to leave the office unattended without setting a forwarder."

"That's weird. I remember doing it. Not sure what happened there."

"Where were you?"

"Out and about. Getting information. Don't worry. It was work-related. I wasn't having my nails done. Anyway, how did you get on?"

"Alright. I reestablished some old contacts, but I can't push them too hard at this stage. They knew Ella. She ran on the edges of the group for a while. I'll hear more later in the week."

"Fine. I'm starving. Shall I cook for you?" I walked towards the door, but Sean placed his arm across, stopping me in my tracks.

"Where were you, Sass?"

I sighed. "In Ashton under Hill."

"Doing what?"

"Sleuthing."

"You're boring me badly. Just answer the question."

"I was chatting to Abigail Catton, wife of Marcus Catton, seducer of Ella Burton."

"Really?" Sean's eyes widened.

"Yes. And it went surprisingly well."

"Then why the reluctance to tell me?"

"I wasn't sure if you'd approve."

"Well, I do. It shows initiative. Get anywhere?"

"Yes. Catton is a creep, and his wife has no time for him. They're only together because of the kids."

"What about Ella?"

"Abi knew little about her. But she gave some insight into Catton. He seems fairly normal, apart from his attraction to schoolgirls."

"Good."

"Can we go in now? I'm starving."

"Sure," said Sean, removing his arm. "I'll catch you later."

"Later? Where are you going? You can't have been home for long."

"Squash with Jack," said Sean. "And I'll be late if I don't shake a leg. He went to the gym straight from work."

"Work? He's only been here for two minutes. When did he decide to get a job? This doesn't sound very temporary."

"Maybe, maybe not," said Sean, non-committally, as he glanced at his watch.

"Enjoy your game. I'll see you later."

"Don't wait up," said Sean, hoisting his sports bag over his arm. "We're watching *Ant-Man and the Wasp* when we've finished."

"Come again?"

"Don't worry yourself. It's a Marvel film. Not your thing."

Sean raised his hand, jumped into the car and drove off. I opened the door and stepped over the threshold with the same now familiar mantel of gloom I'd been wearing all week. It was true. I'd never seen a Marvel film in my life, but I'd tolerate anything for a night out. I tossed my handbag onto the stairs and meandered into the kitchen. Remnants of a hasty snack lay strewn across the breakfast bar. I ran a bowl of water, and cleared up, then turned on the oven before browsing the larder. The contents held little appeal. A cursory examination of the freezer showed that this week's shopping focus was on man-sized burgers and pizzas. And the usually healthily stocked fridge contained half a dozen beers. I searched for something I could stomach and found a solitary carrot in the salad drawer. A few slices of ham and a block of Edam lurked behind a foil takeaway container, and though they were edible, I didn't have the heart.

I gazed at my phone, willing it to ring. But it didn't. An hour and two glasses of wine later, my mobile stayed stubbornly silent. Eventually, I gave in and sent a text.

Dhruv - are you there?

I waited, watching for movement, for something to happen. To my relief, I saw the word 'typing' appear in tiny letters across the top of the screen. Good. Dhruv was online.

Here. What's up? Dhruv replied.

Nothing. Just checking in.

Sass. I can read you like a book. Just come on over if you want company.

Be there in five.

I gulped down the wine, quickly changed and hot-footed it to Bosworth House.

An unexpected change hit me for six as I slunk up the path to Bosworth House. Someone had removed the board from the front window of flat one and replaced it with blinds. I shivered, remembering my last visit inside and the broken body of Veronica Lewis. And though fear snaked up my spine and my heartbeat quickened, curiosity got the better of me. I tiptoed towards the window and peered through the half-open blinds, seeing, to my surprise, a freshly renovated flat ready for new occupants. I closed my eyes, relieved. Visiting Dhruv had been a trial up to now, but this make-over removed all traces of the ghosts of horrors past, exorcising the worst of the memories. I advanced towards the communal door, keen to hear Dhruv's news.

An unpleasant sticky substance covered flat two's intercom, and I wiped it with an old tissue from my pocket before summoning Dhruv. The buzzer sounded, and I advanced inside and towards Dhruv's open door.

Shutting the door behind me, I passed the empty kitchen and headed for the living room, where Dhruv was fussing over the cushions. He plumped them repeatedly and straightened the throws like a man suffering from OCD.

"New neighbours?" I asked.

Dhruv ignored the question, his mind elsewhere.

"Drink?"

I nodded.

"What would you like? I've already eaten, but I can offer you some olives."

"Thanks," I said. "A cup of tea would be nice."

I followed Dhruv to the kitchen and waited while he boiled the kettle with a sullen expression on his face.

"Would you rather be alone?" I asked.

"I'm always alone."

"Oh, dear. No improvement?"

"I don't want to talk about it."

I collected my tea, and we returned to the living room, sitting in awkward silence while I tried to navigate the new taciturn version of Dhruv.

"How can I help?" I asked.

"You can't. Just leave it. I can't process any more well-meaning advice."

"Sorry," I mumbled.

"Why?"

"My poor advice."

"You haven't given me any. I wasn't referring to you, Sass."

"Then who?"

Dhruv glared at me as if I was being deliberately obtuse.

"Okay. You don't want to talk about it. I understand."

"Shall I put a film on?"

"If you like."

"I don't care one way or the other."

"Dhruv. This is horrible. I feel like I'm intruding and don't know what to do or say."

"Welcome to my world. Can we talk about you?"

"If it helps. What would you like to know?"

"How's the lodger?"

"He's alright."

"You're mellowing then?"

"Not really. Jack's decent enough. We pass the time of day occasionally on the rare occasions he's at home."

"Not as bad as last week?"

"Marginally worse."

"I don't see how."

I sighed, frustrated with my position between a rock and a hard place. Whingeing about my trivial problems would curry no favours with Dhruv but refusing to embellish and shutting down the conversation risked venturing into another prickly silence.

"Jack and Sean spend all their time together."

"So?"

"I'm always alone."

"You lived alone in your flat. What's the difference?"

"It's not so bad in your own space. But now I've been relegated to the boxroom in someone else's house, it's getting on top of me."

"Then move out."

"I will. I would have done it before, but Sean said I could stay for as long as I liked. It seems he didn't mean it."

"What do you want from Sean?"

I stared at Dhruv, dumbfounded, not knowing how to answer, my mind racing at the implication behind the question.

"I'm not sure what you mean?"

"Nothing implied. But you don't need me to say you're in an unhealthy situation, Sass. You must realise that by now."

"In what way?"

"You're spending your home life with your single, attractive boss in his house. You might as well be married."

I spluttered into my tea. "Sean and I are just friends."

"You are living and working together. His old friend arrives, and you show all the signs of a jealous girlfriend."

"Dhruv," I say, shocked to the core. "I'm not jealous. Not at all. Just lonely. There's nothing between Sean and me."

"That you don't share bodily fluids is irrelevant. You spend all your time together. He shops and cooks for you, for heaven's sake."

"As I do for him. It's not all one way."

"You're jealous, Sass. Own it."

I stared open-mouthed, tempted to bolt from the room and go home. A flush crept over my cheeks, and my ears burned as I inwardly seethed at his words.

"I thought you, of all people, would understand."

"I do. I'm confronting my challenges, not hiding from them."

"What's that supposed to mean?"

"It's a technique."

"In what?"

"Therapy, as you'd know if you'd bothered attending. If you'd gone for a few sessions, you might have some answers by now."

"Like what?"

Dhruv ignored my question. "Tim Gibbons is employing confrontation therapy in my treatment. Not that he's spelt it out, but I'm not so stupid that I haven't looked online."

"Slow down, Dhruv. All I'm hearing is anger."

"You don't understand."

"Then help me."

Dhruv shook his head as if I were half-witted, then crossed his legs at the ankles and cupped his drink. "Tim says I'm too passive. He thinks I avoid confronting Mill because I'm afraid of what he might say."

"It's understandable. Mill is under the influence half the time and unlikely to listen to reason."

"But not all the time. I told Tim that Mill wouldn't listen to reason, and he said it's because I've stopped telling him how I feel. And he's right. I pussyfoot around the situation, putting Mill's needs ahead of mine. I'm scared to assert myself in case he leaves."

"He wouldn't though?"

"He didn't come home the night before last."

"Where was he?"

"I don't know."

"Did you ask him?"

Dhruv shook his head.

"And Tim thinks you should have?"

"Yes. He said I don't because I'm weak."

"What?" My hackles rose like a protective she-wolf at the thought of such bold criticism from a professional.

Dhruv chewed his lips while mithering at the angry red skin around his cuticles.

"He really said that?"

"Yes. And he's right."

"No, he bloody well isn't," I asserted. "Think about it. In only a few minutes, you've told me that your therapist, a man paid to help you, has accused you of hiding from your problems and called you weak and passive. It's not on."

"He's only doing what I asked?"

"Rubbish. You wanted relationship advice. You hoped to help Mill kick his drinking habit. Instead, your so-called therapist gives you questionable advice that makes you angry and irritable. You've lost your ability to empathise in only a few short days. I hardly recognise you, Dhruv. Something's really off."

Dhruv threw his head back and stared at the ceiling, clenching and unclenching his fists as if trying to quell a temper I didn't know he had.

I tried again. "How do you feel when you leave your appointments?"

Dhruv slowly moved his head and faced me. "Defeated," he said.

"Better or worse than when you arrived."

"Usually worse."

"Is the advice helping?"

"Tim doesn't really give advice."

"So much as criticism," I agreed. "Look, I don't think it's doing you any favours. Not that I know very much. I've met Tim, and he seems okay. But the relationship you two have is toxic."

"That's a little strong."

"Perhaps," I conceded. "But you've deteriorated in under a week, and I trust your judgement more than Tim's."

"He told me to give Mill an ultimatum," said Dhruv.

"That sounds extreme. Was it about his drinking?"

Dhruv nodded. "Yes. Tim said I should tell him to leave

if he didn't promise to quit. He came home a few days ago, covered in something sticky he'd fallen in. I was going to hold my tongue, but he pushed it too far. Mill wouldn't go to bed and left hand prints where he'd bounced from wall to wall. And I let him have it with both barrels. He didn't come home the following day, and I didn't sleep a wink for worrying. It wasn't worth it."

"But he slept here last night?"

"Yes. And I didn't want to frighten him away by giving him the third degree over where he'd been. We booked our wedding venue before all this happened, but I can't see us getting that far."

Tears welled in Dhruv's brown eyes, and he angrily wiped them away. I sat with him on the couch and put my arm around his shoulders. He didn't flinch.

"How much is Mill drinking?" I asked.

"I don't know. He doesn't do it in front of me."

"Beer or spirits?"

"No idea."

"Has he been to the doctor recently?"

"He won't go."

"Why?"

"Mill has never liked medical matters. It was all I could do to keep him in the hospital when his foot went septic. He discharged himself early if you remember."

I nodded. "I do. Here's a thought. Might Mill be poorly rather than drunk?"

"He definitely drinks. I've smelled it on his breath."

"I'm sure he does, but he's back at work, right?"

"Yes."

"Wouldn't they have noticed if his drinking was out of hand?"

"He's fine once he's slept. They wouldn't be able to tell."

"But they'd smell it on his breath."

"I expect they turn a blind eye."

"In a school?"

"What are you getting at?"

"Other things mimic intoxication."

Dhruv's eyes widened, and his mouth fell open.

"Does Mill have any other symptoms?"

"He's clumsy, always banging into things. But he's been like it for a while."

"Since when?"

"Way before his infection."

"In that case, way before his drinking problem."

"I guess."

"Anything else?"

Dhruv shook his head. "Oh, he gets migraines sometimes."

"What kind?"

"The normal. Headaches and visual disturbances. Mill sees lights."

"Auras."

"Exactly that."

"I'm no medic, but you might have been barking up the wrong tree. Sure, Mill drinks, but you should forget all about this therapist and get him to see a doctor."

"He won't."

"That might be because Mill thinks your concern lies with his alcohol consumption. Say you're worried about his headaches and balance problems. You never know. It might work."

Dhruv nodded. "I'll try."

"And I'll follow your advice in return."

"What advice?"

"To see Tim Gibbons."

"Are you sure you should?"

"Too right. I don't like the sound of the counselling he's dishing out. It's best if I check him out myself."

I thrust my hand into my pocket and withdraw Tim's appointment card, quickly checking the date.

"Good. My appointment is this week. Tell me how you get on with Mill, and I'll let you know all about my session with Tim."

"Okay," said Dhruv, his chin up and looking more hopeful than I'd seen him in a while.

I left Bosworth House determined to conduct a background check on Tim Gibbons as soon as possible. Something about his advice was seriously awry, and I was determined to get to the bottom of it.

Chapter Eighteen

"Fat Vi's in ten minutes," said Sean, slamming his mobile on the desk.

"Good morning. Nice to see you too."

Sean glanced at his watch.

"Sorry, I'm late," I muttered. "The traffic was heavier than usual."

"Your car's on the drive."

"Alright. I overslept. I apologise."

"You're slipping, Sass. That wouldn't have happened in the air force."

I clenched my jaw, angrier with myself than with Sean. I hadn't once been late during my time as an RAF police-woman. He was right. My standards were falling.

"Sorry," I repeated. "It's only ten minutes."

"That's not the point. It's no big deal, and you put in the overtime when required, but at least have the courtesy to be honest."

"Fine. I was at Dhruv's last night. We started with hot

drinks and finished with shorts. I forgot to set my alarm. But I was still home before you."

"But I'm still sitting at my desk before nine o'clock," said Sean smugly.

"You're used to it. I rarely drink."

"Lightweight."

"If you say so. Are we meeting Tom?"

"Of course."

"Why?"

"No idea. He didn't say. He summoned us, and I offered to buy breakfast, and that's all you need to know. You fit?"

"I suppose so. Though I'd hoped to make a start researching the life and career of our friendly police psychiatrist, therapist or whatever he is. I'd better not spend too much time out of the office. What's the difference between a psychiatrist and a therapist, anyway?"

Sean shrugged. "Don't know, don't care. There's a sausage bap at Vi's with my name written all over it."

"Seriously, there must be a difference."

"You're asking the wrong person. And what's Mr Gibbons done to require your expert analysis?"

Sean grabbed his car keys and shoved them in the drawer before taking a waterproof from the coat hooks. I glanced outside.

"It's pissing down. Can't you drive?"

"I could, but I won't. I need the fresh air, and so do you."

I opened my handbag and felt inside for the mini brolly I habitually carried before remembering that I'd changed my bag the previous day. "Must we?" I asked.

Sean nodded. "Yep. Take this," he said, pulling a golfing umbrella from under his desk. Sean locked the office, and I passed the umbrella back to him.

"I'd rather get drowned than battle with this," I said as we headed into a windstorm, notably fiercer than the morning breeze I'd encountered earlier.

"I'll do the honours." Sean popped open the brolly, and we walked up the street, huddling beneath as if joined at the hip. My mind drifted back to Dhruv's intimation of the previous night, and I pulled away. If Sean noticed, he didn't say. By the time we arrived at Fat Vi's, I'd made my mind up to move out at the earliest opportunity. Our relationship was unhealthy for both of us and would only deteriorate. It was time for me to stand on my own two feet again. And if I didn't do it soon, I risked my job and security.

We picked up our pace and flew through the doors of Fat Vi's as the heavens opened. Within moments, rain sleeted down, tumbling from above and hammering against the window. Sean strode ahead, and I let the door go, assuming it would shut, but the wind snatched it away and thrust it back with a thunderous clatter. A crack snaked across the glass.

"Damn it," screeched Vi, running towards the front. She dropped to her knees and secured a bolt across the bottom of the door, then stood and did the same at the top. She stood facing us, her arms crossed. "I hope you've no plans to leave. That's staying locked until this bloody storm stops. Look at the state of my cafe. And what is that?"

Vi pointed towards three dark footprints on the floor behind me. Sean picked up his leg and examined one foot, then another.

"Not me," he said.

I stood, rooted to the spot, hoping Vi would let the matter drop. She furrowed her brows and glared at me. Reluctantly, I lifted my foot and peered over my shoulder.

"Jesus," screeched Vi, as her bony arm gripped my wrist

and manhandled me to the door. "Take your boots off and leave them on the mat. I'd put them outside if it weren't teeming down."

Sean wrinkled his nose. "That stinks," he said unhelpfully.

"Thanks," I hissed.

"What have you stood in?"

"How should I know? I wouldn't have done it if I'd seen it."

"Should have gone to Specsavers."

"Give it a rest."

Tom, who had been sitting quietly in the corner by the lavatory, walked towards us.

"Just sit the fuck down, will you, and stop drawing attention to yourselves."

I glanced around the cafe. Sure enough, every eye in the place was on us, but apart from Vi and Tom, that only amounted to six eyes, all of which belonged to elderly women.

"They don't know us from Adam," said Sean.

Tom scowled. "Are you being funny?"

"Not intentionally. What's the problem?"

"Just order something while Vi's still willing to serve Saskia and sit down. Finnegan's on manoeuvres this morning and I don't trust him."

"He's hardly going to turn up here," said Sean.

"I wouldn't put it past him."

Feeling foolish, I stood uncomfortably on my stockinged feet while Vi manhandled a heavy mop and bucket and started cleaning the floor. She watched me from beneath a furrowed brow, shooting disapproving glances with every sweep of her mop. Sean took an exaggerated stare at his watch.

"Sacked all your staff, have you, Vi?"

"The wee scrote's late again, that's all. He'll be along shortly. You can wait until I'm done."

"Charming." Sean cast an insincere smile while I considered leaving and looking for a more welcoming cafe. But the locked door and Vi's Glaswegian bluntness were two hurdles too many for a swift exit. I briefly wondered what Vi was doing so far from home and how she had kept her thick Scottish accent after several decades in the shire.

She stomped past, opened a door behind the counter, and slid the bucket through with her foot. The mop fell with a clatter, but she ignored it.

"What'll you be having?" she asked, fixing a smile on her narrow, lined face.

"A sausage bap and cup of builder's tea," said Sean.

"And you?"

"Would you have any sourdough bread?" I knew my request was unwise as I spoke, but I asked anyway. Vi tried valiantly not to raise her eyes heavenward and failed.

"Not today," she said through gritted teeth.

I glanced at the chalkboard and looked for the least offensive breakfast item. Vi had scribbled a wavy line through croissants and teacakes, and my heart sank.

"Well? I haven't got all day?"

"A boiled egg?" I said defeatedly.

"Aye. I can do that."

Sean smiled and walked towards Tom while I padded behind. He pulled out a chair and gestured for me to sit.

"You okay, Tom?" I asked.

"Not bad," he replied, tinkering with the salt pot.

"Did we keep you waiting?"

"A little. Don't worry about it."

"What's the problem?" asked Sean, cutting to the chase.

"It's your mate."

"Jack? What's he done?"

"Not him. The other one."

"Tea," said Vi, slamming two mugs on the table, both full of an unappealing dark brew with barely a drip of milk.

"Oh, no. I forgot to order," I said.

"Then you get what you're given. Make the best of it."

I stirred the evil brew, feeling slightly sick.

"Too fussy by half," said Sean, slurping his drink as if it were liquid gold.

"Now to business." Tom tried to steer the conversation back to work, but Vi appeared with a plate of eggs and bacon.

"Bad timing," said Tom as she retreated.

"Dig in. Don't wait for us," I said, my appetite now dwindling and hoping Vi was in no rush to complete our order.

"What's this about, my friend?" Sean passed a bottle of tomato sauce towards Tom. He opened it, inspected the crust around the lid, and returned it to the end of the table.

"He's still missing?"

"Are you referring to Adam?"

"Hmmm."

"When you say missing?"

Tom swallowed a forkful of eggs. "Well, missing or gone to ground. We've spoken to his family; they haven't seen him for weeks. The dog's absent too."

"Yes, but didn't you say Adam had just finished a project? He's probably abroad."

"Not without his passport."

"How do you know he hasn't got it?"

"We tracked down his cleaner and took a quick look around the house. The passport was in his desk drawer."

"Driving licence?"

"We didn't find it, but as I said, it was only a cursory look."

"I'm surprised you've bothered. It's not like Adam is a young child or a vulnerable adult. He means more to me than most, and I'm not the least bit concerned about his welfare.

"One bap, one egg," said Vi. Sean smirked as I glanced at my plate, shaking my head as Vi marched towards the counter. She'd cut my toast into soldiers.

"And made from a plain white loaf. You poor thing," he said unsympathetically.

"I'm not fussy," I hissed. "I just prefer healthy food."

"You bicker like an old married couple," said Tom, spearing a mushroom.

My heart dropped at the echo of Dhruv's sentiments.

"She'd be so lucky," laughed Sean.

I dipped a soldier into the egg, swallowing bile as thick gloopy albumen clung to the bread. Snotty eggs were all I needed.

"Anyway, why are you so worried about Adam?" Sean bit into his butty, and a blob of brown sauce splattered onto the plate.

"Because of the cleaner."

"Come again?"

"His domestic. He didn't tell her he was leaving. She turned up as usual, and he wasn't there. Well, Molly has a key, let herself in and went about her business for the first week. But by the end of the second, she started to worry."

"How many times a week does she clean?"

"Twice."

"I see." Sean took another bite and masticated thoughtfully. "That rather changes things."

"We thought so too."

"Did Molly try to contact anyone?"

"Yes. She went round to the neighbours, such as they are. You know the house. One's fairly close, and the other a good way down Broadway Road. Anyway, they hadn't seen hide nor hair of him either. But before that, he'd told one of them he was looking forward to doing a bit of gardening. And that neighbour saw him a day or two later carrying a couple of shrubs which are still on the patio. Or rather, what's left of them after weeks without attention."

Sean stopped mid-bite. "What can I do to help?"

"Nothing. I just wanted to know if you'd seen or heard from Adam since. I figured not, or you would have said, but Finnegan's authorised another more comprehensive house search tomorrow. It seems he's finally taking it seriously."

"Taking what seriously?"

"Adam's disappearance, hot on the heels of Ella Burton's death."

"I thought he said they weren't connected. Not with a three-year gap."

"Correct. But someone kidnapped Adam Harding once before, and we never found out why. We must now face the fact that it might have happened again."

Chapter Nineteen

"Go home and change your shoes," said Sean.

"What?"

"You heard me. Quickly now. I'll meet you back at the office."

"They're fine," I hissed, still mortified by the look on Vi's face as she scraped dog muck from her cafe floor. "I'll clean them in the ladies before we leave."

"Not good enough."

"Your office carpet is so loud and dirty you'd never know."

"Charming, but irrelevant, all the same. We are not going back to the office. Change your shoes like a good little employee, and I'll collect you as soon as I've picked up the car."

"Where are we going?" I asked suspiciously.

"Never you mind. Be ready in ten," he said, tapping his watch.

I stomped back to Sean's house, annoyed at the change to my routine. I had arranged my desk with two monitors some time ago to make it easier to work on two projects at once. Today, I'd planned to carry out paid work with some digging about Tim Gibbons on the side. I wouldn't have time now, which meant delaying the research or letting it encroach on my evening, neither of which appealed. But with a bit of luck and a following wind, Sean's trip wouldn't take too long, and I'd still get an hour or two out of the afternoon.

By the time I arrived at Sean's, my hair was a jumbled mess, and the sky had leaked again. Never mind changing my shoes; I'd need a whole new outfit. I slid my key into the door and slipped inside, dumping my bag in the hallway as I headed upstairs. Grabbing some chinos, a shirt and a pair of trainers from my wardrobe, I dropped them on the bed and made for the bathroom to fetch a towel. As I threw the door open, it met with resistance and a muffled yelp. Shocked, I peered inside to find Jack stark naked, curled into a foetal position on the floor. His eyes met mine, his mouth a mask of horror.

"What the…" I couldn't find the words.

"Oh, dear God. I was having a moment."

"What kind of moment? Second thoughts. Don't answer that."

"It's not what you think." Jack scrabbled off the floor, holding his hands over his groin. I pulled a towel from the rail and thrust it toward him.

"You don't owe me an explanation. What you do in your own time is up to you." I turned to go, and he grabbed my wrist.

"Oh no, you don't," I said, yanking it away and retreating backwards.

"Just listen, Sass. I'm not a bloody pervert. When I said I was having a moment, I meant I was missing my wife."

"I'm not sure that helps."

"Look at my eyes, for God's sake. I'm a great blubbering wreck."

I peered over my shoulder and checked again. Sure enough, Jack's red-rimmed eyes and streaming nose would have given the game away had I not jumped to unsavoury conclusions.

"Do you want to talk about it?" I asked.

"Not in here," he said, adjusting the towel. I retreated a few more paces.

"Later?"

"Perhaps."

"Look. I know we started on the wrong foot, but I'm a good listener. Just say the word if you want to talk things through from a female perspective."

"Okay. Thanks."

Jack scuttled towards his room and firmly shut the door. I tried to erase the excruciating scene from my mind as I squeezed into my clothes, with my skin and hair still wet. But I wasn't risking another visit to the bathroom to fetch a towel. I'd barely got my trainers on before a car horn blared, and Sean pulled up at the top of the drive. I waved from my window to let him know I'd be down in five, and he sounded the horn again. Rolling my eyes, I ran downstairs with my make-up bag in my hand and a hairbrush in the other and made for the car. Sean looked me up and down.

"Not sure about the new bedraggled image."

"Your fault. You knew it was raining."

"It doesn't matter. No one will see you."

"I'm fixing my face. I don't care what you say."

"Up to you." Sean shrugged and pulled the car away.

"Where are we going?"

"To find a friend."

"Speaking of which, Jack seems to be having some sort of breakdown."

"Really?"

"You don't sound surprised."

"I'm not. The poor chap's been through the mill lately. What happened?"

I relayed the bathroom scene in a few short sentences.

"Ah, that's a shame," said Sean. "No harm done though."

"If only I could unsee it."

"How about showing some compassion?"

"I did. I said he could speak to me about his problems anytime."

"Jack thinks you don't like him."

"Nonsense. I never said that."

"You haven't been especially friendly."

I stared at Sean as if he'd landed from another planet. "He's never there. You're never there."

"I'm keeping him occupied," said Sean. "Anyway, think about it. Perhaps you could try a little harder."

Chapter Twenty

I fumed in silence as Sean drove through the centre of Truscombe and towards the edge of the town. And as he pulled onto Broadway Road, an uneasy concern settled over me. "Where are we going?" I asked slowly.

"Like I said. Finding a friend."

"Here we are." Sean pulled the car into a layby and applied the handbrake. "Out you pop."

"We're in the middle of nowhere," I grumbled, releasing the seatbelt.

"Not at all. Adam's place is only twenty yards away."

"And you don't want to be seen."

"Naturally."

"Why are we going to Adam's house when the police are conducting a search tomorrow?"

"To get there first, of course."

"But why?"

"Because something might be wrong. Adam's always looked out for my family and me, and I ought to return the favour."

"Don't you trust Tom?"

"I doubt he'll get anywhere near the house. Finnegan will want his own team, not Kim's cast off's. I'm only surprised that Tom's getting a look in at all. Still, it means we get to hear about it."

"You shouldn't use Tom. He trusts you."

"He's also been around the block a few more times than you think. If Tom didn't want me to know about this, he wouldn't have said a word. That he did brings his tacit approval."

"That makes no sense."

"Tom doesn't trust Finnegan any more than I do."

"He didn't say that."

"Look. Just accept things, Sass. Sometimes it's what you don't say that matters the most."

I shook my head, annoyed at the direction the conversation was taking. I was not good at subtext in the same way that I wasn't good at dating signals. If somebody wanted me to know something, they needed to say it clearly or I wouldn't have a clue. Tom had invited us to breakfast to double-check that Sean hadn't heard from Adam. But in Sean's subliminal world, this implied that Tom wanted him to search Adam's house covertly. The concept was exhausting.

"You can't just break in," I said, my thoughts escaping unbidden.

"I don't need to." Sean wolfishly grinned as he strode down the drive, casting a cursory look over his shoulder as if anyone was likely to pass the lonely road on foot. "This way," he continued.

Sean reached over the wooden side gate and unbolted it from the top. "Ladies first," he said, waving me through. I walked down the side of the house, which opened onto a long, lush lawn badly in need of a cut.

"Now, let's hope Adam hasn't changed his habits," said Sean, tipping a stone planter and moving his hand underneath. He frowned, then approached a colourful pot. Sean repeated the process five times before his fingers closed over a key, and he looked up and grinned. "Got it," he said triumphantly.

Sean approached the sliding rear doors and peered inside. "Nice extension," he said. "Wrong key, though. Must be for the side door."

We retraced our steps, and Sean fitted the key and opened the door. Our hearts stopped at an unexpected bleep from the burglar alarm.

"Oh, God," said Sean. "Tom didn't mention a bloody alarm."

"I told you. You completely misread him."

"Now is not the time. Think Tallis, think." He jabbed a finger into the alarm panel and prodded four digits. The alarm continued beeping.

"Okay. Not that, then. I know." Another four digits and the alarm warbled its acceptance. "He shoots, he scores," said Sean, clicking his fingers.

"What was the code?"

"His birth year, the fool."

"Great. Well, let's get on with it before something else happens."

"You took the words out of my mouth."

"Shall we split up and cover more ground?"

"No. I don't know what we're looking for yet.

"Then why am I here?"

Sean stopped. "For company?" he said.

"Give me a break, Sean. I deserve better."

"Okay. Two heads are better than one. I know I'm speaking in cliches, but it's useful to bounce ideas around. Look. I'm uneasy about Adam's disappearance. But Tom might yet be overreacting. I'd like us to find a good reason for his absence. Look for holiday brochures, guest houses, and route maps—that kind of thing. And yes, we will split up. You look upstairs, and I'll start here. Just be super careful. I don't want to leave any evidence that we were ever inside."

"I know the drill."

"Okay. Off you go then."

Adam had made some structural changes to his home, including an open tread staircase snaking up the far end of the vaulted living area. Though new, it squeaked as I climbed, and I was glad not to be searching covertly. I turned left at the top and found myself in a generous bedroom with an en suite and dressing area. It was likely Adam's room, but the minimalist furnishings made it hard to be sure anyone had occupied it at all. I slid open one of the mirrored wardrobe doors to find tidily hung clothes and an interior storage range, which appeared fresh out of a furniture catalogue. Some hangers were empty, but it was hard to tell whether they had contained clothes in the first place. The drawers told a similar story, and a small bookcase within the wardrobe held an eclectic choice of reading material from classical books to architectural design literature, giving a sense that Adam was both cultured and intelligent. I made a mental note to ask Sean to introduce us once he'd been found. Adam seemed like the perfect boyfriend, and the thought of dating an attractive, eligible man sent shivers down my spine.

I focused my attention away from unlikely fantasies to the task at hand. Adam's bedside cabinet revealed little of interest save a remote-control device, but try as I might, I couldn't see anything to use it on. I was about to return it to the drawer when curiosity got the better of me, and I pressed a red button. A faint hum came from the bottom of the bed as a flat-screen television emerged. Panicking, I pushed a further row of buttons, trying to return it, and the volume swelled to maximum level. Moments later, Sean appeared red-faced with his hands over his ears while I desperately tried to quiet the noise. He snatched the remote from me, jabbed a finger, and the television slid away.

"For crying out loud. Why not take out an advert in the Truscombe Gazette?"

"Alright," I said, smoothing over the bedcover where I'd been sitting. "Have you found anything?"

"Not yet," said Sean. "Let's get back to it. And try not to burn the house down."

The remaining three bedrooms and bathroom held nothing more interesting than an attractive claw-footed bath positioned to make the most of the views over the open countryside. I joined Sean downstairs just as he approached Adam's study door and followed him inside.

"This looks more interesting," said Sean, opening the desk drawer to reveal the passport Tom had mentioned earlier.

I browsed another bookcase as Sean spoke, my eyes drawn to a series of historical mysteries by an author I was keen on. As I pulled out one book for closer inspection, a bookmark sailed to the ground and settled by the cupboard beneath. I opened the door and rummaged through a pile of paperwork inside.

"What's a CRT licence?" I asked, peering at a folded piece of paper with a picture of a boat in the top right-hand corner.

"Sorry"?

"A CRT licence?"

"It's a canal and river trust permit thing. Why?"

"I just found one in Adams's things. It's out of date."

"I'm not surprised. We were always messing around on the water when we were younger. But never mind that. Look at this." Sean held an android phone aloft.

"That's not good. Is it up to date?"

"It's a newish model, as far as I can tell. And flat as a pancake. But it's decent, Sass. Adam should have it with him."

"Unless it's broken."

"Good point." Sean perked up a little. "Ah. And this is his business ledger. Everything seems in good order. He's making a decent living. More than decent. Good enough to fund the improvements to this place, that's for sure."

"Nothing suspicious here then," I said brightly.

"Agreed. It's put my mind at rest though. I guess Adam's popped off on an extended holiday. Well, good for him."

Sean carefully repacked the drawers, and we left the house, returning the key to its hiding place.

"Race you," said Sean cheerfully as we returned past the side of the house.

"Don't be daft. We can't even walk side by side in this narrow space, much less run," I replied. Then something glinted by the back door, and I bent to retrieve it.

"What's that?" asked Sean, looming behind me. I stood up and examined the contents of my hand.

Sean gasped, and his face whitened in front of me.

"It's a St Christopher," I said, holding the tiny gold circle before me.

"I'll take that." Sean gently pulled it from my hand, glanced at the engraving and checked the finely linked chain. He removed his phone, set it to magnify, and looked again.

"This is Adam's," he said, eventually. "He's had it since he was a kid. Someone has damaged the links. See here; they're separated. Adam would never go anywhere without this, which can only mean one thing," Sean continued. "Foul play."

Chapter Twenty-One

"What now?" I asked as we drove back through Truscombe.

"I'd better tell Tom."

"Great. Let's hope you're right about his tacit break-in instructions."

"On the other hand."

"You can't tell him, Sean. But if you don't, what do we do about Adam?"

Sean stroked his chin pensively. "Bloody hell. If it were anyone else, I might leave it until tomorrow. But Finnegan's so useless they might not spot the necklace."

"Did you put it back? I wasn't paying attention?"

Sean nodded. Yes, in a slightly more obvious place. But there's no guarantee they won't walk over it without looking."

"Then you must tell Tom."

"Fuck."

I sat in silent contemplation as Sean scowled at his mobile phone in its resting place on the dashboard as if he was struggling to make a decision. By rights, I ought to be gloating. But Tom was a good contact, and if Sean upset him, we might never get him back onside.

"Here goes nothing. Siri, call Tom."

Siri did her thing, and the phone rang several times before Tom answered. "What is it?"

"It's me Sean."

"I know. What do you want?"

"A moment of your time, if that's not too much trouble." Sean's words dripped with sarcasm.

"Bad timing," said Tom. "I'm in a meeting."

"Call me back then."

"Okay. I should be out in five."

Fifteen was nearer the mark, and we were already back in the office when Sean's mobile rang again.

"Thanks for calling back. Now, you know that little hint you offered about Adam Harding's place? Well, it paid off."

I couldn't hear Tom's reply, but by the subsequent back and forth, Sean's raised voice and multiple apologies, it was fair to say that Sean had misinterpreted Tom's original intentions. Eventually, Sean ended the call and looked sheepishly at me.

"He's a mite dischuffed," he said.

"As well he should be. How did you leave it?"

"I didn't. Tom ended the call."

"That bad?"

"Yes. Tom's not with Finnegan tomorrow and he can't accidentally find the chain. He can only deal with Adam's disappearance tonight if I go official with the evidence. And they'll want to know why I was poking around the house."

"Lie," I said. "Obviously."

"And say what?"

"That you were worried about your friend and already intended to take an afternoon stroll down Broadway Road so you popped in to take a look. It doesn't matter what story you come up with. They can't prove anything."

"Good point. Tom's a little stressed. He's missing Kim's support."

"Has she gone off him?"

"Not at all. But Kim holds no power while Finnegan's in charge and can't back Tom as she used to."

"Shame. I like Tom."

"Me too. But he was unreasonably angry on the phone. I wonder if it was anything to do with his meeting?"

"What meeting?"

"The one he was in earlier. Look. It doesn't matter. What's done is done."

I settled down to my research, pulling up a screen about Tim Gibbons just as Sean reached for a file behind me.

"I don't know why you're bothering with Gibbons, Sass. It's a waste of time."

"Then why are you so insistent on me seeing him?"

"I thought a spot of therapy might help you."

"Me too. I've booked an appointment for tomorrow."

"About time. Good for you."

"That remains to be seen. Tim Gibbons is causing more problems for Dhruv than he's solving."

Sean raised a querying eyebrow, and I updated him on Dhruv's latest issues.

"If Gibbons is good enough for Kim, he should be capable of counselling anyone."

"I disagree."

"Based on what?"

"He's dishing out poor advice."

"In your opinion, as an unqualified psychologist."

"Well, there's only one way to find out. I must put myself back in his hands."

"He didn't upset you the first time you went."

"I didn't know what to expect. And despite what you think, I wasn't especially keen. It's one of the reasons I didn't return."

"And all this because Dhruv and Mill have fallen out."

"Don't you care?" I snapped.

"Sure. But we're not relationship counsellors. Leave it to the professionals."

"What about the Cattons?"

"Who?"

"Abigail and Marcus Catton. Both clients of Gibbons' practice."

"Did I know that?"

"You do now."

"It has nothing to do with the investigation. Not that we're an integral part of it yet."

"But your friend is missing, and Ella's capture must have some bearing on Adam's."

Sean threw his head back and stared at the ceiling as if battling with both sides of his brain. As he opened his mouth to respond, the door slammed open, and Kim Robbins entered.

Sean stared in surprise. "What are you doing here?"

"I want a word," she said, unzipping her coat and hanging it from the hook by the door. She sat heavily before Sean and leaned forward with her elbows on his desk.

"Ah," said Sean.

"Well?"

"Well, it seemed like a good idea at the time. And I owe Adam."

"Just as you owe Tom not to drop him, and by him, I mean us, in the shit."

"I thought he wanted me to search the place before Finnegan arrived."

"In which case, he would have clearly said so. Does anyone else know you were there?"

"Only Sass."

Kim turned to face me." Your partner in crime, huh?"

I badly wanted to tell her I'd warned Sean against it, but loyalty got the better of me, and I kept my mouth firmly shut.

"Well, someone else did know, and now you've put us in a quandary," said Kim.

"I don't see how?"

"A neighbour called the station when the burglar alarm went off. It only came to our attention just before you called Tom."

"Speedy work. Just as well I wasn't thieving."

"Wind your neck in, Sean. If someone has kidnapped Harding again, we must be on it as soon as possible."

"I think they have. Tom's told you about the necklace. The links were stretched as if someone yanked it clean away."

Kim sighed. "We can't wait until tomorrow."

"Fine. I'll call the station and tell Finnegan I went to Adam's to check on him because he's an old mate. While there, I spotted the chain."

"Good. Off you go."

"What, now?"

"Yes, immediately."

"Okay." Sean picked up the phone and began to dial, then stopped mid-way through.

"Are you waiting here?"

Kim nodded.

"You can trust me."

"I don't doubt it."

"But you want to listen to my conversation?"

"I don't care one way or the other. But I haven't finished with you yet."

"Sass. Make a coffee, will you?"

Kim raised her eyes heavenward. "I'll do it," she said.

I smiled in rare gratitude as she headed for the kitchenette with the coffeepot in her hand, then watched as Sean dialled again.

After several abortive attempts, he got through to Kevin Finnegan and gave an abbreviated version of the day's events. A red flush spread over his face as he responded to Finnegan's barbs. "Yes, I will stay away in future," he said, staccato-like, before slamming the handset down.

"Jumped up arsehole."

"It is his case," I said as Kim emerged through the door and shot me a glare.

"He doesn't deserve it," she replied. "But you didn't hear that from me."

"What's the problem?" asked Sean.

"Finnegan's making a pig's ear of things. He's made no progress at all. At least, nothing significant. He's too backwards looking and only wants connections to his prime suspect, Marcus Catton. But if Harding's disappearance is part of a sequence, and I think it might be, then what's his link to Catton? We don't know of one."

"You do surprise me. Someone's not been doing their research."

"What do you mean?" asked Kim suspiciously.

"Never you mind. What's Finnegan's plan? To wait for another disappearance, another murder?"

"Exactly," said Kim. "And that's what I'm here to discuss."

Chapter Twenty-Two

Sean raised his eyebrow. "Go on."

"In the strictest confidence."

"Cross my heart and hope to die."

"I mean it. Something more meaningful than your cavalier approach to Tom's information this morning."

Sean steepled his hands and looked directly into Kim's eyes. "Look. I'm sorry. I misjudged Tom's intentions. But I've never been indiscreet about information. You know that."

"One day, I'll lose my job for telling you as much as I do."

"I thought you already had." A flicker of annoyance passed over Kim's face, and Sean spoke again before she could articulate her disappointment at his ill-judged quip. "Then why do you still need us?"

"Because you can investigate the things we can't touch. And your instinct is as good as it ever was. They should never have let you leave the force."

"The result of an unfortunate marriage, Kim."

"Well, it's our loss."

Their mutual love-in was making me feel slightly queasy, and I glared at Sean, hoping he would read my mind and move things on a bit. He did not disappoint.

"Well, will you tell us what you're here for?"

"Yes, They found a body in Tewkesbury this morning."

"Blimey. Tom didn't give us so much as a hint."

"He didn't know."

"Where was it? Who was it?"

"By the edge of the river. It seems someone dragged the body through Victoria Gardens and placed it in the water. I doubt it moved very far, judging by the tracks on the bank. It may have started in the water but soon found its way back to the riverside, where a dog walker found it this morning. Poor old girl. She didn't realise what she was looking at until her dog started chewing what she thought was an old coat, which turned out to be a human hand."

"Grim," I said, imagining the scene.

"Very. Anyway, I'll spare you the details, but Finnegan's lot went straight down there and returned to give a briefing. Unusually, they let Tom and me participate."

"And you're telling us why?" asked Sean, the colour draining from his face.

"Shit, sorry, Sean. It's not what you're thinking." Kim quickly realised her mistake. "The body wasn't Adam Harding. That's not why I'm here. I mean, it's relevant to our search for Harding, but it's not his body."

"Whose is it?"

"We're not sure. Male, early fifties. Missing a finger on his right hand. Not an injury. It looks like a birth defect, so the forensic pathologist says. But he's too old and too short to be Adam."

Sean visibly relaxed and massaged his tense neck

muscles with his hands. "I thought the worst for a minute," he confessed.

"My fault. I'm sorry," said Kim.

"Then I'll ask again. Why are you telling me? Is it murder?"

Kim nodded. "We think so."

"Cause of death?"

"To be determined. It could be drowning, but there are signs of petechial haemorrhage. And a nasty head wound."

"Just like Ella Burton," I said.

Kim nodded.

"Any other similarities? Evidence of capture, perhaps?" Sean leaned forward, guessing what was coming.

"Yes. The victim had been restrained, probably caged, and certainly held captive."

"Marks on the legs from cuffs?"

"Nothing so subtle. This time the vic still wore a shackle."

Chapter Twenty-Three

I thought about the body as I drove to the Gibbons Gray practice in Cheltenham the following day. Once Kim had left the office, Sean and I debated whether the crimes were connected. We both agreed that Ella and the Tewkesbury John Doe must have suffered by the same hand. But whereas I naturally assumed the same fate had also befallen Adam, Sean was far from convinced. I tried to argue my case but it was impossible while maintaining the level of optimism Sean relied on. He may have been remote from Adam Harding for some years, but I had underestimated his loyalty to his old friend. And though I secretly thought Adam must be dead, Sean wouldn't accept the idea that any harm had come to him. Sean was relentlessly positive that Adam would be found. But even Sean had realised Adam was in some kind of trouble. He could no longer hope his friend would come bowling through the door after two weeks in the Costa del Sol, having forgotten to tell anyone.

I had left Sean pacing the office that morning, frustrated at his reliance on Finnegan and his team to renew their investigation. And unfairly angry with me for not being more positive about Adam's prospects. Sean had barely acknowledged me as I set off for my meeting with Tim.

I arrived in Cheltenham ten minutes early and parked in front of Imperial Gardens before walking to Tim's Montpellier office. Running my hand along the wrought iron rail to the front door, I hit my first snag. A paint splinter deep in my palm that no amount of sucking would dislodge. But I tried to ignore my throbbing flesh as I entered the smart four-storey Cotswold building. I turned right into the reception area, where Tim waited.

"Good morning, Miss Denman," he said formally, offering his hand. I shook it uncertainly and replied in kind.

"Claire's on holiday," he offered as if I ought to know who she was. I raised an eyebrow.

"Our receptionist. Helen and I are managing between us."

"Super," I replied, no wiser about Helen than Claire.

"Come through. We'll use the same place as last time." Tim swept a hand ahead, and I entered his therapy room.

"Coat?" he asked. I nodded and shrugged off my light jacket.

"Take a seat. It's been a while, and I'd like to review your initial responses before taking this any further. How do you feel about that?"

"Fine."

"Good." Tim sat down, opened a brown file and held a piece of paper up. "Hmmm," he continued. "Not terribly enlightening. Can you remember what we discussed last time?"

"Not really." I hadn't intended to be awkward, but I'd still been coming to terms with the effects of my injuries while feeling forced into therapy. I'd shut out the session like a bad dream and couldn't remember any details of our previous conversation.

"Hardly surprising," said Tim. "We didn't get very far. I asked you why you were with me, and you said it was because your supervisor and doctor had insisted. We then touched on your expectations for the counselling process, to which you replied you had none. You didn't know how many meetings it would take to achieve your goals because you didn't have any, nor could you indicate how to measure success because you assumed therapy would fail. Is that a fair assessment?"

I longed to tell him to shove his therapy where the sun didn't shine. He already sounded supercilious and condescending. But I wasn't here for me. It was all for Dhruv, which meant playing the game.

"I'm sorry. I sounded uncompliant. But I was recovering from a traumatic incident and wasn't myself."

Gibbons beamed as if I had prostrated myself at his feet. "Exactly what I thought," he said. "And why I encouraged you to consider other forms of therapy. Many patients are cynical at the outset. It often takes several sessions to see any significant improvement."

And it guarantees you a tidy sum in fees, I thought.

"I understand," I said. "But I found your assessment of a kidnapper's motivations compelling when you spoke at the station, and I feel it's time to put myself in the hands of a qualified therapist."

"You won't regret it," said Tim. "But we must stick firmly to a professional relationship. Neither of us can discuss police-related matters during these sessions or your therapy when conducting business."

"Naturally," I said, craning my neck towards his computer screen, which sat at an angle. I could make out the start of a list of names, one of which began with the letters PAT and could easily belong to Dhruv Patel.

"Okay. I'd like you to sit here where it's a little more comfortable." Gibbons pointed towards a pale leather chair by the sash window. I stowed my bag and reluctantly walked towards it.

"Lean back," he said. "It's a recliner. Adjust it until you feel relaxed." The chair made a faint whirring noise as the headrest moved down. Tim sat to one side, opened his folder, and took out a pen.

"Let's start with some more questions," he said. "Just answer honestly, and don't think too hard about it."

I nodded.

"Right. What do you like about yourself?" he asked.

My heart sank as a stream of negative thoughts snaked through my mind. I bit my tongue to avoid telling Tim I was an abject failure, sacked from a job I loved because the air force medics wouldn't tolerate asthmatics. And my situation had not improved by living in the boxroom of my boss's house because a psychopathic killer had forced me from my own.

"I enjoy investigating," I said lamely, stalling for time.

"I asked what you liked about yourself." Tim's calm and soothing voice was winding me right up.

"I'm fair and tolerant," I said after a moment's consideration. "And I'm kind. I would never knowingly hurt anyone."

"Good. And what don't you like?"

"Generally? Or about myself?"

"Both."

"I dislike rats," I said, shuddering at the memory of the dead rodent Sean had removed from my kitchen floor earlier in the year.

"Why?"

"They remind me of the killer in Bosworth House."

"Do you often think about your experience there?"

"Not if I can avoid it, but that's only possible with suffi-cient distractions."

"Do you live alone?"

"No," I said, "I live with my boss, though I might as well be alone." I could have bitten off my tongue the moment I uttered the words. Tim seized on the unintended truth like a dog with a bone.

"Why is that?"

"I was less lonely when I lived by myself."

"What are your exact living arrangements?"

"Occupying a box room in a house with Sean and his friend."

"How does that make you feel?"

"Isolated."

"In what way?"

I ground my teeth, clenching my fists and hoping Tim didn't notice. Under other circumstances, I might have pointed out the definition in the Oxford English Dictionary. The meaning of isolation should be obvious to anyone with the most basic literacy skills. But the therapy session wasn't real. I was playing a game, and it didn't matter what I said or felt.

"My flatmate and his friend spend a lot of time togeth-er," I said.

"And you feel left out?"

"A little."

"Have you told them?"

"Of course not."

"Why?"

I stared at him, nonplussed. How could he not appreciate the indignity of admitting loneliness? It was a weakness, an abhorrent failure to connect with the human race.

"Because my flatmate is also my boss."

"What difference does that make?"

"I don't know."

"Would he think less of you?"

I pondered the question. "Probably not. He's quite keen on expressing feelings and getting them out there. You know. Therapy, counselling. The woo-woo stuff."

"Do you see therapy as unscientific?"

"Not at all," I said, snapping back to the brief. "I misspoke. Not woo-woo, as in supernatural. But it's not physical medicine. I didn't mean it as a slur."

"There are no right or wrong answers, Miss Denman," said Tim soothingly. "We are just exploring your thoughts."

I involuntarily shuddered. Exploring thoughts sounded dangerously woolly, like going on a journey and blue-sky thinking. It did not appeal to my direct way of thinking. I closed my eyes and waited for his next question.

"What would your ideal life look like in two years?"

"Oh. Good question. I would like to own a home, obviously. And to meet my mum and dad."

I opened one eye and then the other, watching Tim percolate the newly offered information. Let him make of that what he would.

He licked his lips, opened his mouth to speak and closed them again, seemingly lost for words. I smiled inside at his obvious discomfort, with no intention of helping him understand.

"Have you suffered a family rift?" he asked, eventually.

"No."

"Right. But you're estranged?"

"Not really."

"Do you ever see your parents?"

"My mum is dead."

Tim sighed. "But you never felt you knew her when she was alive?"

"Mum and I were very close."

Tim closed the file, put his pen behind his ear, and steepled his hands. "For this to work, there must be some give and take. I'm not a mind reader, Miss Denman. You have the advantage of knowing every aspect of your life. I can only help by teasing information from you and giving you opportunities to explore your problems through therapy."

I glanced at the clock. We'd been talking for thirty-five minutes, and there wasn't much time left. Learning more about Timothy Gibbons could take a while, and if I didn't watch it, he might conclude I was too hostile to benefit from his help. I gave him what he wanted.

"I'm adopted," I said. "And I didn't know my parents, but I've had my DNA tested and a relative made contact a short time ago. I'm trying not to invest too much hope, but I'm getting closer to finding my origins."

Tim flashed a genuine smile. "Good for you," he said. "What are you hoping for?"

"A relationship with my family. I would like them to accept me and perhaps even like me."

"And how will you make that happen?"

"I'm meeting my cousin Callum on Friday. He's offered to help me contact my parents."

"Are you nervous?"

"Of course. My life could change in a heartbeat either way."

"But at least you would know."

"I suppose so." Since receiving Callum's email, I feared

my long-awaited reunion might not go according to plan. But the finality of a complete rebuff had escaped me until now. I bit my lip, almost ready to cry.

Tim glanced at the wall clock. "I think we'll leave it there," he said.

His timing was awful. He was closing the session just as he'd made me feel vulnerable. I could have hit him. I collected my handbag and left the office feeling lower than I had in days and as I exited the building, I felt the weight of a full bladder and ducked back inside. I couldn't possibly make it back to Truscombe without relieving myself. I opened several doors before finding the WC, finished and washed my hands. As I glanced at the small sash window, a thought occurred to me. There was only a tiny chance of success, but with nothing better to do that evening, it was worth the risk. Especially now Tim had released my most negative thoughts, and I felt I had little to lose. I needed something to occupy me and didn't give a second thought to the possible consequences. So, I slid the window catch into the open position and lifted the sash by a finger's width before placing the top of a marker pen into the corner. Then I crossed my fingers and left the room.

Chapter Twenty-Four

Another evening and another note from Sean announcing his absence from the house. For once, I didn't mind. Though a maverick and cavalier in his attitude to the law, even Sean might object to my evening's plan of action. Had he been at home, he might have asked awkward questions, which I might have felt obliged to answer, him being the boss. This way, I could sneak out as soon as dusk fell and make my way back to Cheltenham. But as I was about to pen my reply, I found a further message on the reverse.

BTW - you could be more sympathetic, Sass. Adam is more than just a case. He's a family friend. Keep your negative thoughts to yourself.

I almost reeled at the unfairness of it. I had bitten my tongue until it hurt, trying not to state the obvious fact that Adam was either imprisoned or dead. Sean must be more upset than I'd realised to take it out on me as if I wasn't drowning in my own problems too. I should probably have let sleeping dogs lie, but I scribbled an angry response.

I get it, Sean; I really do. But you need a reality check. And please don't leave passive-aggressive notes. Living here is hard enough right now. Sass.

Bored with healthy food options, I made a Welsh rarebit mix and slathered it over three sourdough crumpets, following it up with a bag of Skittles. Then I lay on the couch, communing with the lizards for a moment before checking my emails. My stomach churned as I recognised my relative Callum's email address. Seconds passed as my fingers hovered over the phone, reluctant to read his message in case he had changed his mind or couldn't make our meeting. Misery had circled my emotions like a predatory beast since my earlier therapy session and was preparing to pounce. I readied myself to meet the potential bad news head-on.

From: Longfellow999#@hello.co.uk
To: SassD32@wideworld.com

Hello cousin!
Just checking to see if you're still okay for Friday. Five thirty is looking too hopeful now. Can we make it six?
All the best
Callum

Relief washed over me, and I typed an immediate response in the affirmative, hit send, and then checked and double-checked the email had left my outbox. To say I was over-invested in this meeting was an understatement. Tears pricked my eyelids at the thought of an impediment to our successful get-together. I felt myself rocking backwards and forwards as I gazed at the lizards as if they might suddenly spring from their tanks to reassure me all would be fine. Then, realising inactivity was stimulating my anxiety, I took the Vax outside and hoovered my car. Once back, I checked my watch. It was still too early to set off, and in desperation, I collected Sean's empty beer bottles and deposited them at the local supermarket bottle bank. By the time I returned, dressed in my darkest gear and with my trusty torch in hand, it was time to get back into the car.

I zipped down Cleeve Hill and sped through Prestbury, parking a few roads away from the therapist in Montpellier. I scuttled down a nearby alleyway and through a back gate I had noticed from the toilet window earlier that day. To my relief, no one had locked it, nor had they discovered my makeshift block keeping the window from closing. I shoved my fingers underneath and pulled. The sash moved noise-lessly upwards, and I allowed myself a smug smile at my ingenuity. The alleyway was in relative darkness, and I scrambled into the building unseen. With my heart in my mouth, I dropped carefully to the other side, avoiding the toilet cistern and an open toilet seat—bad feng shui. I tiptoed down the corridor and through the open door to the reception area. Pausing briefly, I orientated myself before dipping into a bowl of mints not offered earlier that day, crunching one as I navigated to Tim's office.

Tim didn't operate a clear desk policy, and my name graced the brown file on top of his tray. Naturally, I shone the torch and looked inside, disappointed with his sketchy, unopinionated notes about our earlier encounter. I turned towards his filing cabinet, pulling the drawer with gay abandon, only to find it firmly locked. It momentarily put me off my stride, so I tried his desk drawers. He'd locked one, but the top drawer easily slid open to reveal a tidy interior and a disturbingly neat set of stationery items, but no key. I searched every available surface and receptacle for a key to the filing cabinet without luck and concluded Tim must keep them with him. Something to hide, perhaps? My earlier encounter with Tim Gibbons had done nothing to allay my suspicions about how he conducted his therapy sessions. An extensive search was bound to find evidence he was an imposter. But inevitably, detrimental information would be tricky to find.

With nothing more out of place than an old soft mint wedged into the back of his chair seat, I returned to his desk drawer and flicked through a small journal beneath. I hit paydirt a page in, uncovering a list of unencrypted computer passwords a three-year-old could have used. I pressed a button, and Tim's computer fizzed into life as Windows loaded and the password screen appeared underneath a picture of Scooby Doo. I typed the words Great Dane 74 and bingo. I was into the guts of his practice. I navigated through the folders until I found one marked 'Patients'. Then, quickly locating my digital file and Dhruv's, I began reading just as a pair of car headlamps swept the front of the building and a vehicle pulled up outside. My heart almost stopped beating as I froze in fear.

I quickly switched the screen off and dropped to the floor before crawling across the room. Flattening myself against the wall, I peered outside, heart in mouth, to see two merry women emerging from a taxicab feet from the door. Linking arms, they walked away, gently swaying as they giggled. The driver pulled off with a faint screech of tyres, and the room fell into darkness again. Relief coursed through me, tempering my ambitions. I decided not to read anything but put the memory stick I had brought to good use. Mindful of time and data storage, I only downloaded two files. But I couldn't resist peeping into Tim's inbox and was immediately sucked into a mysterious email trail.

Chapter Twenty-Five

I disregarded the first three emails, which belonged, by right, in the spam box. But the heading of the fourth was too tempting to ignore. Generated by Claire, the receptionist, it contained a list of patients. I wouldn't have bothered clicking had she sent it as an attachment, but she'd dropped it straight into the email body, where the familiar name of Marcus Catton immediately drew my attention. Claire had split her list into two columns, one showing Tim's patients and the other Helen's. Scrolling down, I noticed Helen looked after Marcus Catton while both therapists advised his wife, Abi. I already knew she had participated in their email counselling service. She'd told me herself, but I didn't trust Abi's husband and was keen to look at his patient file. An additional email below the list of patients was equally interesting, and I crouched over the desk, scrutinising the trail.

From: Helen.Chalmers@GibbonsGreyPartnership.co.uk
To: Tim.Gibbons@GibbonsGreyPartnership.co.uk
Date: Tuesday, June 14, 2022, 15.16
Subject: Jem Wright

Tim, A quick heads-up before I pop in and see you later, but I'm fighting a losing battle with this patient. He's seriously disturbed, and nothing I suggest is working. I'm starting to think that Mr Wright gets off on telling me his gruesome thoughts. Shout me when you're free, and we can talk.

From: Tim.Gibbons@GibbonsGreyPartnership.co.uk
To: Helen.Chalmers@GibbonsGreyPartnership.co.uk
Date: Tuesday, June 21, 2022, 09.17
Subject: Jem Wright

Hi Helen

Sorry it's taken a week to dig out the paperwork you wanted, but here's the attachment I promised. As I mentioned in our chat, I had a similar case a few years ago, and this approach worked very well. Have a go. We only drop patients as a last resort, and I don't need to remind you that our profit margins are going the wrong way. If your man wants therapy, we must try to provide it, and God knows he needs it.

Chin up, Tim

From: Helen.Chalmers@GibbonsGreyPartnership.co.uk
To: Tim.Gibbons@GibbonsGreyPartnership.co.uk
Date: Monday, August 15, 2022, 15.53
Subject: Jem Wright

Tim

Jem Wright's weekly email has just dropped early, and I am literally sick with nerves at the thought of opening it. And I'm not squeamish by any means. There's just something about him that makes my skin crawl. Thank God he's an email client. I tried to look him up online a while back. Claire did too. Unsurprisingly, we both drew a blank. I doubt he's using his real name. But you should know I'm close to reporting him to the police. I realise we have a duty of confidentiality, but Wright is a ticking time bomb. What do you think? It might be easier if you speak to one of your contacts as you are well connected with our policing friends.

From: Tim.Gibbons@GibbonsGreyPartnership.co.uk
To: Helen.Chalmers@GibbonsGreyPartnership.co.uk
Date: Monday, August 15, 2022, 16.55
Subject: Jem Wright

Hi Helen

Reporting a patient is a little extreme for my liking. We'll talk about it tomorrow morning. I'll be in for a few hours before leaving for the airport. Can you hold the fort for an extra day? They've delayed my return flight, bloody airlines.

Catch up shortly.

From: Helen.Chalmers@GibbonsGreyPartnership.co.uk
To: Tim.Gibbons@GibbonsGreyPartnership.co.uk
Date: Friday, August 26, 10.27
Subject: Jem Wright

Tim - I'm sorry to ambush you on your first day back, but I've reached my tolerance limits with Jem Wright. I'll need therapy myself if I must deal with him any longer. If you want to keep him on, then you can counsel him. I'm done. Sorry, but enough is enough.

From: Tim.Gibbons@GibbonsGreyPartnership.co.uk

To: Helen.Chalmers@GibbonsGreyPartnership.co.uk
Date: Monday, August 29, 11.11
Subject: Jem Wright

> *Helen - Fine, if that's how you feel. But please email and let him know. Give him any reason you like, but pass on my email address, and I'll take it from there. T.*

From: Helen.Chalmers@GibbonsGreyPartnership.co.uk
To: Tim.Gibbons@GibbonsGreyPartnership.co.uk
Date: Thursday, September 15, 2022, 11.25
Subject: Jem Wright

> *Tim*
>
> *It's been a few weeks since I emailed Mr Wright. He hasn't responded or posted his weekly emails, so the problem has disappeared of its own accord.*

Curious about what a patient must have done to make a therapist refuse to continue treatment, I kept a clear head and set all read emails back to unread. Then I took a biro and noted the password to Helen's computer, which Tim had thoughtfully written next to his, and tiptoed into the next room.

Helen Chalmers' office was a chintzy chaotic mess, over-filled with pot plants, cushions and what looked suspiciously like crocheted throws. It was not a place I could easily relax as a patient, and I felt momentarily grateful that I was under the care of Tim Gibbons. Then I remembered how he'd made me feel earlier that day and how Dhruv had been feeling for months, and I wondered if a tidy office mattered after all. A homemade antimacassar shrouded Helen's computer, and the light from the monitor showed a complete lack of care over security issues. Her open computer showed a screenful of patient notes with no effort made to set a screen saver. I tutted loudly, horrified at what delights the cleaner might see whenever she dusted Helen's desk. And Mr Byron Griggs of Lower Slaughter, whose notes were currently on show, would have cringed in embarrassment at the ease of access to reports of his excessive masturbation habit. I minimised the screen and opened Internet Explorer.

I located Helen's patient files in several folders, not all immediately obvious. It was getting cold, and I was running out of time, but I didn't want to leave without Catton's notes. And eventually, I took the opposite approach that I'd used with Tim's files and downloaded the main folders to capture what I needed. The memory stick quickly filled, with only a few bytes remaining. I pulled it out, maximised Griggs entries so Helen wouldn't notice a change, and pocketed the memory stick. Then I retraced my steps to the toilet, took a quick loo break, and reverse-tailed it out of the window, where I fell with an almighty crash into the rubbish bin I had forgotten was there. It skittered down the yard, coming to rest against the neighbouring fence with a thud, followed by the sound of half the contents emptying on the ground. I stood stock still in horror as the next-door rear lights flicked on and the door flew open.

"Who's there?" I crouched in the shadow of the house as the loud-voiced man thumped the fence every few yards as he navigated down his garden.

"Stay where you are. I'm calling the police." I listened, my chest-thumping at the sound of clicking keys. But after a few silent seconds, I figured he was bluffing and stayed quiet. More silence descended. I couldn't hear or see him and hoped he had gone back inside. But an unexpected rattle of the rear gate made me start in fear, and I watched helplessly as the latch moved upwards, glinting in the moonlight.

He must have seen me as soon as he opened the gate. His eyes widened in surprise at the sight of my slight figure, a beanie hat low over my head and my collar high. He sprang towards me, but I was quicker, darting to one side and pushing past him towards the gate. He grabbed my coat, and I faltered, reeling backwards towards him. But with one mighty shove, I threw him off balance, pulled from his grasp and legged it up the alleyway, running for dear life. I didn't dare return to the car in case he saw me but weaved through the streets of Montpellier, across the roundabout and towards Suffolk Square, where I waited it out in the grounds of the art deco flats.

It was after eleven by the time I returned to Sean's house in Truscombe, desperate for company and a few kind words. But the house was in darkness: no Sean and no Jack. I flicked on the kettle and retrieved a cup before noticing another piece of paper below the one I'd left earlier. At some stage in the evening, Sean had returned and written me another note. I picked it up and read it with a sinking heart.

Then perhaps it's time you found another place to live. Sean.

Chapter Twenty-Six

I was in the office, not doing much of anything when my phone rang. I glanced at the familiar number, snatching it up when I realised Tom was calling.

"Tom," I said, relieved to hear a human voice.

"Hey. How's it going?"

"It's okay. How are you?"

"Busy. Where's that boss of yours?" I sighed. Where indeed?? Sean and I had passed like ships at night for over twenty-four hours. It was painfully obvious that he was avoiding me. I'd bumped into Jack once or twice, but he'd said very little, and I was feeling the weight of loneliness like never before.

"In Evesham," I said. "He left me a note." It wasn't actually true. Sean had entered an appointment in our shared office diary simply stating *Evesham Snout*, and I had assumed he was consulting with his druggie informants.

"What's he doing there?"

"I don't know," I lied. Things were bad enough between

Sean and me without me being loose-lipped. "Can I help you?" I asked.

"Not really."

"Great. It's good to feel useful."

"Is something wrong?"

"Lots of somethings."

"Want to talk later?"

I nodded, but the words stuck in my throat, and I gulped down a sob.

"Sass?"

I sniffed. "I'm okay."

"No, you're not. Are you at the office?"

"Yes."

"I'll do this in person instead of over the phone. Be with you in five."

I'd mopped away the worst of my tears before Tom arrived, but one look at his concerned face and another ugly crying fit escaped unbidden.

Tom said nothing but gathered me in his arms while I sobbed it out. And when my shoulders stopped heaving, we stood awkwardly, neither of us knowing how best to break the embrace. Reluctantly, I pulled away.

"I'm so sorry," I said. "You must have a million better things to do."

"My choice," said Tom and I inwardly cringed, knowing he risked a bollocking or worse, at his sudden disappearance from the station. "Now, are you going to tell me what's wrong?"

"I don't know where to start. Or if I should. I mean, you're Sean's friend as much as mine."

"You guys having problems?"

I nodded. "Hasn't Sean said anything?"

"No. He's too busy looking after Jack, not helped by this business with Adam."

"It's hardly Adam's fault," I said, reaching for another tissue. "He didn't ask to be kidnapped."

"Sean knows that. But he blames himself for reasons I don't fully understand."

"I didn't realise he was so upset. It's hard to tell what Sean's thinking. He's rarely serious and takes everything in his stride."

"Not this, Sass. I saw him last night, and he's pretty cut up about Adam. This whole information-sharing business is getting tricky with him so heavily involved."

"Yet you're still keeping us up to date."

Tom patted my shoulder and approached the coffee machine. "Do you mind?" he asked.

"It's probably stone cold."

"Tepid," he said, placing a hand on the jug. "Want one?"

I shook my head.

"The thing is," said Tom, half filling the least chipped mug, "Kim and Sean go back a long way. Their relationship is fractious at times, but there's a deep mutual respect. She values his opinion and his daring, for that matter. And we are so hidebound with restrictions, budgets and politics, that it's bloody hard to get the job done. We both trust Sean and yes, he's a good friend. But he's heavily invested in Adam's welfare, which might make him incautious."

"Are you cutting us loose?"

"No. Quite the opposite. We've discovered the identity of the Tewkesbury victim, and I called to give Sean the heads-up."

"Okay. I don't know when he'll be in next. He's avoiding me."

"By boycotting his own office?"

"I think so."

"What happened?" Tom pulled up a chair and sat opposite, casting a sympathetic gaze my way.

"He wants me to leave."

"I doubt it."

"He wrote it in a note."

"In frustration, probably. Sean's impulsive. You know that."

"Our living arrangement isn't working. We aren't working. Not since Jack moved in. They're out all the time, and they never include me. I'm so alone."

Tom placed his hand over mine.

"I'm sorry, Sass. It's a shame. Sean rates you highly. You've lasted longer than anyone else. I'm sure you can work it out."

"Not unless I move away."

"Perhaps it's time."

I sighed, visions of my trauma in Bosworth House filling me with a stomach-clenching fear. "I'm frightened of living alone," I said.

"I understand. Then you'll need to find a way to make it up with Sean."

"How? He doesn't want me there. Not now that Jack's a permanent fixture."

"It's more that Jack is a useful distraction for him. Sean's not one for sharing his feelings when he can sink a few beers and talk about football instead."

"Oh. Is that what they do?"

"Pretty much. Talk crap, shoot pool, perhaps play the odd game of darts. They just hang out. It's all very light-hearted."

"Not my thing at all."

"Exactly."

"But you go?"

"Occasionally. When I've nothing better to do."

"Are you still swiping right?"

Tom grinned. "Why not? I won't meet a partner through work. The station's too small, and the WPCs are all firmly in the friend zone."

Tom's smile was infectious, and I couldn't help returning it, my mood lifting.

"This is so much better than therapy."

"Don't tell that to Doctor Tim."

"He's not a good counsellor," I replied. "He made me feel awful yesterday."

"That's the nature of therapy," said Tom. "Picking at the scabs of your past will never be sweetness and light. It will help in the long run."

"You're very wise, Tom. Tell me this though. Do you rate Tim Gibbons? He creeps me out."

Tom cocked his head and considered my question. "He's a bit full of himself, strikes me as overconfident sometimes. But it's nothing to worry about."

"Have you checked his qualifications?"

"Of course not. I'm a humble PC. My superiors will have, naturally."

"But can you be sure?"

"I am completely confident. Whatever tree you are barking up, you've taken a wrong turn. You're entitled to your opinion about his abilities, but there's no reason to doubt his qualifications."

Tom leaned forward and wagged a friendly finger towards me. "You need to get a grip, young lady."

"I know. What about this Tewkesbury vic then?"

179

"Sean ought to be here. He won't appreciate me leaving him out of the information loop."

"But he isn't."

"Okay. I'll keep trying his mobile. But in the meantime, I'll tell you this. The Tewkesbury victim is called John Noble. He's a well-known down-and-out with alcohol dependencies. Noble's chief place of abode is Ashchurch, where he sometimes stays with his elder brother, but he's out more often than not. Frankly, the family has had enough. Noble's an amiable guy, but he doesn't work and can't support himself. It's taken its toll. He was last seen about a week ago."

"That's a surprise. I assumed he'd been shackled for longer."

"They don't think so. Noble was captured recently but had barely eaten and must have gone through hell without access to alcohol."

"You'd think he'd have yelled the place down. Someone must have held him securely."

"For sure. The evidence showed he was gagged and restrained. Finnegan is certain it's the same guy who took Ella."

"Guy?"

"Most likely."

"But Ella was slight, and an alcoholic can't easily fight back."

"I take your point, but we're confident we're looking for a man."

"Who is?"

The door opened, and Sean emerged, casting a suspicious glance at Tom.

"Ah, good timing," said Tom.

"Isn't it? Sass, go and get a couple of doughnuts."

"I don't want one."

Sean raised an angry eyebrow. "Just do it."

I grabbed my coat, sick to the stomach at his disregard for me. Sean had never worried about discussing his affairs in my presence. But whatever he intended to say to Tom was not for my ears. I crept from the office, humiliated and despairing, fearful of losing my job and my home.

Chapter Twenty-Seven

I didn't return to the office. I couldn't. Instead, I wandered through the abbey in the centre of Truscombe, sitting for a moment on a bench outside, watching the world go by. But the cheery faces of people hurrying through the little market town did nothing to improve my mood, so I gave up and returned to Carlton Drive, hoping that Jack wasn't in. To my relief, the house was silent, and I sat on the sofa in front of the lizards and bawled. The largest, a bottle green gecko called Douglas, stared at me through slitty eyes, his little flat toes pressed against the glass tank, and I couldn't help but smile. Then he opened his mouth, reminding me of the tongueless maw of Veronica Lewis. I shuddered, feeling nauseous and left the living room, rushing upstairs before throwing myself on my bed and crying it out again. I sobbed for half an hour, and when I had expelled all the self-pity from my body, I tried to view my situation with a rational detachment I did not feel. But my head was foggy with indecision, and I needed to apply myself to something unrelated to my current misery. I'd flipped my laptop closed when I left Sean's office, shoving it in the bag and over my shoulder as if I subliminally knew I wasn't coming back. So, I returned downstairs, collected it from the hallway and resumed my position in the lounge. I fumbled for the memory stick I'd taken from Tim Gibbons' office and clicked it into the USB port. Then I opened the still-switched-on laptop, and the screen flickered to life.

I'd taken a cursory glance at the files earlier that day, but Tom's arrival had distracted me from getting into the guts of the stolen data. And as I opened file after file of sensitive personal information, I cringed at my cavalier decision to steal it. I'd based my suspicions on nothing more substantial than believing Tim Gibbons was a piss-poor therapist. I'd taken the data not only to expose him but also to help Dhruv. Yet as I located Dhruv's name and my mouse hovered over his file, I knew I would never open it. It would be a catastrophic abuse of our friendship. He was entitled to his private thoughts, as I was to mine, and this database of people to theirs. I had made a poor decision. I right-clicked Dhruv's file and deleted it from the memory stick, immediately feeling better. Then I repeated my actions as name after name disappeared, some complete strangers, others like the Cattons known to me. And though sorely tempted to sneak a peek at Marcus Catton's data, I didn't give in and kept deleting. Right up to the point when I reached a file titled Patient X, whose anonymity seemed like fair game. No identifier, no cause for alarm. No way I could ever know to whom it related. So, I gave in and clicked, sorted the files into date order and read.

Case study Patient X extracted from sessions 2 - 5 2021.

Patient response to my initial question about loneliness.

I always knew Mum preferred my brother, but it made little sense. I was quiet and easy to manage, happily fishing for hours on the edge of a riverbank making no trouble for anyone. He was a mini dynamo, always on the go, demanding and resistant to discipline. Yet even so, she loved him more. I bore it for a while, but one day when she left us alone, I took the opportunity to teach him how it felt to be marginalised and lonely. I tricked my brother into the shed at the bottom of the garden, turned the key and left him there for two hours. When Mum returned, I was tugging the door, tears streaming down my face as I pretended to let him out without the key that I'd hidden in the cellar. Ashen-faced, she shot back into the house, retrieving a spare I didn't know we had, released him and gathered him into her arms as he sobbed. If my brother suspected me, he never said. And my mum was utterly oblivious. I felt satisfied at having meted out a crucial life lesson undetected. Throughout my brother's captivity, my senses were on high alert, my heart thumping in anticipation of his discomfort. At the same time, a curious sensation of pleasure surged in waves through my body. It was dark in the shed, with a tiny, dirty window to one side. Our garden was wild and uncultivated, the shed a repository for old unwanted things. The damp wood, heavily webbed ceiling and a floor filled with creepy crawlies had given my brother nightmares for weeks after. He would wake screaming in the small hours, and I listened in anticipation before feeling a familiar disappointment as Mum rushed to comfort him. That incident summed up my childhood. Always the quiet forgotten son.

Therapists note. Evidence of shallow emotions, entitlement & self-centred nature. Manipulative personality disorder? Why is it all centred on childhood? Ask about loneliness as an adult.

Dear Helen. You ask if I have always been lonely. The answer is a simple yes. No one knew or understood me from my earliest memories let alone into adulthood. My time in further education amplified the lengths to which others drove me in my quest to fit in. They never knew how hard I struggled. I held myself well and projected a strong, well-adjusted image. I reached out and was friendly to all. But I never gained their unconditional friendship, spending my time on the outskirts of the various groups. I was never singled out or marginalised, yet remained on the periphery, as if they didn't entirely trust me. Like they knew something was wrong. Because, of course, it is. Even I know that. I don't feel things as others do. Some days I sense emotion. I might be aggrieved, bitter, or disappointed, but happiness eludes me; I can't relate to love. And compassion - well, I'm familiar with the word and what it means, but I cannot find it in me at all. So, yes. Further education was a disappointment but also a revelation.

You asked me what I wanted from these sessions. I want to understand myself. I'd like you to provide a tangible reason why I feel so different to those around me. Diagnose me, if you will. Tell me what I am and whether I might change because my loneliness gnaws like a starving rat. And I think it's because I can't relate to other people. Animals, yes, to a certain extent. But people, not at all. And my only true pleasure in life comes from nefarious acts against the people I long to understand. Why? Because it gives me a power I don't possess, forming a dependency I don't deserve. I know you're dying to escape my childhood memories, so I'll offer you something from my later teenage years. I won't string this out. I captured someone again. There, I said it. Don't worry. She didn't die. Not like the first one, but that was opportunistic and something I am not ready to discuss with you yet. But a chance meeting with a girl allowed me a way to indulge my darkest desires, in total anonymity. She didn't have a clue, didn't know me at all, but I had been watching her for some time, taking careful note of her habits. That's the trouble with routine. It brings a reliable timeline on which someone like me can prey. I knew she'd leave the gym at 7.30 on Thursday night because she always did. And I thought about whether I could take my chance then, but there was no possibility without detection. Friday nights were a different matter. She regularly jogged, and her route took her through the woods, past an abandoned building once used as a swimming pool, now locked for our protection as it still contained hazards. But in the dead of night during one of my nocturnal wanderings, I had snipped the padlock and investigated by torchlight. The filthy premises resembled a reverse Tardis, far smaller inside than they initially appeared. The ancient electrics had been long since removed, and without my trusty torch, the place lurked in utter darkness like a mausoleum. It was perfect.

Friday evening at precisely seven sixteen, I slid a cheap battery-operated cassette player in through the door, left it ajar and waited behind a tree. She arrived bang on time, panting with exertion, her eyes creasing in concern as she approached the building and heard the cries of a baby in distress. She stopped, as I knew she would, and strode towards the door, confident at first, then with trepidation as she considered her position. I thought, at first, that she might run for it, but curiosity got the better of her, and she pushed the door open and peered inside. I was right behind her, placing my hand on the small of her back and shoving her through. Then I grabbed the door handle, threw the bolt and snapped a brand-new padlock through it. She screamed, begging for release. But she could not have seen my face and I left her yelling, safely watching from a distance until darkness fell.

A path ran through the woods, and although not regularly used, walkers and runners would cross from time to time. Someone could have found her that night. If not that night, then over the weekend. But in a massive stroke of luck, her weak cries went unheard until five days later, by which time I had visited often, gaining maximum pleasure from my captive's distress. No one had reported her missing. No one had questioned why she wasn't in any lectures. Her flaky friends had made assumptions about her whereabouts without ever bothering to check. And that made me feel good, less lonely. If someone who regularly participated in so many clubs could be so little missed, then my world wasn't as dark and solitary as it appeared. When they eventually found her and took her to the hospital half dead from hypothermia and malnutrition, thoughts of her captivity kept me going when times were tough. The police briefly appeared, but nobody knew who had lured her to the building or why they had done it. And once again, I remained unsuspected and anonymous, living as if nothing had happened. But of course, it had solidified my feelings as captor, my way of gaining a balm to my loneliness. So, tell me. What do you think as you read this? Am I a lost cause? What must I do to overcome this empty feeling, only relieved by exerting my power over another? Answers, please, and soon.

Therapists note. This response reads like a novel, and I wonder if the patient is testing me somehow. It wouldn't be the first time we've experienced an external audit. Still, it's an unusual way to go about it and doesn't ring true. Surely something as strange as this account would have turned up in the papers. Not that there's any indication about the location, making it impossible to check. I will take the account with a pinch of salt and approach the issue differently. Patient X seems curiously reluctant to discuss his (her?) adult life. Perhaps I'll learn more if I address this directly.

Chapter Twenty-Eight

Reading about Patient X had left me feeling physically sick. I'd broken from the article and resumed my background checks, working from home for the rest of the afternoon in the hope that Sean would arrive, see me beavering away and wouldn't question why I hadn't returned to the office. But predictably, he did not. Sean must have come home after I went to bed, as his car was on the drive when I made a cup of tea the following day. But our paths did not cross, and he was still upstairs when I made the lonely trek to work. I'd felt so miserable the previous night that I'd barely eaten, and my stomach was growling. So, I dropped all pretence at dieting and called into the local store for a duck wrap and a granola bar. Not the healthiest breakfast, but I was past caring. As I scanned my purchases through the machine, an unwelcome pair of eyes settled on me. I looked up to see Miles Savage leering at me with a smug expression on his rat-like face.

I nodded, in no mood to exchange small talk with a reporter, but he placed his items to one side, crossed his arms and leaned on the metal rail, watching me as if he was about to prevent an attempted shoplifting.

I raised an eyebrow. "Yes?"

"You haven't heard then?"

"Heard what?"

"About the body."

It was my turn to stand smugly. I returned the crossed-arm gesture and raised it with a head shake. "Which one?"

"Not Ms Burton," he said.

"Yes, I know about the Tewkesbury victim."

"Obviously. That's not what I meant."

"Sorry?" My carefully cultivated look of disinterest vanished in the face of the unexpected.

"Oh, so you don't know?"

"Of course, I do."

"No, you don't. Talk about late to the party."

"Whatever." I hurled the remaining products through the scanner, inserted my card and flounced from the shop before he could quiz me any further, arriving at the office in the grip of a quandary. I ought to tell Sean that there might be another body in play, but we were barely speaking, and he might already know, in which case I would fall even further in his estimation. I settled for sending a text message.

I've just bumped into Miles Savage in the corner store. He's hinted at another victim.

Sean's reply returned at the speed of an Exocet missile. *Take it with a pinch of salt. He's full of shit.*

I shrugged Sean's lack of interest off as best I could and peeled the plastic from the wrap. I was about to take a bite when my phone buzzed on the desk.

What exactly did Savage say?

He asked if I knew about the body. When I mentioned Ella and the Tewkesbury victim, he said I was late to the party.

Okay. Standby.

I did as he asked, adopting the sitting equivalent while enjoying my unusual breakfast, relieved at the unconfrontational stream of communication with Sean. But I didn't get to sample the granola bar before the landline went. Sighing, I picked it up.

"Sass. Close the office and get yourself to the woods," said Sean.

"Now there's an offer I can't refuse," I replied, regretting the words as soon as they left my mouth, but with friendlier relations established, I'd felt brave.

"This is serious."

"Which woods?"

"Corndean. And make it snappy."

"I will. But can you be more specific? Only there's a fair amount of acreage to cover."

"Sorry. Tell you what. Park up in the layby near Papermill Lane. I'll meet you there."

"Okay. Give me twenty minutes…" But it was too late. Sean had put the phone down.

Stowing the granola in my pocket, I risked indigestion by jogging home, where I'd parked my car outside number twelve. Not only had I lost my bedroom to Jack, but also my regular parking space in front of the house. But for once, it didn't matter. I drove to the layby with Toploader's "Dancing in the Moonlight" playing full blast and was in good spirits when Sean's head popped up from the side of his car.

"Something in my tyre," he growled by way of explanation.

"Shouldn't you get that fixed?"

"In good time. It'll be alright for a day or two. I've bigger fish to fry."

Sean strode ahead, and I was out of breath when we reached Papermill Lane.

"Is this to do with Miles Savage."

"Yes. The little weasel was right."

"Another body?"

"So it would appear."

"Right." I unzipped my fleece as a cloud drifted from above, and the full strength of the morning sun enveloped me. "More details?" I asked, hopefully.

"Soon. Just keep up."

I followed in Sean's footsteps, wondering whether he'd intended his remark as a physical measure or a swipe at my mental effectiveness. But he was in no mood to talk, and I was reluctant to disturb our uneasy truce. As I reached the top of the lane, I saw a seemingly impossible feat of off-road driving, as a police car idled two hundred yards in the distance.

"How did that get there?" I asked.

"Dunno. Shouldn't be possible," grunted Sean. "Still, she's never been one for unnecessary exercise."

"Who?"

"Kim."

"Kim Robbins?"

"No. Kim bloody Wilde. I thought we'd learn the lyrics for 'Kids in America' while we were walking."

"Alright. No need for that."

Sean stopped and glared at me. Then his features soft-ened. "Sorry. You're right. I shouldn't take it out on you."

I stared guppy-like, taken aback at his apology, but Sean didn't wait for a reaction and made a beeline for the car.

Kim saw him, rolled down the window and tossed what looked like a blue nappy sack towards him.

"Put those on," she said.

Sean peeled the plastic apart and handed me a pair of shoe covers.

"Going through the motions, are we?" he asked.

"Absolutely. It's almost pointless, given the circumstances. But you shouldn't be here, so let's not complicate things with unnecessary footprints." Kim had opened the car door and was busy wagging a finger at Sean as she spoke.

"Whatever you say, Kim. So, you've found another body? Only Tom neglected to mention it when we had our little chat yesterday."

"Quite right. He was under strict instructions."

"Sorry, that doesn't make any sense." I had intended to stay quietly in the background but couldn't help challenging Kim.

"Oh, but it does."

"Nope. I agree with Sass." My heart flipped at Sean's unexpected affirmation.

"You'll feel differently in a moment," Kim replied. "Let's go for a little walk."

A few moments later, we regrouped by a fallen tree, around which a small square of police tape flickered in the breeze.

"Take a seat," said Kim, gesturing towards the hefty log. We perched like expectant students at a lecture as she stood before us and opened her mouth to speak.

"Why the secrecy?" interrupted Sean impatiently.

"Give me a chance." Kim scowled and crossed her arms.

"Well, a phone call would have been easier."

"Have you somewhere pressing to be?"

"Actually, yes."

"Fine. I'm sure Sass and I will manage between us."

"No need. I'm here now."

"And naturally, it's all about you, Sean. A fine start to my first post-sickness investigation."

"Your case? What's happened to Finnegan? Have they seen sense and sacked him?"

"No. He's working his case and I'm working mine."

"I don't follow."

"Are you suggesting this dead body is unrelated to the others?" I asked, suddenly realising what Sean had failed to comprehend.

"Exactly that."

Sean shot me a glare. "It still doesn't make sense."

Kim raised her fingers to her lips. "Then I'll tell you. These woods aren't beautiful by accident. The Woodland Trust manages them extremely well. I won't bore you with coppicing techniques; suffice to say that one of the woodsmen got quite a shock while thinning these beauties earlier this week." Kim pointed to several stumps directly ahead of the log.

"See that piece of cleared ground dead ahead?"

Sean and I nodded.

"That's where we found him."

"Who?"

"Not a clue, and we may never find out. No ID, you see. Anyway. One of the woodsmen stepped on a stick which cracked. On closer inspection, it turned out to be a human femur. Long story short, he found human remains."

"In a shallow grave?"

"No. The body wasn't hidden at all. Not deliberately, anyway. But leaves and foliage covered it over time."

"Ah. That makes sense. How did you draw the short straw if it's a natural death?"

"We don't know that it is. But with a dead body on our doorstep and another in a neighbouring town, the pathologist was out of the starting blocks quick-smart. He hasn't finished yet, but we're looking at a death from about three years ago, give or take."

"Then it could be natural?"

"Possibly. But I think Davies is holding back. You know what he's like. He won't commit until he's sure."

"So, a historical murder, perhaps?"

"Could be."

"How does Savage know?"

"Don't," said Kim bitterly. "One day, I'll find out where he gets his information, and God help the idiot supplying it."

"What can we do?" I asked.

"Nothing. It's an internal issue."

"Not that. The third body."

"Ah, yes. My team currently consists of me with part shares in Tom. He's with Finnegan today. I'm working on a couple of theories and could do with some backup. We'll check our records, and I'll try to hurry the analysts along. But I need urgent information on local missing persons— especially those who may not have come to official attention. Sadly, not all missing people are reported. You know what I mean."

"Okay," I said. "I can prioritise that. A description of the body would help."

"I've got nothing. Dai checked the hipbone and said it was male. That's all we know until he finishes the autopsy."

"It helps." I glanced at my phone, wondering how quickly I could return to the office and get on with it.

"You said a couple of theories?" Sean stared at the ground, his mind churning.

"I did. As I said on the phone, this isn't Adam. But that doesn't mean it's not connected with his disappearance. It's less than half a mile to the house where they found Adam all those years ago, and this poor chap might be another victim."

Sean looked up. "Possibly," he said slowly. "But you've never found Adam's captor. And you're only surmising a connection between Ella Burton and Adam. Who's to say this isn't the dead body of the man who held him captive in the first place?"

Chapter Twenty-Nine

Back at the office, Sean sat sullenly behind his desk while I fired up the office PC, eager to get started.

"It wasn't unreasonable," he muttered under his breath.

"What?"

"Sorry. I was just thinking aloud."

"Tell me."

"Kim's fixated on linking the two recent bodies with Adam. I'm sure she's right that the same person murdered John Noble and Ella Burton, but I still don't buy into the connection with Adam."

"To be fair, your opinion changes every day."

"It's not straightforward." Sean slumped in his chair, picked up a pen, and tapped it against his upper lip.

"Penny for them?"

"Are we looking at two different cases?"

"Perhaps," I said. "Adam Harding is definitely missing, which casts doubt on your assumption about his kidnapper randomly dying in the woods."

"I know," Sean admitted. "It was a stupid suggestion, which is why Kim shot it down in flames. I shouldn't have speculated, but that was when I first wondered if we were looking at two completely different scenarios."

"Being what?"

"Not sure yet. But chronologically, Adam was kidnapped and held that year. Another person died in the woods on or close to that time. It might be coincidental."

"Don't forget the death may yet prove natural."

Sean's phone buzzed on his desk. He glanced, held his hand up and opened it, staring wide-eyed at the screen. "Blimey. I wasn't expecting that."

"What?"

"A message from Kim." Sean slid the phone towards me.

DD just called. I'll ring you from the car in a moment.

"That's annoying. I presume she means Dai Davies and the autopsy results are in. Couldn't she just tell us what they are?" I complained, my fingers itching to begin.

"Kim's too canny to put that sort of thing in writing. And Davis can't have whipped up a full autopsy report that quickly. He must have found something interesting."

"Right. Well, it won't make any difference to my research, so I'll crack on."

"Lucky you. I need to be elsewhere. If Kim doesn't ring in the next ten minutes, I'll have to speak from the car."

"Where are you going?"

"Can't say."

"Of course you can't," I said, my voice dripping with resentment.

"It's not what you think."

"None of my business, I'm sure."

"Look, Sass," he began, but the shrill sound of Sean's annoying ringtone filled the air. He snatched up the phone.

"Kim?"

I continued typing, pretending not to care, but irritated that Sean hadn't turned on the speaker so I could hear.

"Grief." Sean let out a low whistle, pursed his lips and listened intently.

"Well, that's put a different complexion on things. I think we can safely label him as another victim. Yes, absolutely. She's working on it now. Email? Yes, if it's easier. I agree. It's a top priority, I promise. Speak soon."

"Wow," said Sean, distractedly shoving his phone in a drawer.

"Tell me then."

"I was right. The autopsy is still in progress, but Dai delivered the headline news. Guess what he found around the victim's left wrist?"

"A watch or a bracelet?"

"Nope."

"Fine. A Fitbit, then?"

"Not that either. The remains of a chunky piece of rope. He's sure someone used it as a restraint."

It was my turn to whistle. "Then we are looking at another victim. Someone taken after Adam, perhaps?"

"Or before."

"Which sounds worryingly similar to the two latest deaths."

"I may need to eat a large slice of humble pie." Sean sighed and cupped his hands over his face, his demeanour suddenly serious.

"Fuck. This doesn't bode well for Adam. Whenever I think he's safe and not part of this sequence, something changes my mind. I don't like our chances of finding him.

Hell, Sass. I've already lost one brother, and the thought of losing one of my closest school friends is too much. Just too fucking much."

I bit my lip, struggling to decide how to comfort him. But he seemed so alone that I abandoned my natural reserve, knelt by his desk and put my arm around his shoulder. "We will find him, Sean. We will, I promise."

He nuzzled into my neck for a moment, then jerked away as if electrocuted.

"Sure."

I resumed my seat, hurt at his rejection, staring at the screen while he regained his composure. Sean grabbed his keys, phone and jacket before heading towards the door.

"Got to go. See you later." I winced as he slammed the door behind him, cringing at the thought of my unwelcome intrusion into his personal space. But almost immediately, the door opened again.

"Thanks, Sass," he said, forcing a smile. "Appreciated. Catch you later."

And then he was gone.

I spent five solid hours researching missing people over the last four years in a twenty-mile radius of Truscombe, seeing only slim pickings. Then common sense prevailed, and I visited the storeroom and unarchived the paperwork from last year's investigation into Amy Swanson. We'd worked the case hard, not only digitally but also using physical newspapers. Ten minutes later, I'd added another half a dozen names to my list. I debated waiting until morning when I'd have another go, but giving Kim an early set of results wouldn't do any harm, so I emailed my findings with a promise of more to follow.

The end of the week was looming, and meeting my cousin weighed heavily on my mind. As I walked through

Truscombe, now quiet at the end of the working day, unending visions of rejection looped through my head, not for the first time. Intrusive thoughts of not being good enough had started within hours of our first contact, and the closer our meeting got, the louder they became. It was increasingly difficult to block their insidious mantra. Though tired and hungry by the time I arrived at Carlton Drive, I was desperate to relax but knew I needed an urgent distraction. A run might have been tempting if I had fully recovered from my back injury, but it was still sore from my unwise intrusion into Tim Gibbon's clinic. A pavement pounding would only set me back further. I was musing over the best way to occupy my time when I opened the front door to a high-pitched whistle and saw Jack waving a dish towel underneath the smoke alarm.

"What's happened?" I asked.

"Nothing to worry about. Got a bit distracted cooking a chop."

I ventured into the kitchen to see a cremated piece of meat welded to Sean's newly purchased frying pan and involuntarily grimaced at the acrid smell of burning.

"Blimey. It's a good thing you noticed. What happened?"

"I fell asleep in front of the TV. Nothing to worry about. I'll clear it up."

I threw open the kitchen door and left him to it, wondering how Sean would view the matter. He'd been supremely laid back about Jack up to now, ignoring the muddles and general untidiness. But if Sean had a spidey-sense, it was smell. He could pick up an odour change at two hundred yards. Perhaps this would be the beginning of Jack's downfall.

I checked the lizards before curling up on the couch.

But after several moments of staring at Jack's half-empty beer glass, accompanied by another surge of intrusive insults from my subconscious, I retreated upstairs. My laptop lay where I'd left it, and I remembered the memory stick and my unfinished deletions. I cleared everything down except the Patient X file, then dipped in for another read.

Chapter Thirty

Therapist's note. Draft reply - Email Tim and ask his opinion before sending.

Of course, you are not a lost cause, although what you have said is disturbing, unpleasant and something you must try to resist. I will, of course, maintain complete confidentiality, though it's only fair to warn you that it is not in your interests to divulge anything criminal. You say that exerting power is the only way to control your loneliness, but I would encourage you to broaden your mind. You have already taken the first step towards rehabilitation by acknowledging your issues and seeking help. Perhaps you could consider your reasons for hurting the girl in the context of underlying causes of abusive behaviour, which we broadly categorise as defensive and offensive. From your recent communication, you did not know the girl who posed no threat to you. Unless she represented another person in your life who might have caused you harm? This suggests you fall into the latter category, and your behaviour is offensive. Honesty is the key here. Please quantify what your need for power fulfils. Does it make you feel better about yourself? Or deliver a feeling of superiority?

I want to address this during our next session to give you a substantive response. To that end, please answer the above questions and briefly describe how you have dealt with loneliness in your more recent adult life. Please be frank about your feelings but don't embellish your account.

Kind regards Helen

(Sent following a slight correction by Tim.)

Patient X Response

Dear Helen

I would thank you for your reply, but it barely qualifies as such. Too brief for the amount I pay you. I was expecting more. However, despite your underlying cynicism, I want your help. I need to reform. I mean it. My life is hurtling towards a precipice, and I fear for my sanity. So, to my considered response, truthfully given.

I don't understand your implication that I physically hurt the girl. I didn't touch her save for the tiniest push. Mother Nature did the rest. I merely trapped her. Yes, against her will. But understand this. I would have let her go eventually. Before she died, I mean. Why did I trap her? I told you that. Holding power over a human being drives away my despair, bringing temporary light into the dark empty void in my life. I suppose you could say it was offensive in both senses of the word. The girl was not a figurehead for an abusive relative or other wicked person. Nobody ever hurt me, at least not physically. It did not make me feel better or give me a sense of superiority, but I found it deeply gratifying. I did it because I wanted to.

Now, how do I deal with loneliness as an adult? I don't, hence the therapy. I realise you know little about me, as I intended. How old am I? Am I rich or poor, male or female? Do I even live in this country? Questions, questions. I am what I am, and giving too much detail might distract you from your task, which is to fix me and soon. So, let me try to provide you with some background.

Sometimes I walk, sometimes I chat, sometimes I get drunk. I read, watch television, and do everything ordinary people do. I work, you know, like anyone else. Yet still, the loneliness of my existence shrouds me like the darkest fog. It overwhelms me, even when I'm surrounded by people. I can never escape it. At best, I look for ways to distract it. I have tried everything you will no doubt advise me to do, like joining clubs and societies, visiting the theatre, and having interminable conversations with friends and strangers. I'm not solitary. People form part of my life. But nobody, however close, can mask the black dog rampaging through my mind. It's because I am different, perhaps even unique. The truth is that my brain was wired differently from birth. So, Helen, what do you think about that? Give me some hope and a decent word count this time.

Chapter Thirty-One

"Sean?" I peered from my bedroom door as the landing light clicked on a few minutes after midnight. I'd tried to dismiss thoughts of Patient X, but his sinister exploits intruded into my thoughts, keeping me from sleeping. I was still wide awake when I heard the soft tread of footsteps on the stairs, preceded by a chink of light beneath my door.

"What is it?" Sean whispered, shielding his eyes from the shadeless lamp bulb.

"Are you okay?"

"Of course. Tired, though."

And he looked it. The unnecessarily bright bulb illuminated the bags under Sean's eyes and his drawn, haggard features.

"Want to talk about it?"

"Not really."

"Are you sure?"

Sean lowered his hand, cast a knowing glance towards Jack's room and crossed his arms. "What's on your mind, Sass?"

"Ah. Well, now you come to mention it."

Sean sighed, but I ploughed on. "I'm in a quandary."

"Go on."

"Let me get my dressing gown."

"Fine. Let's not disturb Jack. Meet me in the kitchen. But be quick. I'm knackered."

I donned my robe and was downstairs in time to see Sean switching on the kettle, his nostrils flaring like a startled stallion. "What's that God-awful smell?"

"Jack."

"I know you don't like him, but there's no need for insults."

"We get on well enough," I protested. "And I didn't mean Jack smells. He caused the smell. Here." I recovered Sean's best frying pan from the kitchen bin. Despite his best efforts, Jack had been unable to save it.

Sean glared in disgust. "I haven't the energy," he said. "It can wait until morning. Now, what's on your mind?"

I considered my response while Sean made the tea. With Sean recently in a better mood, I had disregarded his moving-out suggestion for the last few days, but it was still weighing heavily on my mind. That and Patient X's weird proclivities for capturing people contributed further to my sleep deprivation. Sean passed me an overfilled cup, and we sat at the breakfast bar while I mopped the tea ring with my sleeve.

"That note you wrote the other night."

"Ah, yes. You caught me at a bad time."

"Understood. I can go if you want me to, but I'll need some notice."

"Of course you will. And I'm not suggesting you leave immediately."

My heart dropped, and my face must have reflected my

disappointment as Sean immediately corrected himself. "That's not to say I want you to leave. But you've probably had enough by now. It must be odd sharing when you've had your own place."

"I spent years living in the sergeant's mess. Being around people is nothing new."

"Understood. Stay as long as you want. It's no skin off my nose."

I sipped my tea, still feeling conflicted. Though Sean wasn't shooing me off the premises, his ambivalence about my staying did not indicate any enthusiasm for our current living arrangements. But satisfied he wasn't about to evict me, I changed the subject.

"I've come into the possession of some patient notes," I began.

Sean raised an eyebrow. "Have you been hacking again?"

I smiled, relieved at his thought process. I wasn't sure how Sean would react to my break-in, and with the hacking assumption, I didn't have to tell him.

"What did you find?" he asked.

"Some weird stuff."

"Weird, how?"

"A man fixated on trapping things?"

"Animals?"

"No people."

"Are you suggesting that he might be responsible for the killings?"

"It crossed my mind."

"Who is this guy?"

I shrugged. "I'm not even sure if it is a man."

"Sounds rather vague."

I recounted the transcriptions to Sean, but it must have

lost something in translation. He stared at me through tired eyes. "So, someone of indeterminate gender shut their kid brother in a shed and later played a prank on a passing jogger. Really, Sass?"

"It wasn't like that."

"Are you sure your imagination isn't running away with you?"

"No. It's a horrible account. Frighteningly creepy."

"You should ask Tim's opinion."

"Ha bloody ha."

"I know you don't like him, but he's still a well-regarded shrink."

"You wouldn't agree if you shared my concerns."

"That's what happens when you start hacking computers. Why did you, by the way?"

"Tim's methods are suspect."

"Says who?"

"Never mind. I'll drop the idea if you think there's nothing to it."

"Best do that. You've more important things to worry about. Have you sent that report to Kim?"

"Yes. I discovered a little more from last year's investigation."

"Ah. I hope it didn't bring back too many bad memories."

Visions of a body bag containing the remains of Velda Ribeira burned through my mind, and I visibly shuddered.

"I can see it does. Sean patted the back of my hand. "Tough times," he said. "Still, everyone in Bosworth House has moved on now, except for Dhruv and Mill."

"Even Brendan," I said as a light bulb moment zipped through my brain. "He's living with his uncle, isn't he?"

"So I hear."

"Ella Burton died in Colin Marshall's garden."

"That's right."

"I should talk to Colin. He knows everyone."

"The police already have. Finnegan practically camped in his garden for the first few days after Ella died."

"Still, it can't do any harm."

"As long as you've finished Kim's assignment."

"I have. But Colin might know more than us. He's super sharp on detail. Besides, I badly need the distraction."

"Why?"

"Tomorrow's the night."

"Come again?"

"My cousin. My new family."

Sean stared blankly.

"I did tell you. I had a DNA hit on Root and Branch. I'm meeting a genetic family member for the first time in my life."

"Of course." Sean nodded, but his newfound eagerness did not fool me for a moment. While this was the single most important thing that had ever happened to me, Sean had forgotten about it the moment I told him. Some friend.

"Where are you seeing them?" asked Sean tactfully.

"My cousin's name is Callum, and we're meeting at The Apple Tree."

"Go for it. Good luck. Well, off you go up the wooden stairs, Sass. I'm done. Come back to the office when you've seen Colin Marshall, and we'll take it from there."

Chapter Thirty-Two

I reached Colin Marshall's place just after nine o'clock. The house brooded silently in the street, curtains drawn, and I briefly wondered if he was there. But he seldom went out, and signs of occupation, mostly involving his peculiar habit of drying smalls from his front bedroom window, were in evidence as usual as I parked my car. I'd taken the lazy approach, driving my battered old vehicle a few hundred yards from Carlton Street to Colin's place, knowing the subsequent journey to the office would be even shorter. But I wasn't sure what shape my day would take and I wanted to leave directly from work to meet my cousin, should the need arise.

I reversed into a tiny space, admired my parking prowess and wondered how I would ever get out again, then proceeded to Colin's front door and knocked loudly. Five minutes later, a damp sock flopped against my shoulder as the upstairs window opened, and Colin peered down.

"Yes?" he said in a quavering voice.

"It's Sass. Sass Denman. We spoke a few times last year. Have you got a moment?"

"Ah. I remember. Yes. I'll be down in a few ticks."

A tick became another five minutes and I scrolled through my phone impatiently as I waited to hear the soft shuffle of Colin's feet down the hallway. But I was so distracted by TikTok that the opening door startled me, and I stepped back into the road.

"Are you alright, my dear?" asked Colin, craning his neck forward like an ageing tortoise.

"I'm fine," I replied, stowing my phone in my handbag. "Can I come in?"

"If you want." Colin gestured down the hallway and I shuddered as I walked into the house with the same feeling of impending doom I'd experienced the first time we met. Colin was a nice, kind man with the unfortunate air of a sociopathic mass murderer. Being in close quarters with him always made my skin crawl without reason. No doubt it said more about me than him, but I swallowed my unease and followed him into the back of the house. This time he didn't detain me in the breakfast area but opened the door to his little garden and placed a gnarled hand on the back of a patio chair.

"Sit here, my dear," he said.

I gazed at the rusty iron seat, crisscrossed with spider webs and discreetly wiped them with my hand as I lowered my behind.

Colin's joints all but creaked as he inched himself into the opposite chair. "What's this all about, dear?" he asked.

"Your memory," I said. "But tell me first, how is Brendan?"

Colin chuckled. "He's got himself a young lady."

"Really?" My last memory of Brendan involved several

young ladies, all bought and paid for, but I merely nodded and let Colin continue.

"Yes. She's called Ruthie. A nice girl, quite good looking, lots of puppy fat."

"Is she young?"

"Not young, young. The same age as you, I should think. He's rather keen on this one. I think she's a keeper."

"You'd best buy a hat then."

Colin cocked his head. "No need. I already have one."

"It's just an expression."

But Colin had zoned out and was staring at an empty plant sconce hanging crookedly from the side wall as if it contained riches beyond measure.

"Are you okay?"

"Who are you?"

Colin stared blankly for a moment, then something changed behind his eyes, and his focus shifted back.

"Sorry. What were you saying?"

"I'd like to talk to you about the murdered girl. Did you find her in your garden, or did Brendan?"

"I did," said Colin sombrely. "Poor little thing. It was quite a shock. I might have saved her if I were a few years younger."

"Don't feel bad. From what I hear, nobody could have helped Ella Burton."

"But I heard a disturbance the night before. It's hard for me to get around nowadays, even with my stick. I'd have sent Brendan for a look, but he stayed with Ruthie that night. So I was all alone."

"What did you hear?"

"A cry. Not quite a scream, but it was enough to rouse me and make me think. Then I dropped off again and forgot all about it until the following day. The weather was rotten. It drizzled first thing, and I couldn't face going out in it, but when it dried up after lunch, I ventured down to the lower part of the garden, and there she was."

I stared at the walled garden, wondering what Colin was talking about. He could have easily seen all four corners using the most basic flashlight.

"Where was she?" I asked uncertainly.

"Take a look if you like. Come." Colin stood creakily, stooping as he shuffled towards a wooden door in the far wall. "Through there," he continued. "I'll wait. Come back when you're ready."

I unlatched the door and peered past into an entirely separate long, thin garden at least a hundred yards or more in length. Colin was too frail to tend to his garden and lacked the enthusiasm or ability to pay for a gardener. A path running down the right-hand side of the flowerbeds was relatively clear of foliage. But shrubs and brambles had taken over the remaining space and stood spikily triffid-like, dominating the area.

I made my way to the bottom of the garden, glad to be wearing full-length jeans despite the sunny day. At the bottom, an old shed clung to life, listing to one side with its door hanging open. If the side window ever contained glass, it didn't now, and another dense selection of spider webs peppered the space. I inched towards it and peered inside to see the rusty remnants of once-used garden implements, now languishing unloved in their forgotten tomb. A faint breeze caught a discarded piece of police tape directly in front of the shed, no doubt once surrounding Ella Burton's final resting place. I knelt and inspected the ground. But nothing remained to suggest she was ever there. I examined the garden, wondering how she had found her way into this narrow, confined space, but a quick look beyond the shed revealed an open wrought iron gate. I shimmied past and peered into an alleyway running along the back of the houses. Ella could have come from the west or east, seeking shelter in a neglected garden allowing easy access. Or did it? Testing my theory, I raised a hand and tried to shift the gate, meeting immediate resistance. A quick glance revealed the bottommost bolt was stuck in a hole in the ground and had been there for so long it had rusted over. This natural refuge for Ella offered the same privacy to her captor. I closed my eyes and imagined the scene.

Ella would have been running for her life through the streets of Truscombe, her breathing heavy and laboured. She'd have crouched by the shed panting loudly, desperately trying to still her heartbeat and quieten her ragged gasps. And if her pursuer knew the area, he would wait, bide his time and listen for the desperate girl. The skies would have darkened by then. There'd be little foot traffic in the town. Ella could run, but she could not easily hide. He would have found her and struck like a cobra. I shuddered, then hugged my arms as I tried to cast the memories away. They were too reminiscent of my last few days in Bosworth House. There was nothing more to see, and I wandered slowly up the garden and through the gate where Colin Marshall waited patiently beneath a cloudy sky.

"Did you find what you wanted, dear?"

I nodded. "Yes, for all the good it will do."

"Don't worry. Inspector Finnegan is confident of a satis- factory outcome."

"Have you seen him recently?"

"Only yesterday. They are making good progress."

I didn't have the heart to tell him that Finnegan was full of hot air and that it would be a cold day in hell before he got a result. But then Colin surprised me.

"Have they arrested Catton yet?"

"Did you know him?"

Colin nodded. "Yes. Marcus Catton visited me once or twice while I was still working."

"He must have been young."

"Manners, my dear. I'm hardly ancient."

I swallowed my incredulity. Colin Marshall had retired late and had been knocking on the door of old age for some time. But it would be rude to labour the point, so I bit my tongue.

"What did you think of him?"

"Not much. He was taciturn and as dull as ever. Did you know he went to school here? A good-looking chap, though. I'm not surprised to hear he had followers."

"Ella Burton was his pupil. He should have known better."

"Lines get blurred." Colin stared into his lap.

"Are you sympathetic with Catton?"

"Not at all. But I've seen and heard everything over the years. Things are not always as they seem. Anyway, where's your other half?"

"Sean?"

"Yes. You usually hunt in pairs."

"Not today. Sean's busy elsewhere."

"No change there then."

"I forgot. You knew him at school, didn't you?"

Marshall nodded. "Oh, yes. I knew them all, even those who didn't need anything from me. Mr Tallis was very self-contained. He never asked for help. Not even when he lost his brother."

"Did you know the family?"

"Of course. All the Tallis boys and their father too. Now

Tallis Senior was something else. Extremely bright and a decent sportsman."

"It didn't rub off on Sean," I joked.

The insult was lost on Colin. "The accident affected all three boys, but Sean suffered most. His grades declined sharply, and he stopped competing for a while."

"Competing?"

"Yes. Sean Tallis played tennis for the county but stopped it dead that year; he simply couldn't face it. Turned out Sean couldn't stomach the thought of success with his brother an invalid. If young Bryan hadn't died, Sean would still be consumed with guilt."

"Poor Sean. What an awful dilemma."

"Not really. He needed the death to move on. Draw a line under things if you like. They were all cut up about it. The boys, I mean. Those who were there at the Washpool. A bad day for all, whether saints or sinners, but worse for the Tallises. The guilt always outs in the end."

I nodded, and we ruminated in silence for a few moments.

"Is that everything?" asked Colin eventually.

"Yes. Thank you."

"Come back any time if you think I can help."

"I will," I said, processing our conversation as I left. It was only chit-chat, vague reminiscences of times past. But it wasn't until I returned to my car that the echo of his final comments hit home. What had Colin Marshall meant by saints and sinners?

Chapter Thirty-Three

I changed clothes three times before leaving Truscombe, making unnecessary journeys from the office to Carlton Drive to primp and preen, as if it would make any difference to my new cousin's opinion of me. Assuming he was there when I arrived and hadn't thought better of it. I slowly navigated the hill between Truscombe and Cleeve, inching towards the pub and my destiny, and two damp sweat patches mottled my top by the time I arrived. I wasted another five minutes with the air conditioning on full blast with my arms raised in the air, trying to conceal the evidence of my anxiety. Then I reached for a mint, almost gagging at the sharp rush of sweetness, and my fingers shook as I balled the paper and dropped it into the side pocket of my car. Raising my hands to my face, I rocked back and forth as I screwed up the courage to go inside. But I realised I couldn't do it and sat paralysed, watching an elderly man and his wife leaning heavily on sticks as they made their way indoors for an evening meal, their ageing faces relaxed and happy.

Behind them, a long-haired youth stepped off a skateboard and stood heavily on the rear, snatching the board as it flew through the air before striding to the rear door. He was one of the kitchen staff, no doubt, and his confident demeanour had the opposite effect on me. I gave in to a surge of adrenaline, slammed the gear stick into reverse and high-tailed it from the car park. Driving up Stockwell Lane like a bat out of hell, I braked suddenly to avoid a dog on an overly extended lead blocking the road as he meandered by, sniffing at the tarmac. I beeped my horn, and a woman turned around, glaring at me as she reeled the dog in. I indicated to pass, then stopped. What the hell was I doing? I'd waited a long time for this moment and was just about to run out on the only lead I'd ever had from Root and Branch. Why? What was the worst that could happen? Callum might not turn up, but I would die wondering if I didn't find out. Cursing my cowardice, I performed a five-point turn on the narrow road, nearly ending up in a ditch, and returned to The Apple Tree.

This time I parked in the first available space, sprang from the car and slammed the door before I could change my mind. Striding to the pub door, I opened it confidently to be greeted by a golden Labrador as I went inside. I stroked the dog's head and exchanged a few words with his owner, grateful for the dog-friendly pub, which had allowed a warm welcome from at least one living creature. I found my way to the counter, ordered a slimline tonic, and propped up the bar while I surveyed the clientele. Stupidly, I hadn't agreed on an identifier with Callum. But I needn't have worried. He was several steps ahead of me.

I found Callum sitting beneath a window to the side of the unlit fire with a large piece of paper in front of him bearing the Root and Branch logo. Sitting with his arms crossed and his legs splayed in front, he could hardly have presented a more relaxed demeanour. I hadn't known what he would look like, but my expectations were more in line with a sharp-suited businessman than the ageing hell's angel before me. I briefly hesitated, but he looked up and smiled. "Saskia?" he asked, jumping to his feet.

I held out my hand, and he took it, his grasp warm and confident.

"Find your way to the pub okay?" he asked.

I nodded. "I've been here before. Not for a while though."

Callum leaned forward. "How are you feeling?"

"Nervous."

"Me too."

"But you're part of the family. I'm the interloper." I tried to make my tone jocular, but it sounded peevish, petty.

"Well," he drawled, and a flicker of sadness crossed his face. I realised I'd put my foot in it without trying. "Funny things, families," he continued, shrugging.

"I wouldn't know."

"Who raised you?"

"My mum. I wasn't in an orphanage or anything, at least not within living memory. But my adoption was informal. There aren't any records."

"That's tough," said Callum, lifting his pint. I watched as he raised the drink to his lips, closing his eyes as he swallowed, his eyebrow piercing, glinting above the glass. He wore a black tee shirt, and the top of an inking appeared and disappeared from view as he moved position, unlike his snake tattoo, which weaved its way solidly from wrist to shoulder, with an ever-present glare from its ruby eye.

"Like it?" he asked, following my stare.

"Yes. It's fascinating." I'd never seen a tattoo that looked better than the piece of skin it covered, and my attempt to whip up some enthusiasm had fallen short of the target.

"Not a fan then," he smiled, sharp as a tack.

"Sorry. They're not really my thing."

"No matter. It takes all sorts."

"Indeed."

"Well," said Callum. "What can I tell you?"

"I want to know who my parents are."

"Of course you do. As I said before, I can't be sure. But I can give you a few pointers."

"Anything. Anything at all."

He nodded and flipped over the paper. "This is a rudimentary family tree," he said. "Sorry for the scribbles, but I couldn't get the software to print on one page, so I drew it by hand." He turned the paper towards me. "It's pretty simple. The centimorgans of DNA we each share indicate we're first cousins. I'm William Long's son. He's better known as Billy. Dad has a brother Fred and a sister Sally. If Fred's been up to no good, you're an only child. But you have a couple of siblings if Aunt Sally is your mother."

My heart raced as he spoke. I had a family surname. Not Saskia Denham, but Saskia Long. Or was it?

"Is Sally married?" I asked.

"She was. Uncle Bob divorced her a few years ago now. The randy old goat met a younger woman, and off he went. Sally's all alone now Helen and Spike have gone."

"What's her married name?"

"Chalmers. But she doesn't use it if she can help it. Not that it's official. Sally never changed her name back by deed poll but uses Long wherever possible."

"And Fred. Is he married?"

"Absolutely. To June Sankey. They met as teenagers and have been happily married ever since."

"So, Fred is my dad, or Sally is my mum."

"Nothing's certain, but it's looking that way."

"And there are no other close cousin matches?"

"Not unless one of them has a sibling we're unaware of."

"Could that have happened?"

Callum shrugged. "I doubt it. But you know how things were back in the day. My grandparents kept all talk of scandal on the down-low."

"Can I keep it?" I asked, clasping the hand-drawn family tree to my breast.

"Of course."

"And will you help me?"

"If I can. What do you need?"

"An introduction to the family."

"Ah. I wish I could. But I'm afraid there's a snag."

Chapter Thirty-Four

My heart flipped at Callum's words. I was already too invested in a future with this family to easily take disappointment.

"I realise it won't happen instantly," I said. "They don't know me. I'm someone's dirty little secret. But it could work out in time if I can only find a way in."

"That's not necessarily the problem," said Callum. "Though there are bound to be challenges. The issue is more about me than you."

"I don't understand."

"See this." Callum pointed to an intricate barbed wire tattoo on his left wrist.

I nodded.

"This is my first inking. Bought and paid for with my first full-time wage packet when I left school. I had it done to mark a new chapter in my life."

I saw where this was going. "Do all your tattoos represent important events?"

"You're following. I like that. Yes. I won't bore you with

all of them. And some of my inkings are in places you wouldn't want to go."

He winked as he said this, and my skin crawled ever so slightly.

"But this is my favourite." He reverently touched the snake tattoo, tracing his fingers down its length.

I waited, unsure what to say next.

Callum looked up and stared directly into my eyes. "I had this done a month after my release."

"From where?" The question was a formality. I already knew what he was going to say.

"Prison."

I nodded, fighting the urge to grab my handbag and run. A wholly irrational reaction considering my earlier career as a Royal Air Force policewoman: I had been around plenty of wrong'uns both then and more recently as a private detective. But Callum was family. And my family ought to be saccharin sweet. A loving mother, a hard-working father, and a respectable extended clan all gainfully employed. And here I was, sitting in a pub with a criminal cousin who looked a few steps away from biting bats heads off at a heavy metal concert.

"Makes you think, doesn't it?" he said perceptively.

"Naturally."

"And now you're wondering what I've done."

"I'm only human."

"Good answer." Callum smiled, seemingly unoffended by my newfound hesitancy. "It was data theft before you ask. No violence intended. Sadly, it didn't work out that way."

"Somebody died?"

"No. Life-changing injuries though. If I could go back and change things, I would."

"What happened?" The words were out before I

considered their wisdom. Callum might not answer, or worse still, he would. I operated on the right side of the law, and a relative with a criminal record was a burden I didn't need.

"Money was tight," Callum said, averting his eyes as he gulped deeply from his pint. "I'd been in trouble before as a lad. Let my family down but rose above it. Anyway, I worked hard and wound up in IT. Things were going well; then they weren't."

"Why?"

"When you work hard, you play hard. Too much Charlie at the weekends. We all did drugs. It was a company thing. You were either on the bus, or you were off it."

"Nobody made you." I blurted the words out, unable to help myself. I'd heard it all too many times before.

"Agreed," he said. "It was my poor choice. Anyway, things escalated. Those I hung out with had more money than me, but I had access to a lot of data and, with my skills, an easy way into the dark web."

I stared aghast. "Why are you telling me this?"

"I know what you do," he said simply, reaching into his pocket and tossing one of my business cards onto the table.

"So?"

"So, you'll find out about me sooner or later. This way, I gain your trust and save you the bother of researching me on the internet."

"I didn't," I said, cursing my lack of foresight. I had Callum's name and a vague idea of where he lived. It would have been enough to go on if I'd taken the time.

"But you would have found out eventually. Want to know more, or shall we leave it here?"

"More," I said resignedly, trying to ignore a mental ticker tape of questions zipping through my mind.

"Good." Callum smiled encouragingly. "You've nothing to fear," he said.

I chewed my lip but didn't reply, feeling a warm flush spreading across my body at the excruciating discomfort of my position. Callum carried on, oblivious to my reaction.

"I was spending hundreds of pounds a week at the height of my addiction. I didn't earn enough, and after begging and borrowing from family, Dad found out how I'd spent their loans and kicked me out. So, I downloaded some sensitive company data and flogged it on the dark web. My bosses confronted me. I fled the office and ran right into the path of a passing cyclist. He ended up in the hospital on life support, and I wound up at the police station. Got charged, went to trial, and the rest is history."

I shook my head, still reeling from my stupidity at not checking him out.

Callum leaned forward earnestly. "I want you to know I've been clean for three years. I used my time in Leyhill wisely, and now I'm a different man. I swapped a middle-class corporate life for something that makes me happy. No more trying to impress. No more climbing the greasy pole."

"What do you do these days?"

"I work in an animal rescue centre and paint in my spare time. I tried it in prison, and it turns out that I'm not half bad."

"Voluntary work?"

"No. I'm salaried. It's not high paying, but I don't need much. And my paintings are starting to sell."

"I still don't understand why you're telling me this. We hardly know each other."

Callum flexed his fingers and sighed. "My family disowned me. I spent four years in prison without a single phone call, not one visit. I let them down, but even my mother didn't try to see me. She could have written just once. So, I looked backwards and used my prison time to construct a family tree. I don't know what I thought I'd find. It amounted to nothing much. And when I got back into the real world, I used my hard-earned pennies to get a DNA test done, and that's how I found you, Saskia. You're currently the closest thing I have to family."

Chapter Thirty-Five

I returned to Truscombe on autopilot, my head fogged with Callum's revelations. We had parted awkwardly, me reluctant to agree to another meeting and him showing generous understanding of my position. As well he might. Had I still been serving in the military, a convicted cousin might have destroyed my career. I'd been better off not knowing about his chequered past. I'd hoped for happiness and security in my quest to find family, not to inherit a whole bunch of problems.

I parked the car and crept inside. Sean's and Jack's vehicles stood in the driveway, but the house was still and quiet. Unusually, the boys had turned in early. I climbed the stairs exhausted, changed and flopped into bed, waiting for sleep to take me. But it never arrived, and I tossed from side to side, trying to find a comfortable position. Two hours later, I'd had enough. I plugged in an audiobook, listening through one earbud, hoping it would lull me to sleep. But it didn't. I'd made the mistake of choosing a thriller, which was too gory and well narrated for the soporific calm I had hoped for. I gave in and sat up in bed, peering at my laptop with a vague notion of doing some work. But I was too tired, and after flitting between a screen or two, I found my mouse poised over the Patient X file. Reading it sure as hell wouldn't send me to sleep, but I clicked on the icon anyway.

Tim - Thoughts before I send?

Dear Jem

You ask for hope, and that in itself should tell you that reform is possible. This week, I want you to focus on your loneliness and how we might take active steps to overcome it. Loneliness can bring other problems, such as alcoholism, depression, sleep deprivation and personality disorders, to name but a few. The mental health risks of extreme isolation are manifold. But how does loneliness apply to you? Is it having nobody in your life or being without well-structured relationships? To that end, I would like you to write down all your associations, whether family, friends or work-related. Please include casual relationships. For example, someone you might see regularly, such as a shopkeeper or postman. Describe the extent of these relationships and whether you consider them beneficial.

We can further type loneliness as situational, developmental and internal. We haven't yet touched on how you make your living. Do you work with others? I know you live alone, but is your residence in close proximity to your neighbours? Forgive the sensitivity of the next question, but are you able-bodied? Do you have physical reasons for isolation? Is poverty a factor? Lastly, have you ever suffered from anxiety or depression? If so, do you use any substances to control your symptoms?

(Note - Tim is away at short notice. Response unchecked but I'm sending it regardless.)

Dear Helen

Why are you toying with me? You've written nothing so far that I couldn't easily find on an amateur psychologist internet forum. Please don't generalise. I'm paying for your consideration of me and only me —my symptoms, my issues and not a re-jigged paragraph from an article on the world wide web. You've given me nothing to work with, and I've no intention of answering your insulting puerile questions. Of course, I drink. Doesn't everyone? Even occasionally self-medicating if times are tough. But I am not an alcoholic nor depressive in the true sense of the word. Being lonely makes me sad, but being sad doesn't make me lonely. You are missing the point entirely. I am and have always been lonely, whether in company or not. Of course I chat with my local postman. God knows I see the man most days, and we share a word or two. Does it make me feel less alone? Of course not. You see, I'm like Lonesome George. I bet you're wondering what I'm talking about.

Here's a quick natural history lesson for you, Helen. Think the Galapagos Islands; think an old Pinta tortoise hatched in 1910, nearly a hundred years old and the only one left of his species. He died, of course—a natural death. But for several decades, old George was the only one of his kind, the rest extinct, gone, dead as the proverbial dodo. That's how I feel, Helen. Unique, unlike anyone else. How will anyone ever understand if I can't convince you of my isolation? You must come inside, Helen. Enter my world. So, here's a little homework for you.

Imagine your hands clenched around the bars of a cage—a large, rusty cage in a dark place. The silence is deafening, and as your eyes grow accustomed to the dark, you see four stone walls and a narrow shaft of light revealing a pitted concrete floor. You see a leg burning raw with pain, and you wonder why, so you reach down and touch a cold metal cuff biting into an ankle. You watch as the leg twitches in shock after injuries gained from tripping over a metal bowl before collapsing to the floor. You crouch, narrow your eyes and see a hand feeling its way around the cage before alighting on a plastic plate containing a crust of bread. And then you turn around and hear the faintest scrabbling coming towards you and see the glint of a pair of eyes bulging from a whiskery face. Is it night or day? Will the paltry food and drink containers be refilled? Or will the rat get there first?

But you are not the captive, Helen. You are the jailer. Put yourself in my position and tell me how to stop these thoughts, this fascination for control. These urges that keep me from sleep and intrude unbidden into my day. I try to ignore them, but they are always there, whispering, whispering, whispering.

So, Helen. Over to you.

Chapter Thirty-Six

Bosworth House stood sullenly before me as an early morning rain shower leaked from the sky. So much for an Indian summer. September was shaping up to be the wettest on record. The day had seemed fine when I woke from a fitful slumber a few minutes before six. Full of unwarranted energy after barely any sleep, I'd texted Dhruv to see if he was awake. He was equally sleep deprived and eager to invite me to breakfast. Against my better judgement, I walked over.

Pulling my damp collar higher, I confidently strode towards the front door of Bosworth House as if a madman had never attacked me on the premises. My normal apprehension had vanished, and my skin no longer crawled when I glanced right towards the other ground-floor window. My recent visits to Dhruv had quelled my former fears, and though I would never forget my ordeal, Bosworth House was no longer my enemy. I buzzed, Dhruv answered, and before long, I found myself sitting at his breakfast bar while he poured pancake batter into the kind of high-quality cookware I could only afford in my wildest dreams.

Dhruv welcomed me with a toothy grin, chatting as he had before all the trouble with Mill. And for a fleeting moment, I wondered if things were better. But the flat was strangely still as if Dhruv was all alone. I opened my mouth to ask and decided against it, not wanting to spoil his much-improved mood.

"Here," he said, flipping a pancake onto my plate. "Eat while it's warm." He turned to the grill, removing six pieces of perfectly cooked bacon. "Help yourself."

I did as he asked before adding a healthy drizzle of maple syrup. "Delicious," I said, all thoughts of my criminal cousin and Patient X momentarily forgotten in a burst of deliciousness.

We ate quietly for ten minutes, Dhruv shovelling pancakes into his mouth as he cooked. Bit by bit, the batter disappeared. We finished and took two steaming mugs of tea into the living room. I kicked off my shoes and curled up on the couch.

Dhruv glanced at his watch. "I've only got half an hour," he said ruefully. "The monthly audit won't run itself."

"Too bad. I could sit here all day," I replied, feeling unusually calm and temporarily at peace with the world.

"No work today?"

"Plenty. But Sean's in a half-decent mood and I might be able to stretch a point."

"Ah, good. Progress then?"

"A little. I'll still need my own place, but the pressure's off for now."

"You could come here."

"Never. I've come to terms with being attacked now that

creep has departed this world, but moving back is a non-starter. Who's leaving, anyway?"

"I am."

"No. Surely not. Is it Mill? Please say you haven't parted ways."

"Not yet. But it's only a matter of time. I won't stay here without him, though I could just about afford it."

"You seemed so much happier. I thought things must be improving."

"They're exactly the same. I'm just getting used to it."

"Where is Mill?"

Dhruv shrugged. "I don't know."

"Hasn't he said?"

"No. But he often stays out all night. I've stopped asking."

"Did you talk to Mill about seeing a doctor?"

Dhruv nodded. "I did, but he refused."

"Please don't give up on him," I blurted, suddenly realising I couldn't imagine Dhruv without Mill.

"Then you try. He won't listen to me."

"I bloody well will."

"Then bloody well do."

"Fine. I'll call him later."

"Just be prepared for him to hang up."

I sighed. A distressed Dhruv was bad enough, but he'd gone beyond caring, which was more dangerous. He really might leave Bosworth House if not the town, and a selfish voice inside my head kept reminding me that Dhruv was an entire half of my tiny friendship group.

"Never mind me," said Dhruv. "What gives in your world?"

I quickly recounted the previous night's events with

Cousin Callum, and Dhruv whistled aloud. "Well, well," he said. "That's a turn-up for the books."

"Isn't it just? And not in a good way."

"But you know much more about your family now."

"That's the trouble. Callum's done time and his mother and father are so intolerant they've disowned him."

"Ah, uncles and cousins are easily ignored. What about your parents?"

"Either Fred and June Long, who are childless or Bob and Sally Chalmers, who have divorced—acrimoniously, I might add. If the latter, I have a sister Helen and a brother Spike. Spike! I mean, who looks at a tiny baby and calls it Spike? It's practically child abuse."

"Or possibly a nickname?"

"Perhaps," I grudgingly conceded. "But I'm not feeling it, Dhruv."

"Shallow, Sass," he mouthed, "shallow."

"I know it seems that way, but I'm super protective of my good name." I crossed my fingers as I spoke, remembering my foray into Tim Gibbons' place a few nights before. Squeaky clean, I was not, but I wanted my nearly perfect record to remain intact.

"Okay. A teeny bit judgemental then," said Dhruv. "Come on. Think of the benefits of having a family. And I know you'll regret it if you give up now."

"Hmmm. I'll need to know a little more about them first."

"Did your cousin mention where they lived and what they do?"

"We didn't get that far. But I assumed it was close to Truscombe. Certainly, somewhere in Gloucestershire."

"Then do some research and check them out. It's not as if your cousin can help with an introduction."

"I know. I will. But do you know what I'd love to do right now?"

"Go on."

"Phone my mum." My voice wobbled as I spoke. Dhruv perched beside me and administered a bear hug.

"You can call mine," he offered. "I know it's not the same, but she'd understand."

"I miss Mum so much. My adoption doesn't matter. Mum chose me and was always there in times of trouble, always. And it makes me wonder if genetics matter. I could never love another woman as much as my mum, even if I shared fifty per cent of her DNA. So why bother?"

"Because you're you," said Dhruv, ruffling my hair affectionately. "You're naturally curious." He thrust his hand into his pocket, withdrew his wallet and extracted a twenty-pound note. "This," he said, slamming it onto the coffee table, "is how sure I am that you will have found where they live and what they do for a living by the end of the week. Match it, and the winner chooses where we go for dinner this weekend."

"You're the best," I said, leaning in for another hug.

"Not really. I'm about to evict you." Dhruv tapped his watch face and pointed to the door. "Begone, Saskia."

"I'll walk you to your office."

"Very well. No dragging your heels."

Chapter Thirty-Seven

My first act on reaching the office was to make a steaming cup of coffee. The second was messaging Mill. Brevity was in order if I didn't want a rebuff, so I typed a brief text and pressed send.

Are you teaching today?

His reply took five minutes, and I was deeply distracted with the Root and Branch search engine when it arrived.

No. Why?

Can we meet?

Not really. I'm in Stroud.

Ah. What are you doing there?

It was a cheeky text to which I didn't necessarily expect a reply, at least not a courteous one, but Mill answered without hesitation.

I'm up at the college invigilating exams. Lucky me.

Wow. Sounds interesting.

Not really. Just a side hustle for a bit of extra cash.

I wondered why he needed it, but that would be a question too far.

Can we talk?

I suppose so. Why?

This time I took my time to reply. Honesty might shut the conversation stone dead, but I couldn't say what I needed to by text.

I opted for the former.

Can we speak about Dhruv?

Nothing happened for a while, for many whiles. The little tick indicating an acknowledged text showed loud and clear, but the welcome buzz of a response never came. I sighed and resumed my research. Then my phone unexpectedly rang, and I grabbed it.

"Hello,"

"It's me, Mill." It seemed forever since I had last heard his lilting Irish tones, and I couldn't help but smile.

"Thank you for calling. I wasn't sure you would."

"I nearly didn't."

"Fair enough. How are you?"

"I've been better. Things are tough, but you know that."

I nodded, then realised he couldn't see me. "Dhruv has told me bits and pieces, not anything personal. He won't tittle-tattle, but he's terribly worried."

Mill barked a laugh. "Dhruv's a shocking gossip, and you know it."

"Okay. But not salacious gossip. What's happening to you both? I was expecting an invitation to a wedding, not this."

Mill sighed, loud and long. "We're not getting along."

"But why? He still cares. Don't you?"

"It's not that simple."

"Nothing worthwhile ever is."

"Yes, but that's the critical point, right?"

"What?"

"Whether it's worthwhile."

"Wow. If that question crosses your mind, it's already too late. What changed?"

"I did. And Dhruv."

"You've fallen out of love?"

"No. But we've gone in different directions. He's into all this happy-clappy stuff. Frankly, I can't stand it."

"Understood. I'm not a fan, either. And you?"

"I had a health scare."

"Have you seen the doctor?"

"Yes, regularly. There's nothing wrong with me now. There was, but now there isn't."

"Then what's holding you back?"

"Has Dhruv told you about my fondness for the hard stuff?"

"He mentioned it."

"I'm not an addict, Sass. I went too far, did some stupid things, saw the error of my ways, and now I'm in control again."

"Then everything's alright."

"No, it's not."

Mill paused, and I waited as the silence grew uncomfortable, and I bit my tongue to stop myself from filling it with drivel.

It worked. He resumed the conversation.

"As I said, I did some silly things. Two silly things, I bitterly regret, one being Steven Hicks."

"The physics teacher?"

"The very one."

"You were unfaithful to Dhruv?"

"Just the once, but once is enough."

"Are you and Steven still together?"

"We never were. It was just one night."

"Then there's hope. Dhruv need never know."

"Except for one small thing. It happened on a work night out, very publicly, and everybody knew—everybody. It was an overnighter. The gossip was rife, and half the staff witnessed my morning walk of shame. I managed one week back at school before handing in my notice."

"Jesus. How long ago was that?"

"Earlier this year."

"Dhruv has no idea."

"Not a clue. He thinks I've been going to work, and I haven't said otherwise because I can't without explaining why."

"How are you making rent?"

"I've burned through my savings, such as they were."

"I don't know what to say."

"How about I'll keep your secret, and I won't tell Dhruv."

I considered his proposition. "You know I can't do that. He's, my friend."

"Then I'm screwed."

"Come on, Mill. You must have known how I'd react. Your subconscious has forced you into a position where your only option is to come clean."

"Hmmm. I guess. How long before you squeal?"

"That's harsh. And you know Dhruv deserves better."

"Better than me, that's for sure."

"Do you love him?"

"Of course I bloody do. But I've royally fucked up. It's over, and I know it."

"Just talk to him. I'll back off until the weekend. At least I'll try to. If he calls or texts, I'll answer. But otherwise, I'll leave well alone until Monday. That gives you a few days."

"Right. Thanks for the chat. All that remains is for me

to figure out how not to fuck it up further." The phone went dead, and I internally debated whether Mill's sarcasm was warranted. But one glance at the daybook completely distracted me from my internal monologue. A long, rambling message in Sean's spidery hand said, *Sass - out for the foreseeable. Kim & Ferret are not speaking. K's Tewkesbury informant has uncovered something near the river. I'm heading over to investigate. Smoke me a kipper and all that.*

I smiled at Sean's reference to our shared fondness for TV's *Red Dwarf* before a frisson of annoyance elbowed the happy reminiscence away. Bloody hell, Sean was off on his own again, leaving me with only bare bones of information. Yet again, we were running in different directions. Yet again, he had left me to mind the office like an obedient Stepford wife. I tossed the daybook aside and began rummaging through Root and Branch again. Work could wait. I had a family tree to research.

Chapter Thirty-Eight

The more I considered Sean's desertion, the more it wound me up. Between five-minute bursts of focus and teeth-grindingly stressful imagined conversations about what I would like to say to him when we caught up, I managed to add a few facts to my family tree. But my heart wasn't in it. I was fed up with staring at the office walls while Sean went solo on all the interesting jobs. God only knew when he would reappear, and though there was work to do, I wasn't in the mood. I poured myself another coffee and sat at Sean's desk, mimicking his laid-back Friday afternoon posture of legs crossed at the ankle and head lolling back on cupped hands. But there was a knack for balancing on Sean's chair, and when I briefly plunged backwards, I readjusted my stance and sat upright while quietly seething. I stared at the phone, willing it to ring for someone to talk to, but it remained stubbornly silent. Then, without thinking, I tugged the handle of Sean's top drawer. It slid open cooperatively, and luck smiled when I realised he had forgotten to lock it. It took about a second to discount the urge to close it again. Instead, I yanked it wider and had a good rummage. Nothing seemed noteworthy until I found his old Filofax, a mud-coloured moleskin affair now beginning to disintegrate. Sean used it mainly for addresses and telephone numbers, with a handy pocket at the end for business cards. I withdrew half a dozen and speed-read through them, finding a brand-new card for Callie at the back of the pile. My lip involuntarily curled at the sight of her rank and I acknowledged to myself that I didn't much like her. I knew it wasn't fair, considering we had only crossed paths once or twice. But Callie's constant belittling of Sean and attempts to control him with threats of pulling the budget jarred. No decent woman would behave that way, especially while wielding an imbalance of power. But it wasn't until I turned the card over that a visceral hatred turned my stomach to mush as I stared defensively at four short words. *Thanks for last night x*

God-all-fucking-mighty. Sean surely couldn't be starting that up again. He'd always been open about Callie's volatile relationship with her husband and was clearly flattered by her continued interest in him. But Sean was smart enough to know better. Any contact with Callie would come with strings. And she didn't like me any more than I liked her. A renewed relationship with Callie bore clear and present danger to my continued employment.

I sat with my head in my hands for several minutes then logic kicked in. Perhaps the card was an old one. Sean might have saved it for old-time's sake. But on closer inspection, I could see the business card was in pristine condition. I strode to my desk and rifled through my box of contacts. Tom's newest card exactly matched Callie's, meaning it must be recent. A glance at Sean's desk calendar confirmed an appointment with Callie earlier in the week that I hadn't noticed before. What in the hell was he playing at? No wonder he was so disjointed, his mood up and down. I re-packed the Filofax and returned it to the drawer. But if I had been distracted before, I was overwhelmed now. Work and research went out of the window, but I didn't want to go home and run into Jack. With nothing else to occupy my thoughts, I pulled the memory stick from my laptop case and opened the last Patient X file.

Chapter Thirty-Nine

Tim — see below. This is what I'm talking about. It's too disturbing. I realise you won't read this for a while, but you must take a look as soon as you can. I'm disregarding the patient's last comments. Talk about the tail wagging the dog! But I'm out of my depth with this client, and nothing I say will make any difference. This is my final shot, and I'm sorry if you think I'm being too harsh. Frankly, it would be better if my email caused offence and the patient found another therapist.

Dear Jem Wright

You must realise I cannot participate in your proposed suggestion. It benefits neither one of us. And the scenario you portray is so unlikely I can only conclude you are exaggerating. Perhaps even intentionally presenting symptoms a lay person might envisage in a psychopath or sociopath. At least in the world of fiction. Was that your intent, or have I misunderstood? I sympathise with your inability to conquer your loneliness, but your reactions are so extreme I wonder if you are making fun of me for reasons unknown.

I can only help you if you want me to, and your response to my questions suggests otherwise. You have resisted all my attempts to open a dialogue and find the answers that might help me diagnose your condition. Communication between therapist and patient is paramount. Email counselling will fail if we cannot settle into a mutually beneficial relationship. Perhaps it is time to consider face-to-face appointments.

If you wish to continue as we are, we must make immediate progress. Your primary concern is loneliness, but I detect anxiety, self-doubt, and perhaps even self-loathing. This week I would like you to think back to your childhood, to a time when friends surrounded you. How did that feel? What could you do in your adult life to replicate that sensation? Before you answer, please consider my part in your treatment. What can I do to help you? And what do you want from me?

Dear Helen Chalmers

Oh dear, a bare B minus for you. Average to poor on the homework front, which is a generous mark considering you didn't answer, let alone engage with the subject matter. But I fear you are tiring of me, so let's move on. I will ignore your hurtful suggestion of malingering on my part, and I will stop sparring with you.

How can you help me? Well, that's a good question, and it made me think. I've tasked you with curing my loneliness, but we both know you're unlikely to succeed. So, what did I want when I reached out? Forgive my use of that horrible expression. It conveys my situation curiously well. I suppose I wanted to talk to someone without exchanging actual words. We will never meet. That would mean revealing my identity, so email therapy is as good as it gets. And to a certain extent, I've enjoyed our little chats.

They have fallen short of my expectations, but I can be my true self this way and discuss my inclinations anonymously. It's like having a pen pal to bounce ideas off. A distant enough relationship that extreme frankness doesn't matter and feelings don't get hurt. So, I would like you to be there and simply listen. Comment by all means and I will heed them or not as it takes my fancy. Too one-sided for you? Sorry, but I'm the paying customer, and that's the way it is.

Now, I've been thinking about my early years, those formative times when friendships grew, changed, and adapted. I can visualise a moment in my mind's eye that might fit your agenda. It was a summer's day, and I was twelve or thirteen, gadding around during the holidays. I was on the hill with my friends, playing by the Washpool. Everyone was there, all the regular gang, messing around as kids do. We were immature by today's standards. Nowadays, pre-teens hang around town smoking or doing drugs. Back then, we fished, sailed and aimlessly dicked around. But on this particular day, we'd reverted to our younger selves and were playing a game of hide and seek. I remember standing there, the sun full on my face, watching as we squabbled over who would be it. And I realised we were as close as a pack of friends ever could be. Comfortable in each other's presence and knowing each other inside out. Does that sound good to you, Helen? It's a pleasant memory, isn't it? The exact opposite of solitude. So now you'd like me to tell you how I felt about it. Warm? Happy? A little fuzzy flicker of gratitude? Nope. I found it threatening.

You see, it wasn't future-proof. The camaraderie was only an illusion of solid friendship waiting in the wings to be splintered, fractured by the passing of time. I could see ahead even if my friends could not. And I was determined not to be the one left behind.

Fast forward an hour, and that snapshot soon nested in my head beside another darker one. A subverted moment where everything changed, with lives forever altered. A day of heroes, monsters and a drowned child. Sunshine smothered by clouds. Was I happier in the warmth of the sun's rays or the subsequent pall of gloom? The latter, of course, for I was in control. I saw death at close quarters. It nipped at my ankles but took another, leaving me in thrall to its power. Perhaps you're right. The loneliness stems from that moment, from an unspeakable secret known only to me.

Thanks, Helen. I feel much better. It's good to talk.

Chapter Forty

I came home again to an empty house. When was it any other way? But I didn't fancy rattling around without company, with Patient X's revelations churning through my mind. I needed to talk to Sean urgently, but a nervous trepidation stopped me from calling his phone. I brooded, allowing the twisted words space to roam, examining the problem from all angles. Patient X, whom Helen later referred to as Jem Wright, had been at the Washpool. And, if I wasn't mistaken, Sean's younger brother had died there. Had Patient X witnessed the death? And who was he? Was Jem his real name? And was it a man at all? Sean might know. He'd remember who was there that day.

I replayed our earlier conversation in my mind, recalling Sean's softening expression as he thought about his younger brother, grateful for Adam's heroics while saving his brother's life. But who had stood on the periphery gloating at Bryan's death? And might they bear some responsibility for it? Patient X certainly implied it. I jotted down everything I remembered, chasing fleeting glimpses of names I couldn't quite put my finger on. And then I gave in and telephoned Sean, risking his wrath if he was still hard at work or provoking lonesome sadness if not. But the mobile clicked straight to the voicemail, and my heart sank. I left a brief message, not daring to elaborate, and made for the kitchen.

It took a while for me to notice Jack's absence. I realised he wasn't at home, but the kitchen bore no signs of his usual mess: no pots and pans, leftovers, or crumbs scattered across the work surface. Sean's parka hung forlornly from the coat hook, together with an old umbrella. But Jack's coat wasn't there, neither were his spare boots. I raced upstairs and tapped on his door. Silence. Then I checked the bathroom, opened the window, and glanced out the back in case he was in the garden. He wasn't. With both cats away, nothing could impede my natural curiosity, and I slowly rotated Jack's bedroom door handle and went inside.

My former room was full of filth. The duvet lay crumpled at the bottom of the bed, and the sheet had a worryingly yellow tinge in the middle. I threw open the curtains and peered into the sliding wardrobe seeing empty coat hangers and a plastic bag in the corner. I picked it up and looked inside, almost vomiting at the remains of a week-old Chinese takeaway. 'Dirty pig', I muttered as I took it downstairs, opened the back door and tossed it into the bin. Jack was long gone, but why? And did Sean know anything about it?

When I entered the living room, I soon discovered the answer finding a folded note addressed to Sean lying on the rug where it had fallen from the mantlepiece. I opened it and read the message.

I'm in with a slim chance of getting back with the missus. Going home to try. Thanks for everything. I'll be in touch.

And just like that, Jack had gone. It was a tremendous relief, but Sean and I had been through so many ups and downs in the last few weeks I was no longer sure whether Jack's absence would make any difference to our relationship. I considered asking for my old room back but realised I wasn't unduly bothered. It was time to go it alone again and cheered by this thought, I made myself dinner and sat down to eat. An episode of *Midsummer Murders* later, I checked my watch. It was after nine o'clock, and there was no sign of Sean. Yet again, he'd been out all day. I debated whether to feed the lizards, noting that their tank was unusually grimy. But Sean had changed their food yesterday, and I decided not to interfere. They'd be alright until tomorrow morning.

A long bath, a good book and a decent night's rest took me through until the next day. I'd fallen asleep with my curtains open, and sunlight streamed through as I rubbed my eyes and glanced at my phone. It was half-past six, and although the weekend, I was wide awake, so I showered, dressed and made myself a bowl of porridge and a cup of tea. I'd almost finished and was chuckling at a talking collie on TikTok when I glanced towards the back door, noticing an unwelcome space where Sean's shoes ought to be. I cleared my breakfast things away and tiptoed upstairs, listening outside his closed door for any signs of life. But the room was deathly silent, and I risked popping my head around the door for a look. Sean's quilt lay evenly across his bed, his curtains neatly drawn, but he clearly hadn't slept there overnight. Where was he?

I tried calling Sean's mobile, but it went straight to

voicemail again. I repeatedly continued until I had worked myself up into a futile loop of senseless repetition. Bereft of ideas, I called Tom.

"What's up?" he said as the phone connected.

"Have you seen Sean?"

"No. But then I don't live or work with him."

"Ha bloody ha. He's been out all night."

"Sean's a big boy, Sass. Cut those apron strings."

"I'm serious. He's been gone since yesterday morning, and I've heard nothing. No text, no message, nada."

"Where did he go?"

"To Tewkesbury. He was checking out something for Kim."

"I didn't know. I'm with Finnegan most of the time."

"Can you ask Kim if she's heard from him?"

Tom sighed. "Can't you call her?"

"She can take or leave me. I'm never sure what to expect. Best you do it."

"Okay. I'm not sure when Kim's next around, but I'll get in touch when I can."

Tom rang off, and having nothing better to do, I carried my laptop to the office and continued plodding through my family tree.

I was on my second cup of coffee when Kim rang.

"What's this about Tallis?" she barked.

"He didn't come home."

"Really."

"Yes. Has he been in touch with you?"

Kim paused at the other end and tapped her fingers against the phone. "No," she said finally. "And he promised he'd let me know."

"Know what?"

"Whether Big Ken was a reliable source or a hallucinating druggie."

"Big who?"

"It doesn't matter. You only need to know that Big K is a friend of the force. He said he'd seen someone by the canal on the night of the murder. I thought it was worth following up."

"Then why didn't you?"

"Politics. This thing with Finnegan. You know how it is."

"So, you sent Sean?"

"It's easier. Big Ken moves around. No place of his own, you see."

"A down and out?"

"Not exactly. It's hard to explain. Ken has issues, and sleeping rough is one of them. Not that it's necessary. He's far from destitute. Let's put it this way. Big Ken is knocking on in years and not the free spirit he aspires to be. Too old, too fat, and too many bad habits."

"A drunk?"

"Surprisingly, no, but he likes his drugs."

"Off his head then?"

"Not hard drugs. Ken's intelligent and, for the most part, law-abiding."

"Do you know what he saw?"

"Unfortunately not. Ken left me a message, but I was too busy wading through your list of missing people. Thanks very much, by the way. We're close to identifying him."

"The man in the woods?"

"Yes. We've got a match through dental records and have extracted some DNA, but there's further checking to do. Belt and braces before we make a formal identification."

"Care to share?" I asked lightly, taking advantage of Kim's more relaxed mood.

"Not yet." Kim shut me down dead, and I sighed loudly. "Look," she said. "There's no point in naming names. It won't mean anything. But our corpse was a young man in his twenties reported missing by his concerned family when he didn't return from the pub a few years ago."

"Where did he live?"

"Evesham."

"Now there's a surprise."

"Yes. It's a tight geographical area, isn't it?"

"Hmmm. Any connection to Ella Burton?"

"Not that we know. But it's early days."

"And Marcus Catton? He taught there too?"

"I know. It's on my radar." Kim's tone veered towards sarcasm.

"Fine," I said, defeated. I was much less interested in Kim's three-year-old corpse than in my colleague's current whereabouts. "Back to Sean. Where might he be?"

"Try the Black Bear if he's still with Big Ken."

"I thought you said Ken didn't drink?"

"He doesn't. But he calls in for a chat most days."

"Okay. I'll take a look," I said. I was about to ring off when a surge of irritation provoked an outburst I hadn't intended.

"Actually, I won't. You sent him, Kim. Get your officers out there."

"I beg your pardon?"

"I know nothing about this informant of yours. Or where Sean went or what he might have found."

"Yes, but you're the only one mithering about it like an overgrown nanny."

Kim had not taken my home truths well but I was fretting about Sean and had no intention of giving ground.

"Well, you should be worried too. Sean's been gone a whole day without a word. I've left two dozen voice messages, and nothing. I mean, it's not as if we're living in a safe part of the world. Three dead bodies and a missing architect aren't bad by anybody's standards. Perhaps it will be four dead bodies by the end of the day? That should give Miles Savage plenty to write about."

"Oh, would you calm down? I'll send someone now. But Sean won't thank you for it. Just remember that."

Chapter Forty-One

I was cramming the remains of a duck wrap into my face when my mobile rang. I glanced across to see Tom's name on my screen, but with a mouth too full to answer, I let the phone ring out. By the time I had washed my hands and resumed my seat, he had called again. I dialled back, but annoyingly, it went straight to the voicemail. Two rounds of telephone tennis later, the office door squeaked open, and Tom strode inside, his face drawn.

"Tom," I said, greeting him with a hug and a smile.

"You'd better sit down."

My heart dropped as I watched his tense jaw flex while he considered his words.

"What is it?" I asked, beating him to it.

"Another body," he said gruffly.

My hands gripped the edge of the table as my heart rate quickened.

"Oh God, no."

My tongue stuck to the roof of my mouth. Barely able to breathe, I stared open-mouthed like a fish on a riverbank.

I couldn't speak, couldn't form the words. And as my face flushed beetroot red, I realised I was in the early stages of a panic attack.

Tom gripped my hand and reached for the plastic cup of water I kept by my PC.

"Drink this," he said.

I took it with a trembling hand, and the routine act of raising it to my lips helped stem the rising tide of anxiety.

"Who is it?" I asked, my stomach clenching in fearful anticipation.

"Big Ken."

"Oh, thank God. It's not Sean."

"No. But we still don't know where he is."

"What happened to Ken?"

Tom shook his head wordlessly while running a finger around his collar. "I don't know yet. There's a little shelter in the Ham Ken used in fine weather. They found his body there."

"Foul play?" I squeezed the words out, still barely able to speak but starting to get a grip on the situation.

"Yeah. Judging by the injuries, someone hit him over the head. The old boy must have struggled. There's blood everywhere."

"But no Sean."

"No Sean."

"Do we know if they met?"

"Sorry."

"Have your officers been to the pub to find out if Sean spoke to Ken?"

"They're on their way now. Believe me, they'll be all over Ken's haunts until they learn more."

"How long has he been dead?"

"I don't know. Dai's there now."

"Oh, my God. I don't know what to do."

"Nothing. Stay here and don't get involved. Shall I call Dhruv?"

"No."

"I've got to get back to the station. You shouldn't be alone."

"It's okay. I'll call Dhruv when I'm ready."

"But you'll go home and get some rest? Promise?"

I promised, but with my fingers tightly crossed behind my back.

Chapter Forty-Two

I didn't go home. I couldn't face the prospect. Instead, I waited until Tom had gone, then sat shivering as I contemplated the significance of yet another body. I rang Sean, knowing it was futile but needing to hear his voice on his voicemail message. It came within seconds, as curt and sharp as ever, and I hugged the phone to my ear, willing him to be safe.

Pacing around the office, I contemplated Sean's last known movements. Whatever the question was, Tewkesbury was likely the answer. But in a market town of over twenty thousand people, he could be anywhere, doing anything. *Think, Saskia, think.*

I strode towards the whiteboard at the back of the office and removed details of our current case with my cardigan sleeve. Too bad it was a light colour, which amplified the red ink now streaking across the wool like a swathe of blood. But that was a worry for another day. Time was not my friend if I wanted to do something constructive. I removed the marker lid with my teeth and drew a mind map, putting a question mark in the centre with arrows pointing to Sean, Ella Burton, Big Ken, and the body in the wood. Then, after further thought, I added John Noble and Adam Harding, too. In a square beneath the question mark, I drew a list of people beginning with Marcus Catton and ending with the mysterious Jem Wright. The list of suspects grew with an ever increasingly unrealistic set of people vaguely connected with the case. Even Tim Gibbons didn't escape my notice, as unlikely a candidate as he was. But I wasn't risking a single detail. Then I perched on the desk and studied my handiwork. It made no sense at all. Nothing did.

Turning to my laptop, I reviewed the data I had studiously stored after every new lead. Contemplating those who had helped and those who might have something to add, I jotted more names. Abigail Catton was an obvious choice, but so was Colin Marshall. And more importantly, he was close at hand. My head was swimming, and I couldn't face any more work. If I went home, I'd sit around moping all night, so I grabbed my handbag and made for Grosvenor Road.

I hadn't accounted for Colin having company, but as I strode towards his house, I could see someone ahead of me letting themselves in his front door. By the time I reached the property, they were safely ensconced inside and I faced the prospect of disturbing the household. Ordinarily, I would have walked away but this was too important. I hammered on the door, which eventually opened to reveal an attractive young woman with a moon-shaped face. She wore an oversized jumper with a picture of a zebra on the front.

"Yes?" she asked pleasantly.

"Ruthie?" I replied.

"Do I know you?"

"No. But Colin mentioned you during my last visit."

She stared, perplexed, and I offered my hand.

"Saskia Denman. I'm a friend of Colin's."

"Oh. That Saskia Denman. Wow. I mean, I've heard of you, but wow." Ruthie's voice trailed away, and I cringed internally, knowing she was thinking about the horrors of Bosworth House.

"It's all in the past," I said brightly.

"You're so amazing. Brendan said you are one of the bravest people he has ever met."

"That's kind. Brendan is a very nice man."

"He's poorly though. That's why I'm here. Colin doesn't want germy hands over his legs."

My eyes involuntarily closed as I tried to resist the image of Brendan helping his uncle with personal care. It didn't sit well.

"Is he expecting you?" Ruthie continued.

"No. I called on spec. But I need to ask him something. Is he available?"

"Yes, as long as you don't mind me getting on with things while you talk. I have a pottery class in half an hour."

"No problem."

I followed Ruthie to the living room, where Colin Marshall was sitting on a high-backed chair with his trouser legs rolled up to the knee. Shiny, tight sores with a nasty yellow tinge covered his lower shins.

"Surprise visitor," said Ruthie brightly as she waved me through the door.

"Ah. Miss Denman? Did we have an appointment?"

"No. I called on the off-chance."

"I see. Well, sit down then. I'd offer you a cup of tea, but I'm somewhat indisposed."

"I'll make it when I've finished," said Ruthie, squirting a

tube of white cream onto her hands. She rubbed them together before gently massaging Colin's legs.

"That's more like it," said Colin. "You can tell your young man that he's far too rough."

"Silly," giggled Ruthie.

I forced a grin, unduly irritated at the inaccurate description of Brendan, who was older than me and on the slippery slope to forty.

"There you are, all done," said Ruthie, cleaning her hands with a tea towel. Colin reached for his trouser legs, made a token effort to roll them down, then groaned as he held his hand to the small of his back.

"Sorry, Uncle. I'll do that for you."

Ruthie knelt in front of him again while I contemplated the etiquette of deciding when your fiancé's relatives became yours. They hadn't been together for a year, and she was already calling him uncle.

"Right. Let's pop the kettle on," said Ruthie as she strolled towards the kitchen, leaving us alone.

"Well?" said Colin.

"Ruthie seems nice."

"Told you so. She's a fine addition to the family."

"I'm glad you like her. Brendan deserves to be happy."

"He does. But you're not here to talk about that, are you?"

"No."

"What can I do for you then?"

"I don't know. More information, I suppose. I don't know what you can tell me you haven't already said. But matters are pressing and lives are at stake."

Colin raised a greying eyebrow and stared doubtfully.

"Sean's missing," I blurted out.

"Tallis?"

262

"Yes."

"I don't know where he is, I'm afraid."

"I know. No reason why you should. They found another body in Tewkesbury."

"I heard."

"No. A second one. Only discovered today."

"Christ all fucking mighty."

I stared aghast, not knowing who was more shocked by the blasphemous swear catapulting from Colin's mouth. But he slammed his hand over his lips before spluttering a heart-felt apology.

"Saskia. I'm sorry. Excuse my potty mouth."

"It's fine. I'd have said worse."

"No. It's not good enough. Bad manners."

"I truly don't mind. God knows I served in the military long enough, and profanities came thick and fast in that environment."

"Even so."

I interrupted his guilt fest. "Look. Too many bodies, too little time. And none of it makes sense. But I've seen a recent email. Something I shouldn't know about. A person who might have been around when Sean's brother died."

"How is that relevant? It was a tragic accident."

"I know. But it might be a means to identify the onlooker."

"I'm an old man, and my reasoning isn't up to much. You'll need to explain in simple terms."

I sighed, my stomach clenching with guilt. "Someone with nefarious intentions wrote something I saw that should have been private. I helped myself to some information I shouldn't know. Don't judge me. Now this person might have something to do with these murders or not. I can't be sure. But I know they witnessed a child die at the Washpool, and there can't have been many such deaths. So, if you could tell me exactly who was there that day, I might be able to start ruling people out."

"I see." Colin steepled his hands and nodded towards the fireplace. "There's a notebook and pen in that cubbyhole. You'll need to use them. I'm having a difficult day." He waved a gnarled, arthritic hand towards me, and I gratefully smiled as if I didn't have a fully functioning note-taking app on my phone.

I resumed my seat opposite while he gazed into the air, searching his memories.

"Sean and Mike Tallis and Adam Harding, obviously," he said, eyes closed, still hunting the past.

"And Marcus Catton," I added.

"Of course. Now, let me think. Who else?" He leaned forward and snapped his eyes open. "Graham Strong, that's who. And if Strong was there, then Morgan Williams would have been too. Those boys were joined at the hip."

"Great stuff," I said, jotting down the names. "Didn't someone mention girls?"

"Yes. Little Lou Calver and…" Colin Marshall clicked his fingers and winced in pain. Placing his hand under his armpit, he continued. "Annie or Aggie, someone or other. I can't remember. They were friends. You'd need to ask."

"Who?"

"Good point. Are you in touch with Mike Tallis?"

"We message occasionally through MyPerfectLife, but he's down under. The time difference doesn't make for easy communication."

"I see. Graham Strong moved to Ireland and I don't know where Morgan lives now. As for the girls…" Colin shrugged and smiled weakly.

"God. That only leaves Marcus Catton. I doubt he will speak to me."

"Seems your only choice."

"Have you remembered everyone? I thought there were more?"

"And so there might be. But I've tried, and I just can't. My memory is not what it was. And I wasn't there that day. It's all second-hand. If you'd asked about the fishing competition earlier that month, I could have given you chapter and verse."

"That's an unusual sport for a school."

"It was extra-curricular and run by the janitors, for a while at least. No one had the appetite for it after young Bryan died. A great pity. Those boys spent so much time messing around on the water. Fishing on the Isbourne or further afield on the Severn."

"That's a distance from Truscombe."

"One of the dads had a boat."

"Nice. Do you know who?"

"Sorry. No idea."

But as he said it, an image slid into my memory—something I'd seen recently and conveniently close at hand.

"Thanks for your help," I said, getting to my feet. "Duty calls."

"I hope you find your friend."

"Me too," I vaguely replied as I exited the house. Then, stopping only to pick up a torch and some trainers, I set off for another night of house breaking.

Chapter Forty-Three

It wasn't dark or especially scary. But breaking into Adam Marshall's house without Sean beside me held little appeal. Still, if memory served, the item I wanted would be easy to reach and perhaps provide valuable insight into where the perpetrator might be hiding. Adam was missing. Sean was missing. The same person might be responsible for both disappearances, in which case anything in their homes might be relevant. And anything that stood between me and asking Marcus Catton for help had to be worthwhile pursuing.

I retraced my steps from the previous week, past the side door, and into the garden, where I collected the key from its hiding place. So far, so good.

I remembered to use the side door, slid the key inside, and waited for the warble of the alarm with my finger poised over the panel to enter the code. Then my mind went blank. Completely empty. I could see Sean, almost hear him repeat the number—a date—Adam's birth year. Ten seconds ago, it had echoed around my head, but now that I needed it, the digits had crumbled away like cliffs after a storm. I stood silently, willing them back, but it was no good. I wiped a prickle of sweat from my forehead and waited with bated breath, hoping the alarm might malfunction. For an interminable second, I thought it had. Then the alarm screeched a warning, and I leapt back a foot in shock. *Shit. What to do?*

The room sensor flashed a pulsing red light in time with the angry warble, and I paced a step forward, another back, spinning around as I contemplated my next move. Then I took a deep breath and tried to rationalise my situation. The alarm would go through to a control centre which would trigger a check and a notification to the householder or their next of kin, which would be fruitless. Adam was missing, and what remained of his family was far away. So, there was no immediate danger. It would take some time for control to notify the police, who would put a household burglary some way down their list of priorities. If I could keep a cool head, I had a good ten minutes to continue my search. Ignoring the racket around me, I headed straight for the study and dropped to my knees, precisely as I had before. A quick rummage in the cupboard and the document I'd remembered lay in my hand. I switched on Adam's desk light and cast my eyes over the paper. I was right. The Canal and River Trust licence gave access to the River Severn, which joined the River Avon at Tewkesbury. This licence was out of date, but if Adam had purchased another, his abductor could have taken it at the same time and be using it now. And judging by the bodies stacking up along the river, the assailant might be living on a barge. But how would I find it?

Quietly musing on the subject, I turned back towards the bookcase and noticed a framed photograph on the middle shelf. Four adults, three men and a woman, well into their thirties, were toasting an occasion with glasses of something sparkling. I recognised Adam from Sean's description, and for a moment, my cynical heart fluttered at his handsome face and strong jawline. I'd considered him a weakling, a weedy compliant victim, but he was a regular guy, attractive and eminently dateable. My breath quickened as I imagined meeting him. Our eyes would lock across the room, and he'd ask me to dinner. Then I cringed in embarrassment at my Mills and Boon daydreaming. *Inappropriate, Sass.*

I tore my eyes from his face, peering at the woman beside him, as my mouth fell open. It was Abi Catton, cosying up to another man, no doubt her erstwhile husband, Marcus. I'd known Adam and Marcus were childhood friends but never realised they'd continued to see one another. Gripping the photograph, I cast my mind back to my visit to the Catton house. Had I mentioned Adam? Did I know of his abduction at that point? Damn it. I couldn't remember, which meant another trip to Ashton under Hill.

Chapter Forty-Four

Abigail Catton resignedly nodded as she opened the door to me at eight forty-five the following day. I'd risen with the lark, alone in an empty house, and jumped straight into the car. Then I drove to Evesham and wasted time eating a supermarket breakfast to avoid arriving unsociably early. I was lucky Abi was there at all. Had her children not been sick in bed, Abigail would have been doing the school run, but without kids of my own, I hadn't considered it.

Abi glanced at her wristwatch before flashing a weak smile. "I suppose you had better come in."

I followed her into the magnificent kitchen diner, where she gestured towards a bar stool nesting underneath the counter. I hopped aboard and waited for an offer of a coffee. It never came.

"Well?" she asked, with none of the friendliness of our previous visit. I examined her face, which seemed to have aged by a decade in a week. Her red-rimmed eyes were sunken, her make-up scrappy. Not poorly done, I decided. But she'd applied it some time ago and slept in it. Her pillow must need a good wash. Abigail's hands shook as she fumbled in a kitchen drawer before removing what looked like a shimmering metallic marker pen but was, in fact, a vape. She pressed a switch, took a drag and the room filled with the aroma of blackberries. I pulled away from the cloud, trying to stifle a grimace.

"Sorry, but I need it," she said, her voice quivering.

"Are you okay?"

"Do I look okay?"

"No, actually. That's why I asked. You seem different."

"You could say that."

I waited for her to share, but Abi Catton sucked on the e-cig as if her life depended on it, as a plume of sickly vapours swirled around her.

I resisted the urge to speak and let her quietly puff away until she looked up and stared at me, eyes shining with tears.

"What is it?"

She shuffled towards the kitchen door, her feet barely leaving the tiles, and listened for a moment before shutting the glass-panelled door.

"They haven't worked it out yet," she said.

"The children?"

"Yes, poor little sods."

"Is it Marcus?"

She nodded.

"He's gone?"

"Yes. Fucking horrible timing. He left the day after my boyfriend told me he was seeing someone else and wanted a monogamous relationship."

"Wow. I was only here a week ago."

"Thanks, albatross."

"When did it happen?"

"Two days after you left. I could have taken one rejection or the other, but not two at once. I'm a bloody wreck. Can't sleep, can't eat. Bought this stupid fucking vape on a whim. And now I'm addicted."

"You're not. It just feels that way. There's too much going on. Use it while you need it."

"It's probably full of carcinogens."

"Doubtful. Shall I make you a drink?"

"No. Help yourself if you'd like one."

I slithered from the stool, grabbed a cup, and found the bits necessary to make myself tea, then used the boiling water tap in the centre of her kitchen.

"Nice," I said, watching the steam rise from the scalding hot water.

Abigail scrunched her face, unimpressed with something she'd seen many times before. Then she put her head in her hands and spoke in a muffled voice.

"I wish it had been the other way around."

"What?"

"That Phil had left first. Then Marcus might have stayed."

"But he was only here for the kids."

"I thought that. It turns out I miss the company more than I thought."

"Where has he gone?"

She shook her head. "No idea. He just took a bag and left. Marcus said he couldn't go on living like this. Not with me staying out all the time, which I didn't, by the way. A couple of times a week at most. Typical. He can go off with a school child for years but can't deal with my open affair."

"It seems unfair," I said. "But in some ways, understandable."

Abigail narrowed her eyes. "Not to me. Anyway. What do you want? I should be tending to my kids."

"I came to ask you about Adam Harding."

"God, yes. I saw his name in the papers the other day. But I couldn't make head nor tail of the reporting. I knew him a little."

"A little?"

"Superficially. Adam and Marcus were at school together."

"Did they stay in touch?"

"Lightly, yes. We went for dinner once or twice. They lost contact when Marcus ran off to Ireland. At least, I assume they did."

"And you?"

"What about me?"

"Did you know Adam in your own right?"

"I just told you. He was my husband's friend."

"Was?"

"As in, Marcus has gone, and Adam is missing. Nothing more suspicious than that."

"Do you know any of Adam's other school friends?"

"No." Abigail clenched her mouth over the e-cig but didn't puff.

"Sure?"

"Positive."

"Does Marcus fish?"

"What a bloody odd question."

"Does he?"

"Yes."

"And has he any connection to Tewkesbury?"

"Yes."

"What is it?" I snapped unintentionally. I liked Abi

Catton and wanted to go easy on her, but getting information was like pulling teeth.

"Time for you to go," she said, getting to her feet.

"Sorry. My impatience was rude and inexcusable. I didn't mean it."

"Maybe not. But I'm done. I can't sleep, my kids are sick, and what does it all matter anyway?"

I left her side to pop another teabag in a cup and let the magic steam tap do its thing.

"Drink that," I said, thrusting a Star Wars mug towards her.

"I don't want it."

"Drink it anyway."

She took a slurp and scowled.

"My partner is missing. Someone has Adam, and all roads lead to Tewkesbury," I said. "Tell me what you know."

"I thought they'd have found him by now. Is he dead?"

"Adam?"

She nodded. I shrugged.

"Bloody hell. He's a nice guy."

"So I gather. Will you help me?"

"Yes, but how?"

"Tell me about your husband's connection to Tewkesbury?"

"Marcus walks there sometimes. Across the Ham and along the Back of Avon. There's a pub he likes."

"Name?"

"Sorry. I don't know."

"Does he meet anyone?"

"Not that he's told me. He goes there to get away from things. It's an old childhood haunt."

"But nowhere specific?"

She shook her head and I tried again.

"Could he be living there?"

Abigail looked up. "It's possible. He always said he'd like to live by the river. Had some foolish idea about converting a barge."

"That's promising."

"Why?"

"In case he knows where Sean or Adam are."

"If he did, he would say. Marcus might have some dubious morals when it comes to young girls, but he's not a monster. You're not suggesting…"

"No. I'm not. But was there anything untoward between them?"

"Adam and Marcus? No. They didn't see enough of each other."

"Was Marcus ever violent?"

"Never. He could be cold, but my husband never raised a hand to me. Not once. You're barking up the wrong tree if you're going to Tewkesbury, hoping to find Marcus. He won't know anything."

"I'm sure you're right."

Abi Catton walked me down the hallway, but a further thought occurred as I passed an ornate mirror. "Where did you go to school?" I asked.

She hesitated for a moment and I thought she wouldn't answer. But as I crossed the threshold and made for the street, she muttered behind me in a voice too faint to be sure. "Truscombe," she said as the door slammed behind me.

Chapter Forty-Five

My car stuttered past the turning to Alderton, and I hurriedly changed gears. Driving on autopilot had never been a problem, but my mind was so overwhelmed with information about missing and murdered people I couldn't even use a car properly. And Tom's call bringing both welcome and alarming news about Sean hadn't helped. They were finally taking his disappearance seriously. Kim had approached Callie, who had ordered all hands on deck, budget constraints forgotten. Whatever Sean had done to earn her thanks during their meeting, which, despite the situation still rankled, had paid dividends. Though Finnegan objected, she had taken personal charge and given Kim the authority to lead the hunt for Sean. According to Tom, Finnegan had complained that it was part and parcel of his case and that he didn't need another inspector muddying the waters. Callie had intervened, publicly questioning his progress and flushing beetroot red, he'd skulked into the corner while Kim set out her plan.

Tom had said Tewkesbury was currently swarming with

police officers, both undercover and uniformed. If Sean were there, they'd find him. But I had my doubts. Kim had centred her men around the Severn Ham, where Big Ken had lain dying, with another contingent tracing his last known movements around the town. And though it made sense, there were worrying gaps like why she wasn't pursuing Marcus Catton, who ought to be a prime suspect. Come to think of it, so should any of Sean's school friends. And then I remembered how much I had discovered through nefarious means that Kim didn't know, and I couldn't tell her. My only choice was to see it through myself.

My phone pinged as I reached the Teddington round-about. I glanced at the dash where I'd mounted my archaic hands-free system, which skewed permanently left to see it was from Dhruv. For a moment, I considered letting it go to the voicemail. Mill should have spoken to him by now, but it would be awkward if he hadn't. Then again, what kind of friend would I be if I let a minor inconvenience stand in the way of our relationship? I jabbed a finger at the mobile, cursed as it demanded my pin, and pulled it from the cradle. The phone fell to the floor. I swerved, the Mini driver behind me beeped and raised his middle finger, and I pulled into the side of the road and clicked my hazards on. Traffic buzzed around me as I squeezed my hand beneath the seats and felt for my phone. Dhruv had disappeared by the time I reached it, and the mobile had defaulted to my running app for some unfathomable reason. I cleared it and pressed recall. Dhruv answered within seconds.

"When did you know?" he demanded.

"Know what?" I wasn't taking any chances.

"About Mill."

"A couple of days ago."

"And you didn't think to tell me?"

"I did. But Mill said he'd do it himself."

Dhruv tried to respond but choked on a sob.

"I'm so sorry, Dhruv. I wish it hadn't happened."

"We were getting married."

"I know."

"Our life wasn't perfect, but we were happy."

I squeezed my eyes closed, remembering the first day I'd met Dhruv at Bosworth House. He'd been a happy-go-lucky chatterbox, full of joy.

"I know. When did he tell you?"

"Last night."

"You should have called me."

"I couldn't."

"I understand."

"Do you? He broke my heart, Sass."

"I've been there. It happened to me in Cyprus. Still saddens me now." I bit my tongue as soon as the words left my mouth. The last thing Dhruv needed was a lesson in how long heartbreak lasted. "Where's Mill now?" I asked, changing the subject.

"In the spare room."

"He stayed at the flat?"

"Yes. It makes a change, doesn't it? Bloody ironic. All the times I've wanted him home, and now it's over, he's claiming house rights."

"It's definitely over then?"

"How could I ever trust him again?"

"Do you still love him?"

"Forever." Dhruv's voice broke and a tear trickled down my face. Thank God I was on audio, where he couldn't see me blubbing like a baby.

"Can't you work it out?"

"How? He's been lying to me for months."

"Only to protect you."

"Himself, you mean."

"I don't. Mill regrets his behaviour."

"Not as much as I do."

"Can't you give him a chance? Get couple's therapy?"

"I'm done with all that crap. I've spent hundreds of pounds on counselling sessions, all wasted. None of this was about me, my behaviour or how I handled Mill's issues. It all comes down to a drunken shag on his part that he couldn't own."

"Perhaps he's not as strong as you."

"I always thought he was better. I admired him and aspired to be good enough to deserve him."

"It's hard to be on someone's pedestal. There's a long way to fall."

"What do you think I should do?"

I considered the matter. I was a big fan of happy-ever-afters, but Dhruv's feelings were raw and Mill's complex. They had a long way to go. "Do nothing," I offered. "Live with it for a while; come to terms with your feelings."

"With Mill in the house?"

"Will he move out if you ask him to?"

"He'd rather not. Mill's been sofa surfing and has no money. But why should I pay his share of the rent after what he's done?"

"Tell him to go then?"

The line went quiet. "Are you there, Dhruv?"

"Yes."

"Well?"

"I can't do it."

"Then you've no choice but to continue as you are. Take your time."

"Can you come over tonight?"

"I'll try, but I can't promise."

"Please."

"It's Sean. They haven't found him."

"Still?"

"Yes. It's serious. He's truly missing."

"Where are you?"

"Travelling to Tewkesbury. I have a lead."

"Hand it over to Tom."

"I can't. I gained it illegitimately."

"What have you done?"

"I can't tell you. And it doesn't matter anyway. But I must work alone. No choice."

"Sounds dangerous, Sass. Selfishly, I'd rather nothing awful happen to you."

"I'll be careful."

"Then I'll see you tonight."

"Tell you what," I said. "Let's say I'll be at yours at six o'clock. And if I don't turn up and you haven't heard from me, feel free to call Tom. Tell him I'm aiming for the waterway. Does that make you feel better?"

"As much as anything could right now."

"Okay. It's a date."

Chapter Forty-Six

I parked my car in front of Victoria Gardens and meandered through, casting an eye towards the water where they'd found the body. The police tape had long since disappeared and no evidence of the crime scene remained. Instead, dog walkers crisscrossed the lawns and the boat-shaped planter burgeoned with autumn flowers. I gazed at the waterway while watching the bird life, momentarily grateful for the calm tranquillity. Then I thought of Sean. Where the hell was he? How could a strapping six-foot man disappear, leaving no evidence of his whereabouts?

I continued my journey alongside the canal, weaving through the town and casting an appreciative eye on the buildings and alleyways steeped in history. Back in the day, much of my walking route had fallen within the abbey grounds, and medieval architecture dominated my view. On any other day, I'd have found it inspiring. But today was for serious matters.

A red-painted moored barge hoved into view in the

distance, and I recognised it as the static information barge I'd seen on the internet. Adam's lock and moor licence was now only available online. I could hardly email and ask questions without the inevitable refusal on data protection grounds. I needed to speak with a human being, hence the information barge. The door was open, and the welcome smell of bacon permeated my nostrils as I entered, approaching a counter behind which a whiskered man was taking a bite from a foil-wrapped sandwich. My mouth watered. He hurriedly re-wrapped his lunch, and I fixed my best smile.

"A fine day isn't it?" he said, wiping his mouth.

"It's lovely."

"Have you travelled far?"

"Not very."

"Then how can I help you?"

I took a booklet from the counter, turned it over and noted the price; £3.99 wouldn't break the bank, and handing over money always softened a request for information. "This, please," I said.

"Ah. Local history. Are you interested?"

"Always."

"You should visit the museum. It's small but well worth seeing."

"I will. But it's the waterway that fascinates me. How many barges are usually moored here?"

"I couldn't say. You'd need to check with the marina."

"Okay. But learning more about the barges and river life while I'm here would be useful."

"What can I tell you?" The man looked up with a smile, eager to please but not fully comprehending my question, which was fair as I was taking my sweet time getting to the point.

"Are the barges used by holidaymakers or for residential purposes?" I asked.

"A bit of both. That one there," he said, pointing dead ahead. "Now that's for hire. I borrowed it myself a while back. Took a lovely trip to Stratford with the missus and Herbert."

He pointed to a photograph taped to the side wall of a middle-aged woman cradling a collie.

"Lovely looking dog," I said, and he beamed.

"I've had him from a pup. He's getting on a bit now. Arthritic, like me."

I gazed at his swollen knuckles and smiled sympathetically.

"But some people live on the water?"

"Oh yes. More are getting off-grid every year, as you young people call it.

"Is it expensive?"

"It's as dear as you make it. See that black and white vessel over there?"

"Liberty?" I said, peering at the peeled white lettering running down the side.

"Aye. She's a forty-foot trad and as cheap as chips."

"How much?" I said, wondering how to calculate the chip value of a barge.

"Twenty-five, thirty thousand pounds at a push."

"Hmm. Seems reasonable."

"As long as you don't forget to factor in mooring costs."

"Of course."

"But that's your no-frills narrowboat. You can spend as much as you like at the top end."

"How about that one?" I pointed to a pale green barge slightly farther ahead.

"Now you're talking. She's a fancy-pants wide-beamed cruiser. Usually moors at the marina."

"Nice. Could I rent one?"

"Of course. Take this." He handed me a leaflet with a gaily painted vessel on the front titled "Best British Barging Holidays."

"Thanks, but I meant for home rental, like a flat."

"Yes," he said uncertainly. "I believe there are one or two. Private landlords, most probably. It might take a while for a boat to come available for rent."

"But it's possible?"

"Yes. As I said, best check at the marina."

"That will be my next stop."

I turned to leave, then remembered the photograph of Marcus Catton I had misappropriated from Adam's house. Anything was worth a try.

"Have you seen this man, by any chance?"

He reached for the photo and smiled. "Yes. Nice chap. Hasn't been here long but always says hello."

"Where is he?"

"Parked near the Back of Avon. Small barge—like the liberty. Can't remember the name, but I pass him most days."

"How can I find it?"

The man stroked his beard and mused. "I know," he said, snapping his fingers. "Can't remember the colour for the life of me, but there's a ship's wheel painted on the side. You can't miss it."

And with that, I dismissed all thoughts of going to the marina and headed straight for Catton's boat.

Chapter Forty-Seven

Marcus Catton's temporary home bobbed gently on the water as I approached its starboard side, wondering if I had the courage to jump aboard. The entrance to the vessel gaped open beneath a plastic canopy, and the door was most definitely ajar. Entering was tempting, very tempting. But Catton was a prime suspect and unlikely to cooperate if questioned.

Fortunately, we had never met, and I could watch him without risk. So, I familiarised myself with his narrowboat by pacing back and forth a few times until I had glimpsed enough of the inside to know that the bedroom was as far away from the living area as it was possible to get. Luck had been on my side. Net curtains covered only one window, allowing a decent view inside and the moving shadow beyond the obscured bathroom window told me everything I needed to know about Catton's current position within the boat. Surveillance completed, I tore myself away from the oddly named Silver Sea Slug, passing through the nearest alley and onto the high street, where I spent a pleasant hour in a nearby cafe. The food was tasty, and two flat white coffees later, I had formulated a plan. I would wait until dark, hop aboard and have a good poke around the living area while Catton slept soundly at the other end. Beyond that, I was unprepared. Nor had I considered how I would make any further progress if he hadn't squirrelled an obvious clue on the barge. But I had little else to go on, and as Tom had rightly said, plenty of uniformed officers were patrolling the town.

Grabbing a magazine and a bottle of water, I settled on a bench twenty yards from the boat with a bird's-eye view and spent the next few hours alternating between magazine gossip and the ever-depressing news app on my phone. Bored and on the verge of plugging in my earphones, I glimpsed something ahead of me and looked up to see Marcus Catton focusing a pair of binoculars on the building in front. I watched for a moment, unsure of what to expect then quickly snapped a few photographs before he stopped what he was doing and went back below. He'd only been there a matter of minutes, but it was enough to spook me. What was he looking for? Had he trained the binoculars my way before switching direction? I hadn't been paying enough attention. Perhaps I'd been rumbled? Then I reassessed the situation using logic and remembered that he didn't know me, had never met me, and couldn't possibly recognise me. I was safe.

The day turned to dusk and I grew sleepy as I waited for nightfall. And to escape the cold, I popped into the nearest public house for a warming brandy. It did the trick but without the hoped-for burst of energy. I was close to giving up and going home. One more call to Sean's mobile changed my mind. Nothing. Tumbleweed. I knew I couldn't walk away to a comfortable bed with my partner still missing. Then my mobile buzzed, and Dhruv's name appeared above a text message.

It's ten past six. Where are you?

Still here. Sorry, I won't make it to you tonight.

Disappointed. Are you okay?

Yes. But about to go back into the cold.

To do what?

It doesn't matter. I'll call you tomorrow.

What time will you drive back?

IDK

Then I'll phone Tom in an hour.

No. Don't do that. Say, midnight.

Urgh. That's late. Guess I'll wait up. Nothing better to do.

No need for that.

Oh, yes, there is. Contact me by midnight, or Tom will be my next call.

Fine. I will. Take care, Dhruv,

You too.

I terminated the conversation feeling a swell of undue pressure. Dhruv was looking out for me, but I still didn't know when I'd finish. Midnight seemed too soon, but he'd forced me into a corner, and I had to say something to stop him from dragging Tom into a situation he would disapprove of. Truth to tell, this intrusion into Catton's privacy went way beyond Tom's approval. He'd likely arrest me. I left the pub, resuming my former seat, and slumped back against the hard wooden bench with my coat collar raised high against the light autumn breeze. The lights of a dozen barges twinkled across the waterway as the waterfowl settled down for the night. Lucky them.

A succession of mindless mobile games saved me from the depths of total boredom and by ten thirty, darkness had well and truly fallen. I'd managed to stay awake long enough for a second wind and approached the next hour eagerly, right up to the moment Marcus Catton confounded my plans by appearing again, dressed from head to foot in black and sporting a balaclava. If he had not been carrying a torch, I might have missed him. But the beam helped, and I jumped from my vantage point and melted into the shadow of the towpath, heart thumping in my chest. Catton walked quickly, his tall frame loping towards the north end of town. I tracked him along Back of Avon, keeping a safe distance behind, alert, optimistic, and professional. Then a sudden dip in the pavement left me careering into a large black bin which fell to the floor with a thump as the contents spewed across the pavement. Ahead of me, Catton froze. I lay spread-eagled on the ground for a second before rolling into the wall. Catton turned and shone his torch directly at the bin, swirling the beam from floor to wall to floor. I lay barely breathing as he advanced a few paces towards me. But my cover held. He grunted and turned away.

Peering past the upturned bin, I watched as he faded from sight, quickly scrambling to my feet. He must not get away. But one step forward and my best intentions exploded in a world of pain. I'd sprained my ankle as I went down, and it hurt like holy hell. Gritting my teeth, I pushed myself onwards, my left foot dragging as I applied my weight to the right. Tears rolled down my face as the pain raged sharply with every step. Catton was gaining ground, barely in sight, and I knew it would all be pointless if I lost him. Then suddenly, he stopped outside a building, a vast warehouse. He slipped inside and I sighed in relief. I knew where he was.

The pressure was off, and I could take my time. I limped, rested, limped, rested before reaching the weather-beaten door where he'd disappeared. A jagged hole gaped above the doorknob, which hung limply by a single screw. The door stood ajar. Had Catton vandalised it? I hadn't heard him, but I'd been too preoccupied with my pain to know for sure. A burst of common sense hit me just before I entered the building. I hesitated, then messaged Dhruv with my exact coordinates and a short text. *Tell Tom.* And then, for better or worse, I entered.

Chapter Forty-Eight

The door opened into a cavernous open space, pitch black with a musty odour that made me gag. The old building creaked and groaned in the stillness of the night and I stood, stock still, trying to find my night vision. It didn't work, at least not quickly enough. I reached into my jacket for my trusty torch, removed the cotton scarf from around my neck and wrapped it over the lens. The light was bright enough to see without drawing undue attention but too dim to make out the extent of the downstairs room. I picked my way across the floor, crunching unfamiliar objects, tasting dust particles, and flinching at every sound. I soon found myself at the back of the building near an open door with a rising staircase. Torch in pocket, I took the first tread as slowly as possible, but no matter how carefully I went, the stairs squeaked their objection to my presence. Up I climbed, heart in mouth, desperate to know what Catton intended to do.

I passed the first floor, still dizzy with pain, listened,

heard nothing, and climbed again. My cumbersome routine continued the same way until the fourth floor when a soft beam and a light tread roused my attention. I pulled open a half-closed door, looked inside, and saw one figure, then another while trying to rationalise what my eyes were telling me. The kneeling figure in the middle of the narrow room gazed at his blood-covered palm, which noticeably shook in the dim light. He was suffering, wracked with pain and oblivious to the other man bearing down upon him like a hunter tracking his prey. I froze as Marcus Catton tiptoed towards the stranger, wielding a weighty implement in his arm, ready to swing. Instinctively, I grabbed my torch, sprang towards Catton and thwacked him on the back of the head as hard as possible. He dropped like a stone. The stranger looked up, gazed towards me with a confused look as if he were about to pass out, brushed his fingers over a wound on his temple and held his hand towards me. I rummaged in my coat and relit my dented torch before placing it on an old desk where it illuminated the scene before me. The shadowy man was now vaguely familiar. "Adam?" I asked uncertainly.

"Thank God," he replied.

I cleaned up Adam as best I could with a dried-out packet of wet wipes and a used tissue. He didn't object as I cleaned the blood from his temple and examined the wound.

"You'll need stitches," I said. "I'll call someone."

He reached for my hand and held it momentarily. A frisson of electricity sparked through me as I stared at a perfect hairline framing a handsome, unshaven face. Battered and bruised, he might be, but Adam Harding was making my body react in ways it had almost forgotten. I tried to speak, but my breath came in rasps.

"Give me a moment," he said, his voice husky. He shook his head as if trying to focus.

"Catton's hurt you badly." Trust my voice to resume normal service while stating the bleeding obvious.

"It's okay. I'll live."

"What happened?"

"He came at me. Then tried again. But why? I thought he was my friend."

"Of course." I felt for the photograph of Adam and Marcus now crumpled in my pocket and decided that now was not the time. "I'm sorry. Everyone has been so worried about you."

"Who are you?" he asked, his voice low and brimming with gratitude.

"Saskia."

"Saskia," he repeated in a whisper.

"Yes. I'm a friend of Sean's. He's missing too."

"Sean Tallis?"

"Yes."

"Oh, God."

"What was that?" My head involuntarily jerked upwards at an unexpected noise—a thumping sound directly above me.

"I don't know."

"Stay here. I'll take a look."

"No. Don't go alone. Wait for a moment. I'll come with you."

I hobbled to my feet, wincing in pain. Adam smiled sympathetically.

"Hold on," he said. Then, clutching his head, he swayed as his legs buckled.

"Sit down," I commanded. "You might have a concussion."

Adam didn't argue. He shook his head from side to side and placed it in his hands.

"I'll be back in five," I whispered before limping from the room.

Chapter Forty-Nine

I braced myself as I stood at the foot of the next set of stairs, knowing that I was nowhere near the top and that reaching the source of the banging would take a super-human effort and involve considerable pain. And for what? It could simply be a regular noise from the pipes. Then I gave myself a reality check. The building was abandoned, unlit, and with no power supply. My sensible self knew I should leave and get help. Adam, though injured, was safe for now. Catton was down but could wake at any moment. And with an ankle injury and still healing from last year's attack at Bosworth House, I was in poor shape to be prowling around a large, unfamiliar building. Memories of Bosworth House left me momentarily paralysed into inac-tion. Then the noise, which had stopped, faintly resumed. Placing a shaking hand on what remained of the stair rail, I heaved my damaged body forward, plodding one foot at a time until I had climbed another two flights of stairs, arriving at a chillingly dark landing. I reached for my torch, and my heart lurched as I realised, I'd left it downstairs. I'd need to use the phone light instead and I flicked it on, noting the thin red line indicating a rapidly diminishing battery. Holding the phone aloft, I noticed three doors off the landing where I'd expected another large room. They must have been offices back in the day when the building was in use and full of workers.

My musings were interrupted by a faint clang from the right-hand door. With a low battery and a volatile situation below, I needed to act, and it was now or never. I gingerly opened the door and stared into the pitch black beyond, trying to pick out a shape in the corner of the room. My eyes settled on a reinforced cage. Something once intended for housing large animals but rebuilt inside a warehouse and adapted to cage a man. Someone was inside, still banging pitifully on the metal struts with a broken ceramic chunk that looked like a piece of a dog bowl. Whoever it was hadn't heard me arrive and was still oblivious to my presence. They lay there, clanging the bars on autopilot, facing inwards. Heart in mouth, I ventured closer. Then dropped to my knees and whispered.

"Hello. Don't be frightened. I'm here to help."

The figure froze before rolling over, and I jumped back in alarm at the sight of a pair of frightened eyes staring above a blood-stained gag. Blood trickled down his forehead and nose, and an angry purple bruise flared across his cheek. But despite the damage, I knew him. And relief washed over me.

"Sean. My God. What happened?"

He mumbled through the gag, words incomprehensible. Through the gloom, I saw one of his hands cuffed to a ring in the middle of the makeshift cage. Sean got to his haunches, teetering off balance.

"I'll get you out of here, I promise."

Sean's eyes narrowed in pain, but he raised a faltering hand and jabbed it towards the door.

"You want me to go?"

He shook his head and pointed again.

"Turn around. I'll release the gag."

Sean sighed and shook his head before moving painfully forward. As he drew closer, I realised the gag was a black mask covering his lower face and fastened with a tiny padlock.

"Christ. Marcus Catton is one sick fuck."

Sean mumbled again.

"What?"

He pointed to the padlock on the cage bars and jabbed his finger towards the door again.

"You want the key?"

Sean nodded.

Left or central door?

He pointed hard left.

"Okay. I'm on it."

Trying to ignore my ankle, now swollen and hot with pain, I dragged myself towards the left-hand door, wondering how I had missed the chink of light shining beneath. For a moment, I thought I was hallucinating. But the light was real. Shit. Was someone inside?

I placed my hand over my heart, trying to still my rising panic. Duty called, and Sean was in dire straits. All should be well downstairs, or I would have heard the disruption. With a deep breath, I opened the door and peered inside.

The first thing I noticed was the low hum of a battery-powered generator. The second, to my relief, was that the room was devoid of people. It was safe. Someone had been sleeping here, and a camp bed lay in the corner of the room by a TV set and a camping stove. A large desk and a metal filing cabinet occupied the left-hand side, and a dusty armchair finished the accommodation. I stared, perplexed, caught off guard at the scene, feeling a misguided sense of safety at the normality of the furniture. Until I noticed a pair of blackout curtains hanging from the windows. Whoever stayed here had tried to avoid being seen.

I made for the desk and pulled open the lower, large drawer, surprised to see it full of medical supplies. Its partner opposite contained packet food items. I glanced around the room. No fridge, no kettle. Probably an occasional sleeping place, but now was not the time for speculation.

Throwing open the other doors, I found stationery items, a dog lead, keys with a tag bearing the words Merry Maid, and a second large bunch of keys of varying sizes. They should be what I needed.

Retracing my steps, I staggered towards Sean's prison in all kinds of agony, wondering how I would ever get downstairs. While I'd been out, he'd positioned himself as close to the front of the cage as possible, ready for a quick escape. Grabbing the keys, I fumbled, trying one after the other in the lock. The first three did not fit. With one free hand, Sean thumped the cage in frustration, then held it out, palm uppermost. I shrugged. How did he expect me to pass them through the mesh? But he pointed to a raised section along the front, and I tugged at an almost hidden metal lip and pulled it down. A hole big enough to fit a dish appeared, presumably made for delivering food. I passed Sean the keys. He took one, then another, before successfully unlocking the handcuff from the floor. He massaged his wrist, and the pitiful remains of my phone light picked out a bleeding welt which would need urgent medical treatment. Hands now free, Sean fumbled to release the padlock at the back of his head. But wounded and at such an odd angle, he stood no chance.

"Give them to me," I ordered.

Huffing, he passed the keys back through the hole.

"Turn around."

Sean stood obediently, and I realised that this must have become part of his routine. Unmask, eat, drink, and mask up again. Jesus. What an awful time he'd had.

With only a few tiny keys to try, I finally released the mask just as my phone died.

"Fuck. Sean. Are you okay?"

He sighed as he fumbled to remove the headgear. "I've been better. Quickly. Get this overgrown rabbit hutch open before he comes back."

"He won't. You're okay. I slugged him over the head. He's out cold."

"Thank fuck. I still can't come to terms with it. All those years and I never had a clue."

"Weird. It seemed so obvious to me. Ah ha."

The lock opened with a satisfying click, and I stood momentarily in the pitch-black room, awash with relief, before releasing the door.

"Let's get going," I said. Then something thumped me in the small of my back, and I fell headlong into the cage.

Chapter Fifty

I had fallen onto Sean, and we careened to the floor in time to see a hand snake out and apply another padlock. A shadowy figure retreated towards the door, pulled it open, and dragged something through. Then he approached the cage once more.

"Mobile," he said, opening the hole. I couldn't see much but sensed that he was standing back.

I felt for the now useless phone and handed it over—no point in making a fuss over something I couldn't use.

"Good," he said, noting the blank screen.

Silence fell, and I reached for Sean's hand. He firmly grasped mine and squeezed. "What now?" I sighed.

Something clicked, and a shaft of light appeared at the back of the room, illuminating the space and revealing a man sitting on a chair by the side of the door. I gasped as Adam Harding grinned back, his arms and legs crossed as if he were about to enjoy a movie.

"I don't understand." I stared dumbly at Sean as his

features twisted in pain. "Is he in cahoots with Marcus Catton?"

Sean shook his head. "This has nothing to do with Catton."

"Actually, you're wrong." Harding smiled wolfishly, a hard note of arrogance marring his handsome features. "Life is full of unfortunate coincidences. I've sailed up and down this river for months, safely anonymous while finalising my plans. Would you like to know what they are? Of course, you would. Who doesn't love holiday stories? Well, I'm off to Amsterdam in a couple of days," he continued, checking his watch. "Across the channel by private boat. No need for anyone to know I'm still alive."

"What's that to do with Marcus Catton?" Caged or not, Adam had piqued my curiosity, and I needed answers.

"Catton moored next to me a few days ago. I didn't notice who he was at first. Then he spotted me and dropped by to let me know everyone was looking for me. I should have realised they'd report me as a missing person. But time was of the essence, and I needed to leave Truscombe quickly.

I nearly killed Catton there and then, but he was far too close to home. So, I told him I was living off the grid because I'd witnessed something I shouldn't have seen and needed to lie low for a while. I made him promise not to say anything. We were old friends, and I should have been able to trust him. But Catton can't keep his mouth shut when he drinks. He grew suspicious of my story and blabbed about me in the pub. People started talking, and I came to hear of it. But not before he'd started spying on me."

"You should have left Tewkesbury. It's far too close to Truscombe," said Sean.

"I had a few loose ends to tie up," Adam replied. "A medical issue."

"What?"

"None of your business. I needed drugs and getting them took a few weeks."

"Just let us go. You can be long gone by the time we raise the alarm."

Adam grimaced. "I would have given you a quick death for old time's sake, Tallis. But now I'll leave you here to rot."

"Why would you do that to an old friend?" I asked.

"Because he's a fucking psychopath." Sean spat the words as his eyes filled with tears.

"That's fair," said Adam. "I do enjoy this kind of thing." He waved his hand towards the cage. "No point in denying it."

"I should have hit you harder." Sean snarled, clenching his fists.

"And I should have cut your face," said Adam. "Still, you're not getting any more food, so you won't get a chance to repeat that little stunt."

I gazed at Adam's temple wound and Sean's still weeping cut. "Did you do that?" I asked, gesturing towards Adam.

Sean nodded. "For all the good it did."

"Exactly. All you achieved is doubling my pleasure. Now two rats are trapped in a cage. But she's easier on the eye."

My heart quickened at the compliment, and I changed the subject, disgusted at my body's betrayal. "Why would you do this to an old school friend?"

"Friend? Don't confuse growing up together with friend-ship. Friends don't abandon each other when times get tough."

Adam glared at Sean, lip curled, his disdain on full

display. "And anyway, your partner is too nosy for his own good. Catton spilt his guts to an old man in the pub and Tallis or one of his contacts found out."

"But all those others. You killed so many people."

"Not by choice. They got away."

Adam's voice broke. For a moment, he looked small and alone. Then he raised his head and grinned. "I wanted to keep them. Watch them, see them adapt to captivity. It makes me feel alive."

"But you had everything. A successful job, a wonderful life."

"What the fuck do you know about my life? I was lonely. So lonely. I'm the only one of my kind. I can't find a kindred spirit. No wife, no life. And my best fucking friend didn't want to know me."

"For God's sake, Adam. We were schoolmates, not lovers." Sean's voice quivered with contempt.

Adam stood, grabbed the chair, and hurled it at the cage. It bounced off and skittered across the floor. "You bastard," he screamed.

"I'm right. Did you have the hots for me, big man?"

I heard one cracking knuckle after another as a grimacing Adam stood in the centre of the room, trying to calm his rage.

Moments later, he licked his lips and approached the cage, keeping a wary distance from the door. "Perhaps I should take you with me," he said, looking directly into my eyes.

I gulped. Now that he was closer, I could see a soullessness in his dark eyes, a hidden cruelty beneath the surface.

"Did this happen because of your past? Did your captivity break you?"

Adam stared blankly, and then his face creased into a

smile. "Bless your sweet little heart," he said. "Things aren't always as they seem."

"Sorry? You'll have to explain."

His eyes narrowed at my command, but he disregarded the tone.

"I heard they found a body in the woods," he said.

"Another of your victims?"

"In a manner of speaking. The young man had been with me for a while. A good few months. He could have stayed long-term but succeeded in doing what your partner could not. He faked an injury, tricking me into the cage and shutting me inside before running away. But I hadn't figured out the optimum food and water required to keep someone alive, leaving him too weak to survive. He didn't make it, thank God. Which I hadn't realised by the time they freed me. I steered clear of my predilections for a while and tried to rise above my urges. It could all have gone badly wrong, and I'd had a lucky escape. Prison would have been unfathomable." Harding visibly shuddered.

"So, you were the captor and not the victim?"

"Of course. And nobody knew. They fell for my story about a cyber-stalking maniac hook, line, and sinker, including you, old friend."

Sean clenched his fist, and I stroked his arm. "Don't react," I said, but Sean was too angry for restraint.

"I'll fucking kill him."

"Now, now." Adam's voice dripped with sarcasm.

"Tell me about Ella Burton," I said.

Adam grinned. "I went looking for Ella," he said. "By that time, I'd been alone for years, and taking a new captive occupied my every waking thought. I'd tried therapy, taken drugs, and abused alcohol for a while, but nothing sated me. My urges raged, and I knew I'd give in eventually, so I

decided to plan my move properly. I occasionally saw
Catton and his silly wife and knew all about Ella. He'd
watched her from afar, so I knew she'd fallen on hard times
and would be the perfect victim. No one would ever miss
her. And if they did, they'd assume she was living rough or
in some squalid drug den. So, I took her, rented a house
with a basement using a false name, and assembled one of
these." He waved towards the cage. "I kept her there for a
few weeks and fed her once in a while. Ella was canny and
tried to befriend me. I liked it. Our arrangement could have
worked out, but she offered her body, and stupidly, I agreed.
It had been a while. A man has urges, other urges. But the
stupid bitch hit me on the head and broke free. Just as well,
it happened in the middle of the night. Running through
Truscombe with a pounding head and a fleeing captive was
not my idea of a good time. But I knew Truscombe like the
back of my hand, and she didn't. It was always going to end
badly for her. I caught up with Ella at the back of
Grosvenor Road, took a rock, and hit her over the head. I
was about to finish her off when I heard footsteps. Someone
was walking down the alleyway and too close for comfort. I
ran for it, not knowing if she was still alive.

I'd been thinking of moving on for a long time. With a
head wound and someone who might identify me, the time
was right to go. I could keep a low profile on the barges and
planned to keep moving. But my first mooring was directly
outside this fine place." Adam smugly gestured while
sporting a fake smile.

"And you decided to stay here?" I offered.

"No. Someone else already had—a stupid drunk,
though not too dim to have set up a makeshift home here. I
noticed a light in the upstairs room on my first night in
Tewkesbury. Naturally, I investigated and found another

perfect victim. Long story short, I ordered the usual large animal cages online, wired a few together, and readied myself for his inevitable return. I particularly enjoyed this one. People are so pitiful when dependent on alcohol, aren't they? He cried like a child for days, repeatedly banging his head on the frame. It was fascinating to watch. But I hadn't anticipated the damage a heavy, desperate man could do. One night, he broke free. I was on deck and saw him just in time, tracked him through Victoria Gardens and finished him off. I left for Stratford the same day."

"Then why did you risk coming back?" Sean growled.

"I forgot my passport. I'd already forgotten it once and had to sneak back to my home in the dead of night to recover it. But I had so much to think about that I left it on the desk next door with some other paperwork. That's what happens when you leave in a hurry. I could have risked it, but it wasn't worthwhile for the sake of a quick return visit."

"And that's when you ran into Marcus."

"Yes. And into you, Sean, my old friend."

"Fuck off and die."

"Make me."

Adam Harding gloated, hands on hips. Then his face changed in a flash at the unmistakable sound of police sirens in the background. He strode towards the window. "How?" he asked.

I shrugged carelessly. "Prior planning prevents piss poor performance," I smirked.

"No matter. I'll take the back way." He took the keys, momentarily held them in mid-air and dropped them on the floor, visible but far out of our reach.

"You callous bastard," said Sean as Harding strode towards the door.

"Oh, you don't know the half of it. Here's a parting gift,

Tallis. Something I should have told you years ago when we were still friends. I didn't save your brother. Quite the contrary. I held the little fucker's head under the water until he drowned. He was taking up too much of your time. So I fixed it. You're welcome."

And with that, Harding was gone. Sean howled like a banshee behind me, his hands on his head, knuckles clenched. Then the door slammed open, and I expected to see a blue uniform. Instead, Marcus Catton stared woozily ahead, blood streaming down his face and neck.

"Over there," I yelled, pointing to the keys.

Catton said nothing but slumped to the floor on his knees.

"Get up," I screamed.

He shook his head but fell to one side until his hands closed over the bunch. Then, shuffling on his hands and knees, he approached the lock. Two minutes later, we were free.

Chapter Fifty-One

Sean sprang ahead of me, screaming for Harding. Muttering my apologies to Catton, I followed behind, trailing down the stairs, desperate to keep up but hobbled by my ankle injury. Below, Sean's feet echoed through the warehouse as he raged towards the rear, searching for his former friend, injuries and hunger forgotten. Behind me, Marcus Catton silently panted as he fought through his pain to get out of the godforsaken building. I arrived at the bottom and collapsed into the arms of a police officer.

"Are you Miss Denman?"

"Yes. He's getting away."

"Who?"

"Never mind. Go to the rear staircase."

"Let's get you out first."

"No. Just go. Now."

He stared uncertainly, then bolted. Catton joined me and placed an arm under my shoulder, still mute. I leaned against him, and we supported each other as we plodded outside.

"Sass. You look awful." Tom bounded up, followed by Kim Robbins.

"What's going on?" she demanded. "This better be worth my time and officers."

"Don't start," I snapped, in no mood for her cynicism. "You got Sean into this mess, and now you can stop him from getting banged up for life."

"You've found him?"

"Yes. Adam Harding had Sean trussed up in a cage. Sean's going after him. There'll be another death if you don't get there first."

"Where?"

"Back stairs of the warehouse."

"You, you and you." Kim pointed to her officers. "You heard the lady. You're looking for two men. Go."

I watched them scramble towards the building as Kim spoke into her radio. "Ambulance, Back of Avon. Now."

"I don't need an ambulance."

"You both do. Who's this?"

"Marcus Catton."

Kim pulled a face in recognition of the name.

"What's he doing here?" she asked, removing a pair of handcuffs.

"Oh no, you don't. This man's a bloody hero," I said.

Kim nodded and reached for her radio again. "Anything?" she asked.

"No. We're inside. No sign of life."

"Shit, he's got away." My heart lurched at the thought of a weakened Sean pursuing his psychopathic friend.

"Where are they going?"

"I don't know," I hissed. And then I remembered the keys I'd seen in the office room. A bunch that Adam had pocketed just as he'd dropped the cage keys.

"He has a boat. The Merry Maid."

"Call the marina. Find out where they've moored the Merry Maid," she barked.

I shivered against Tom, who had wrapped a metallic thermal blanket around my shoulders. "The ambulance won't be long," he said.

"I don't want it."

"You need to rest."

"Can I sit in your car?"

"Sure. Come on."

I limped the few yards to where he'd parked it, clambered inside and reclined in the front passenger seat, gripped with anxiety. Tom sat beside me and a few moments later, his radio crackled. "The boat is at Wharf launch," said Kim.

Tom punched the name into Google Maps, reversed the car and screeched away while I clung to the door handle, trying to locate the seat belt.

"Sorry, Sass," he said.

"Just get there."

Wharf Launch was only a few minutes away. Tom weaved through the back streets of Tewkesbury and slammed the brakes on just as he reached a sloping jetty to the river. He parked on double yellows and ran towards the water. I limped behind as Tom vaulted a wall and leapt onto the boat. By the time I reached him, Tom had Sean in a headhold, with Sean straddling Adam Harding, now lying on the deck, his face battered and bloodied, groaning in pain with a tooth visible on the painted planks. Tom released his grip on Sean and cuffed Adam while I ran to Sean's side, cradling his head. He sobbed on my shoulder as a dog howled from below deck.

"Take him away," commanded Kim as she boarded the barge.

Chapter Fifty-Two

One Month Later

"How did it go?" I asked as Sean entered the office, his face set grimly.

"Alright."

"More detail?"

"I'd rather not, Sass. It's still pretty painful."

I nodded. Sean, always more open to therapy than me, had been seeing Tim Gibbons as a private patient for several weeks. He'd taken it seriously, relived his ordeal, and opened himself to painful memories. It would help in the long term, but now it hurt like picking at an open wound.

The irony of him attending the Gibbons Grey group was not lost on me. I had spent sleepless nights trying to decide if I should tell him that Adam Harding used the same services under the false name of Jem Wright. But that would mean revealing my nefarious nocturnal activities, which Sean might tolerate, but only if he could see the emails. I knew their contents would be too raw, and Sean needed protection from temptation. So I deleted the evidence and kept the knowledge to myself. Tim Gibbons would feel bound by client confidentiality and Adam had admitted enough for the police to gain an easy conviction without my help. Marcus and Sean had given first-hand evidence; DNA left on the warehouse cages, and both Tewkesbury bodies tied Adam to their deaths. But a subsequent investigation uncovering an empty rental property where Adam had held Ella Burton had sealed the deal. There was no need for me to divulge any more. Adam's future, or lack thereof, should be a done deal.

Sean nodded to my suitcase tucked beneath my desk.

"You still leaving me then?" he asked.

I nodded.

"You don't need to."

"I know." He was right. Things had been so much better since Jack's departure. But I had become dependent on Sean, and it was time to make my way alone in the world again.

"I'll drop you off," he said.

"It's only two o'clock."

"I'm giving you an early finish. It's not every day you move home. Got your keys?"

"Here." I dangled them in front of me, still wondering at the wisdom of my decision. Moving into a new place was usually exciting, but this time was different. I was distinctly unenthusiastic.

Sean loaded my suitcase into his car and we drove five minutes across town to a small enclave of new-build maisonettes, just close enough to walk into town and far enough out not to be part of it.

I let myself in, and Sean deposited my case in the lobby.

"Unusual," he said, opening a door leading to the downstairs bedroom, bathroom, and dressing area.

"Wait till you see upstairs."

We ascended the stairs to my new living room, overlooking the open countryside to the rear.

"Wow."

"And this." I ushered him through to a perfectly functional but tiny kitchen.

"You'll be happy here," he said.

I nodded doubtfully.

"Take this." Sean passed an envelope towards me.

"What is it?"

"That's a good question. Let's call it an opportunity. But it's up to you."

I gingerly opened the envelope and withdrew a '*Welcome to your new home*' card. *Good luck. All the best, Callum.*"

"How did he know?" I asked.

"Your phone rang when you were in the bathroom last week. Your cousin wondered why you weren't returning his calls."

"You should have told me. It's a total invasion of my privacy."

"Why? Callum sent the card to my address, and I've handed it to you. I didn't give him your new address in case you reacted like this."

"Good. Because it's all too complicated. What's this?"

I pointed to an address scribbled on the card.

"Do you trust me?" asked Sean.

"I guess." My voice quivered. I didn't know where this was leading, but I couldn't say no without offending him.

"Fancy a drive?"

"Not really. I was hoping to settle in."

"And you will. We can pick up a few provisions on the way."

I gazed at the kitchen and realised Sean was right. I hadn't brought a single edible item with me. It was a half-hearted move and I was unprepared.

"Go on then."

Two minutes later, Sean drew up and parked in a bay by the side of the road.

He turned to me and chewed his lip. "I know you've given up on your family, Sass. And I get it, I really do. But your cousin was trying to contact you because he says he's certain he knows who your parents are."

My heart fluttered at his words and a sick dread filled my stomach. "I can't do this right now. Too many other things to think about."

"True. Yet there will never be a better time."

"But they might not accept me."

"I know. It could go horribly wrong. But at least you'll know."

"Do I have siblings?"

Sean shook his head.

"Then my parents are Fred and June Long."

Sean smiled and nodded to a painted sign reading *Longs Greengrocers* on a double-fronted building ahead.

"I sure hit the parental lottery big time."

"Does money matter?"

I shook my head.

"Then onward to your destiny."

"I can't."

"I'll be right here, Sass. I promise."

Butterflies filled my chest as I opened the passenger

door and crossed the road, taking baby steps. I glanced back at Sean, who smiled encouragingly. For a moment, I stood with my hand on the door, paralysed with indecision. Then, taking a deep breath, I turned the handle and stepped inside.

The Devil Comes to Bylands: Prologue

Sunday, April 1, 2018

I track my quarry from the battlements, her slight form hunched against the dusk as she stamps across the grass with theatrical purpose, arms clamped across her chest. A flick of a lever adjusts my binoculars, pulling her petulant face into sharp relief. Her scowl deepens as I watch. She's reasonably attractive if you're generous, with looks that wilt under scrutiny – entitled, overindulged, under-formed. Resting bitch face in full bloom, but no laughter lines or crow's feet. A life untested by real consequences, and it shows.

I press a button, and the infrared LED casts its invisible glow, amplifying the dwindling light. Perfect for bat watching, which I had intended to do this evening, until she put on her little show. Another minor adjustment, and I see everything: the small mole near her cheekbone, the crude swathe of regrowth bisecting her yellow hair. A fat, dark band of neglect – half-hearted like everything else about her. Dye it or don't but make a choice. There's nothing more offensive than a task abandoned midway.

She sinks to the grass near the gated entrance, arms looped around her knees like a child pretending to think. Then predictably, dramatically, she wipes at her eyes and bows her head. A gesture she thinks shows vulnerability. I've seen her sort before. But she's not the only one with a decision to make.

I've been watching her for days. She arrived last week and hasn't stopped sulking since. She is spoilt, sullen, and sapping the atmosphere like a black hole of misery. Her mother, a woman hollowed out by appeasement, flutters in attendance, trying and failing to win her over. Their unhappiness is self-inflicted, and I've observed its progression like mould in a petri dish.

Tonight, their tension came to the boil. I heard the quarrel through my window, her screech splitting the silence as I tried to conclude a complex experiment – their angry words an irritation until I realised the opportunity it offered. I quietly opened the sash, kept to the shadows, and listened. They argued about Brian. The mother disapproves of her daughter's fiancé – a foolish, futile emotion. These enforced separations never end well. A bouquet delivered to reception had prompted another flurry of accusations. The mother tried to reason, which was predictably useless, and when that failed, she lost her temper, calling out Brian with a stream of invectives. An unforced error. She'd surrendered the moral high ground, and the girl, unsurprisingly, weaponised it. Their paths split: the mother storming one way, the daughter another.

Slinging my binoculars over my shoulder, I climb to the battlements. I advance to the crenelations, surveying the grounds for signs of the mother. She's gone, as expected –

likely drowning her inadequacies in something alcoholic and overpriced at the bar. She's left the girl exposed and alone, still muttering to herself near the gate, presumably rehearsing some grand exit. I recall her last words: a shrill threat to return to Brian's house. The mother's response, "good riddance," uttered wearily without drama, resigned to a lengthy bout of sulking.

The recent hotel renovations have been a blessing, with fewer guests and no distractions. The hotel, being isolated, offers long windows of quiet with a road distant enough that cries don't carry. Once the girl steps beyond that gate, anyone who sees her will assume she has left of her own accord. If I time this carefully and take the shortcut through the yew hedge and down to the gatehouse, I can intercept her unseen.

My heart accelerates, not from fear, but from anticipation. This is a rare opportunity: a live test subject with minimal risk, real data, and the chance to refine my techniques on a thinking, reactive participant. The ethics are unimportant. Curiosity and an experimental study of human suffering override every other consideration.

She stirs, unfolds, brushes grass from her knees and rises. I lower the binoculars, my pulse steady now. Purposefully, I descend the worn stone stairs, each footfall swift but careful.

It's time. The variables align, and I hurry towards my prey.

The Devil Comes to
Bylands: Chapter One

Friday, April 11, 2025

"Coffee?" asked Sean, raising an immaculately waxed eyebrow in my direction. I looked up, noting with disgust the application of a small amount of liquid eyeliner below his dark lashes.

"For God's sake. Is that makeup?"

Sean wiped his eye in feigned surprise. "Oh, that," he said.

"Well?"

"Sheena thought it would suit me."

"Wow. Say goodbye to good taste and hello to emasculation."

"You're just jealous," said Sean defensively.

"I'm really not. If I wanted to cross-dress, I'd make a proper effort."

"This isn't some profound gender change, Sass, and it's not about making a statement. Sheena wanted to jazz up my appearance a bit. And because I am comfortable with my masculinity, I let her. What's a bit of makeup between lovers?"

I shuddered at the thought of Sean bumping uglies with his latest squeeze. I'd never met a more self-obsessed, vacuous creature than his girlfriend, Sheena, who judged everything by appearances and social media validation. She housed her vast makeup kit in a handbag the size of a bucket, which also contained a portable ring light for something she called content creation. I am no stranger to the internet, but I have stayed well away from TikTok and all the other social media platforms with which everyone else seems strangely obsessed. If Sean wants to fall into that rabbit hole, then good luck to him. But I won't be joining in. I fleetingly wondered if they filmed themselves in bed and found myself blushing bright red.

"What's wrong?" asked Sean, his eagle eyes scanning my volcanically hot cheeks.

"Coming down with something, probably," I muttered.

"Then stay away from me. I don't want your germs spoiling my romantic weekend with Sheena."

"Though you don't mind her parents hanging around."

Sean scowled. "Can't avoid that. They're paying."

"Or her two little friends?"

"Retract your claws, cat," said Sean. "Do I detect a little jealousy?"

"Not at all. If I were going away for a dirty weekend, I'd be leaving the family at home."

"Be fair. If you were going away for a dirty weekend, it would be a heavy dose of wishful thinking."

"Wow," I said, feeling the sting of his words hit home. It had been many years since I last dated, and the longer I stayed single, the more my self-confidence seemed to evaporate. Sean knew this was my Achilles' heel and sensed that he had gone too far. He held his hands up, palms facing towards me.

"Sorry, low blow," he said.

"Whatever. I'm sure you'll have fun."

"And you will have a great weekend too. What are you up to?"

I fixed him with a pointed stare. "I'll be in the office. You scheduled some weekend work."

"So I did. Well, that will keep you busy until I return."

"And when will that be?"

Sean smiled wolfishly. "It depends on how well we get on."

"Don't be daft. You said Sheena's parents have already paid for the break. It must have an end date."

"Ah. But what's to stop us from hanging on for a few days once the parents have returned to bonnie Scotland?"

"Do you know how much it costs for a one-night stay at Bylands?"

Sean shrugged.

"I'll show you." I spun my laptop around and deposited it on his desk.

"Bloody hell. That's daylight robbery."

"Bylands is pricey. You'll be rubbing shoulders with the great and the good."

"My kind of people," said Sean.

"Yes, I'm sure they'll appreciate your new style."

Sean smirked. "Anyway, what were you doing on the website? Fancy booking a room yourself?"

"Not unless you give me a hefty pay rise. And since I'm barely making minimum wage, then no. I was interested in how the other half lives. I knew Sheena's parents were well-off, but a long weekend at Bylands is a whole other league."

"It's a birthday treat. They don't do this all the time."

"How old is Sheena?"

"Twenty-five this weekend."

"That's not even a landmark birthday."

"That's what Arthur said."

"On first-name terms, are we?"

"Naturally. They like me. Why wouldn't they? Arthur has invited me to his local golf course during the summer."

I snorted, remembering Sean's hapless attempts at crazy golf. In fairness, we were both hopeless. "Good luck impressing him with your slicing skills."

"I'll use the driving range to practise before we go."

"I wouldn't waste your time. You'll need more than one lesson. Anyway, why did Arthur give in?"

"Say again?"

"To Sheena. As he rightly says, reaching twenty-five is no great shakes."

"Times have changed. Anything with a zero or five deserves a lavish gift and a pricey trip away. They all do it. Jean wanted to go to Marbella, but Arthur refused to travel abroad. So, Sheena settled on a spa trip to Bylands."

"How very gracious of her."

"Now, now. Sheena's a nice girl when you get to know her."

I raised a cynical eyebrow. I had only met Sean's girlfriend a few times and, despite my best intentions, disliked her at first sight. The feeling had been mutual. Apart from a perfunctory greeting whenever she swanned into the office, she left me largely to my own devices, preferring to regard me as Sean's employee rather than his friend and former housemate. A touch of insecurity, I suspected.

That and the fact that I had little interest in the latest brand of primer and a total ignorance of fashionable handbags.

"What time are you going?" I asked.

Sean glanced at his watch. "About ten minutes," he said. "We're meeting at the Martingale Arms. Arthur has booked a Bentley."

"Grief," I said, feeling momentarily envious. "Isn't Marty's a little downmarket for the McBrides?"

"They're not snobs."

Though tempted to say that Sheena showed every sign of it, I swallowed my retort. "Well, I hope you have a lovely time."

"I will. Look, don't spend all day at your desk tomorrow. Take a break, have an early finish."

"It's Saturday. I'm already working overtime, and I don't need your permission to do less of it."

Sean frowned, looking hurt. "I know, and I appreciate your efforts. But do something nice this weekend. Don't make it all about work."

"You're right. Perhaps I'll call on Dhruv and drag him out for a cocktail."

Sean chewed his lip. "He's busy," he said.

"Have you seen him?"

"Yes."

"Lucky you. I've called and texted a few times. Anyone would think he's avoiding me."

"Just busy, I suppose."

"I guess. Pity though. I'd have loved a few hours putting the world to rights with Dhruv. Is Mill with him?"

Sean nodded.

"A quiet weekend then. Damn."

"Call Tom."

"I don't want to cramp his style. He's back on the dating app."

"Why? He never follows through with an actual meet-up."

"Weird, but understandable."

"It's annoying," said Sean. "Tom bothers me. He should finish what he started."

"Are you taking a swipe at me?" I asked, snapping down the lid of my laptop.

"No. That comment was purely about Tom."

"Are you sure?"

"For fuck's sake, Sass. If I wanted to have a pop at your failed attempt to meet your parents, I'd say so. It's your choice. If you'd rather take an anonymous stroll around their shop and come out with a pound of root vegetables, that's up to you. Not my problem, and I haven't judged you for it."

"Do you think I'm a coward?"

"I think you're confused, and like Tom, you prefer the process to the outcome."

"Whereas you would stroll in and have them eating out of your hands."

"Sass, it's your decision," said Sean gently. "They're your parents, and you know best how you feel. If you're not ready, that's fine. You know where they are, and you can deal with your situation when the time is right. Or not at all, if that's what it comes to. Either way is fine by me."

I lowered my head, ashamed of my outburst. "Sorry," I muttered.

Sean stood up and approached me, then enveloped me in an unexpected bear hug. "Friends?" he asked.

"Friends. See you next week."

Sean grabbed his keys and flipped a mock salute before leaving the office.

I stared at the whiteboard, covered in bullet points for tomorrow's research, and huffed a sigh. Sean was off for a weekend of luxury while I was on lizard duty, followed by a lonely meal for one. Some things never changed.

Grab your copy...
vinci-books.com/bylands

About the Author

Jacqueline Beard crafts chilling crime thrillers and gripping mysteries that peel back the idyllic veneer of rural England to expose the darkness beneath. With roots in East Anglia stretching back to the 1500s and now settled in Gloucestershire, she draws on history, place, and the complexities of human nature to weave tales of suspense and deception.

A former military servicewoman and long-time estate agent, Jacqueline has a sharp eye for understanding ordinary people's virtues and secrets. Since 2017, she has penned two historical mystery series before turning her hand to regional crime fiction, with a thrilling new series set in the haunting beauty of the Cotswolds.

Her books are for readers who crave atmospheric tension, psychological depth, and shocking twists that linger long after the final page. Whether exploring the shadows of the past or the crimes of the present, her stories deliver the unexpected, revealing just how far people will go when pushed to their limits.

When not plotting her next sinister tale, Jacqueline will be researching her expansive family tree or wandering the Gloucestershire countryside with her dog, perhaps uncovering inspiration for her next dark and twisting story.